SHADOWS THROUGH TIME

Melanie Robertson-King

King Park Press

Published by King Park Press

House image: Melanie Robertson-King
Grandfather clock: Wolfgang Eckert (Pixabay)

Poem The Listeners by Walter de La Mare (Public Domain)

ISBN: 978-1-990371-16-5

DEDICATION

For those who have experienced shadows through time...

ACKNOWLEDGMENTS

Thanks to Joanna Penn and Joseph Michael for their informative workshop on ChatGPT. It turned out to be a great brainstorming partner.

Additional thanks to Joseph Michael for his informative Scrivener workshops. I now do all my writing using it.

Huge thanks to my eagle-eyed proof/beta reader Nancy Chapman.

If I've missed anyone by name, I apologize.

Special thanks to my husband, Don, who continues to support and encourage me, and provides a shoulder to cry on when things don't go well. He redesigned my website making it mobile-friendly and taken charge on the domestic front giving me time to write.

Chapter One

MARCH 25, 1832

Charles Whitmore pulled open the heavy oak door of the tavern, and the smell of damp wool and pipe smoke, mingled with the warmth of the crackling fire, greeted him. As he stepped over the threshold, the low-lit room came into view, with men who had been speaking in low voices pausing to look at him before returning to their discussion.

"Crumbled like a child's toy," one said, slamming his mug onto the table. "Stone and timber all neat and proper until it gave way without warning. Buried three men before they had a chance to cry out."

"Wasn't shoddy work," another said. "Greaves builds sound; everyone knows that. But those markings ..." He lowered his voice before he continued. "Scratched into the beams, carved into the stone; nothing from any draftsman's handbook I've seen."

Whitmore lingered near the fireplace, pretending to warm his hands. He hadn't yet met the architect he was to apprentice under, the renowned Greaves, but already his name travelled like a curse.

A third man spat into the sawdust on the floor. "Fortune? Looked more like folly. Now there's nothing but a heap of rubble on Kingston's Main Street, and widows left wondering why." The suspicion in his voice was palpable, hanging in the air like the smoke from his pipe.

Whitmore's stomach knotted. An accident; it had to be. Houses failed. Beams split. Yet, the way these men spoke, the unease in their voices gnawed at him:

symbols, strange and deliberate, woven into the bones of a building.

The voices from the tavern still clung to him as Whitmore crossed the lane towards his boarding house. Talk of shoddy work, of corners cut. It needled him. Greaves seemed every inch the capable architect, yet the story whispered over tankards would not let him rest. Was it possible the two images were real? The trusted leader and the careless man? The mystery deepened, and Whitmore found himself drawn further into the intrigue.

Whitmore paused at the doorway and took out his journal. He hesitated, quill hovering, before scrawling a single word.

Uncertain.

Whitmore shut the door of his compact boarding house room, the faint rattle of the latch louder than he expected. The aroma of fried onions and lard from the downstairs kitchen hung in the air, mixing with the tang of lamp oil. He struck a match, the flame dancing in the dim light, and brought it to the candle's wick, the soft glow illuminating the room. He dropped onto the chair at the small desk by the window, the flickering light casting eerie shadows on the walls.

For a long while, he stared at the blank page of his journal. The voices from the tavern echoed in his mind. The men's grumbles, their talk of Kingston, of a wall that would not hold, and of Greaves's cursed symbols. He dipped his pen, and the ink blotted before he moved the nib.

> *This night I overheard much ill spoken of Mr. Greaves*, he began. His script was careful, as if each letter needed to steady his own unease. *They say he builds as he pleases, with signs no man of the trade understands. Some whisper of the ruin at Kingston, where good stone fell and lives with it. I know not the truth, but their mistrust is plain. He carries it with him like a shadow, a mystery that I*

cannot unravel.

He paused, tapping the pen against the margin. A shiver, more pronounced than before, passed through him, not from cold, but from his memory of that conversation.

Whitmore closed the book and set his pen aside, his body weary and his mind troubled. Sleep would not come easily, but he lay down fully dressed, the discomfort of his clothes a constant reminder of the unease that had settled within him. He gazed at the ceiling's cracked plaster until the candle guttered out, the darkness of the room mirroring the shadows in his thoughts.

Chapter Two

JUNE 17, 2023

Nicole rolled onto her side, facing Mitch, and propped herself up on her elbow. "Mitch, are you asleep?"

The covers beside her moved, and he groaned. "Not anymore. What's up, babe?"

Mitch rolled onto his back.

"Well ... um, do you regret giving up your apartment overlooking the harbour in Belleville? Moving out here away from everything?"

"No. What makes you ask that?"

"I don't know. It's just you were so close to everything there. Most of your customers were in and around the city."

"I'd live in a tent if it meant living with you."

Something dripped onto Nicole's arm. "We replaced the roof, right?"

"Yes."

"We might have to get the roofers back. Something just dripped on me."

"The amount of money we paid them for the job, and the materials used. It better not be leaking." Mitch rolled towards the bedside table and turned on the lamp. When he turned back to face Nicole, his face paled, a stark contrast to his earlier nonchalance.

"What is it?" she asked.

"That's not water," Mitch said, his voice tinged with unease.

Nicole looked at her arm. A red stain soiled the sleeve of her white cotton nightgown. She leapt out of bed, her heart pounding, and looked upwards. The same colour stained the ceiling and dripped down onto the bed.

"Stay here. I'm going to go see what's causing it." Mitch yanked on his flannel sleep pants, grabbed a flashlight from the drawer in the stand beside the bed, and dashed to the stairs leading to the third floor.

Mitch opened the door to the space above the one he and Nicole shared. He switched on the flashlight and swept its beam about the room. A dark patch stained the underside of the roof, and a slow drip struck the unfinished wood floor. The location aligned over their bed.

Cautiously, he approached the spot on the floor, knelt and pressed his index finger into the red pool. The substance was sticky. Mitch raised his hand to his nose. After his accident the year before, he knew all too well what blood smelled like. This had the same metallic tang and faint coppery sharpness. This wasn't fresh. It was old, and old blood didn't drip, which meant it shouldn't be wet.

Nicole had inherited the house from her aunt when the woman died. From the day the couple married until now, they had poured time, money, and love into restoring the old house and making it their home. Until tonight, nothing strange had occurred since they moved in.

He needed to conduct a further investigation, but not at this hour. The flashlight didn't illuminate the room that well. He needed power and clarity — his heavy-duty work lights and ladder from the workshop he built near the back of their property. At the moment, he couldn't go any farther.

As he turned to leave, a sudden chill surrounded him. He froze. The air was at least ten degrees colder. It was as if he had walked through something or someone. Mitch closed the door behind him and stood in the corridor. A faint sound reached him. Muffled but audible. He wasn't sure what it was, but as he moved towards the stairs, it became louder. Crying. It was someone crying. Nicole?

What was that?

Nicole swung her legs out of bed and crept into the hallway. The sound again — soft, distant, child's crying. It was impossible because no children were living in the house. At least not in the here and now. She couldn't make sense of it, but the sound was unmistakable.

She tiptoed towards the nursery door, her heart pounding so hard she was sure it would give her away. The sound might stop if she got too close. She may have imagined it, but the weeping persisted. She placed her ear against the door, hoping for clarity. The sound remained elusive and indistinct, yet real.

Mitch dashed down the stairs. When he reached the bedroom level, Nicole stood frozen in place in the hallway outside the nursery. "Are you all right?" Mitch asked. His voice made her jump.

"I should be asking you," she said, turning towards him. "You're as white as a sheet. What did you find upstairs?"

"Blood," he said, his tone grim. "I need to go back in the morning with my work lights and a ladder. The flashlight wasn't bright enough."

The soft crying exploded into a loud shriek.

Nicole staggered as her knees gave out, and she clutched Mitch's arm to steady herself.

"I heard the same thing upstairs," he said, holding her close. "At first I thought it was you."

"I'm going in with you," she said, her voice trembling but firm.

Mitch nodded, turned the knob and pulled the nursery door open. Nicole clenched his arm as they entered. Snowflake, the hobby horse, wasn't moving, and Clara, the china head doll, was in the rocking chair by the fireplace.

The cradle, though, rocked back and forth as if someone was trying to soothe a restless infant.

Nicole's breath caught. She waited for a vision —

a glimpse from the past. She had had them before in this house and at Kembleford Manor, but nothing came of it.

Only the cradle, swaying in the silence.

Chapter Three

MARCH 26, 1832

The grass remained wet with morning mist when Whitmore reached the Brighton site. The house rose from the ground like a great skeleton, its timbers stark against the pale sky, and scaffolding lashed together at hasty angles. Workers moved about with the ease of those long accustomed to the rhythm of stone and timber. Their talk carried on the damp air, but their eyes flicked often to the lone man standing apart.

Mr. Greaves.

His coat, a stark contrast to the dust, his posture a silent command. When his gaze met Whitmore's, it was as if he had already delved into his life.

Whitmore approached, holding his hat in his left hand. "Sir, Charles Whitmore. You asked for an apprentice?" He extended his right in an invitation to shake hands.

For a long moment, Greaves said nothing, only studied him. Then, with the faintest smile tugging at his mouth, he gestured towards the rising wall. "Every house is a conversation, young Whitmore. The stone speaks, and we, if we listen properly, answer. Do you hear it?"

Whitmore swallowed and nodded. "Yes, sir. I suppose that's why I'm here, sir. To learn."

"Good." The word came like a benediction. Greaves stepped closer, lowering his voice as if confiding a secret. "Most see only a wall, but a true builder creates shape, memory and destiny. That is what we raise here."

As he moved away to speak to the crew, the men straightened as though drawn to his presence. Their grumbling fell silent under his calm authority. Greaves didn't need to raise his voice. Every syllable seemed to find its mark.

Whitmore stood, a sense of unease settling over him. The whispers in the local tavern had been clear. Collapse. Ruin. Men crushed in Kingston. Yet, as he looked at Greaves, magnetic and self-assured, a seed of doubt crept in. Did a man such as this cause such a catastrophe?

He finally met the man he was to apprentice under on the building site on the outskirts of Brighton. Whitmore watched the man's hand move across the vellum, his pencil tracing uncanny sigils. And he remembered the ruin in Kingston and the tale of the dead carried on whispers in taverns.

And yet, in the dust at his feet lingered the faint tracings Greaves had drawn earlier, curling symbols Whitmore didn't recognize. They belonged to no measure, no drafting mark, no geometry he had ever studied. Strange. Alien.

The clearing exuded the loamy scent of damp earth and sawed timber, the latter neatly stacked nearby for the upcoming stages of the construction project. Elias Greaves, his sleeves rolled up, stood next to the foundation, a sketch clutched in his right hand. Sweat glistened on his temples, and the wind tousled his dark hair. His eyes blazed with a fervour that just a handful understood, a sign of his steadfast commitment.

"No, no, no," he lamented. "This wall must curve." He pointed his long index finger towards the northeast corner. "Just here, ten feet from the edge. A perfect crescent. Not a bay, and not a bow, but a crescent." His innovative spirit shone through; his vision was clear.

The mason stared at him with a dumbstruck expression on his face. "But the rest of the house is square, sir. Rectangular. That curve won't ..."

"Conform?" Elias cut him off, amusement in his voice. "Indeed, that's the point. This house does not have to conform. It's meant to breathe."

Elias's young apprentice, Charles Whitmore, stepped in cautiously. "Mister Greaves, the supports for such a curve, especially when the tower is just above, might need us to make adjustments to the substructure."

"Then, that's what we do, young Whitmore." He turned back to his book of plans, flipping to a page that showed a cross-section, a hidden support channel running beneath the room. "It's all here. Calculated and tested." His confidence in his calculations and leadership was unwavering.

What Greaves didn't add was that he had performed the calculations by candlelight, or that he'd dreamt the crescent room after walking the grounds under a full moon. The men didn't need to know those details.

Charles leaned over the plans. "This part here under the stairs — it's hollow?"

Elias smiled at his young apprentice. "What would be the point of solid ground beneath a staircase when a narrow passage would just as easily traverse it? There are more paths through a house than those we see, young Whitmore."

The mason muttered something unintelligible under his breath and returned to stacking bricks.

Above them, scaffolding creaked as workers hoisted beams into place. The central tower rose like a sentinel over the clearing, skeletal for now, but already commanding attention. That part of the construction was Elias's pride and joy.

Charles watched him for a moment, then said, "They say this house'll outlive us all."

"They're right," Elias said, a tender tone in his voice. "If we build it true, it will remember. Houses are like people, young Whitmore. They absorb everything. Joy, grief, secrets, and more. And if we shape them well, they keep those memories safe until someone is wise enough to ask the right questions."

The younger man shivered despite the heat.

As Charles Whitmore packed up the tools and prepared to leave, Elias remained on the scaffolding, one hand pressed against the curved wall.

"Mind your step on the way out, young Whitmore," Greaves called, not looking down. "This house does not take kindly to the inattentive."

He hesitated for a moment, then nodded. "Of course, sir," the apprentice said before walking away slowly, the strange phrase sitting deep within his chest. He was both in awe of the house's design and the architect's words, yet a sense of unease lingered in his mind.

Charles trudged down the path towards the rim of the clearing. Thick mud covered his boots, and his thoughts weighed him down even more. Behind him, the house's skeleton loomed against the subdued colours of twilight, the unfinished tower catching the last light. Somewhere up in the framing, Elias Greaves still talked. To himself, the trees, or the house, Charles didn't know.

He adjusted the satchel containing his tools, slung it across his shoulder, and glanced back.

The place was ... extraordinary. No, it was absurd. Strange angles, hollow places where solid foundations should be. A staircase that led up and then back down again on the other side of a wall. A narrow arched door where no hallway existed — yet. A tower room with only two small windows, both aligned with the setting sun on the summer and winter solstice. Who builds like that? The design was a puzzle, a mystery waiting to be solved.

"Who *thinks* like that?" Charles asked.

Greaves did. That's who. That man lived half in the real world and half elsewhere. His other world was of dreams and blueprints layered with meaning no one else saw. Charles had spent enough time with architects to know the type. Mathematicians wearing waistcoats, pragmatists with plumb bobs and rulers. Elias Greaves was something else entirely.

That man was a conjurer with a measuring tape.

Charles stopped at the tree line and cast one last look at the house behind him. There was something about it, even unfinished, that pulled at him. A sense of motion in the stillness, as though the house were waiting and watching, its very silence filled with a strange, eerie energy.

A chill crept up his spine despite the heat. He shook it off and pulled a folded page from his pocket. He sketched a cross-section of the crescent room himself, a room Greaves had insisted on building. It made no structural sense, but somehow, it was right. Even on paper, it emitted a strange harmony. The lines hummed beneath his fingertips. He folded the page and returned it to his pocket.

“Madness,” he said out loud. He turned down the path, disappearing into the trees, wondering if, years from now, anyone would remember the name Greaves. Or whether the house would simply stand, its secrets hidden, until someone went looking.

Chapter Four

JUNE 18, 2023

Nicole watched as Mitch made his way to his workshop at the back of the property. He hadn't taken the time to eat breakfast before heading out to get his ladder and work lights. She wasn't certain if she wanted to know what he had found in the room from which the blood dripped.

She had changed out of her blood-stained white nightgown and put it to soak in cold water so that the stain wouldn't set. After that, Nicole settled for one of Mitch's t-shirts, a baggy and comfortable fit on her, but snug on him. The familiar scent of his cologne enveloped her, bringing a sense of comfort and intimacy.

During the renovations, they opened the utility room, where the appliances once stayed and made it part of the kitchen. The wood stove that Nicole loved remained along the back wall, a comforting constant amidst the changes. They had replaced the old appliances with modern, energy-efficient ones. Somehow, Mitch had found the set of five designed to match the wood stove at one of his suppliers. Nicole fell in love with them from the moment she set eyes on them. The room was now retro and roomy, proof of their hard work and dedication. Fresh paint covered the tin on the walls and ceilings, and they stripped and stained the wainscotting, a visual representation of their transformation.

Nicole checked her nightgown. The stain had come out. She put it in the front-load washing machine, then gathered towels and their bedding to make a full load.

By the time she started the load of laundry, Nicole was eagerly expecting Mitch's return. She knew he would be on his way back soon, his huge ladder balanced on his shoulder. She waited by the back door, her heart fluttering with excitement, and opened it for him as soon as she saw him approaching.

Mitch set the ladder down, then returned to his workshop for the bright construction lights. He'd need them to illuminate the room where the blood appeared to originate. But, had it come through the roof, seeped through that floor and then dripped onto their bed? That thought sent a shiver down his spine.

With his long extension cord coiled around his shoulder and a work light in each hand, he made his way back to the house and up to the room where he'd found the wet spot the previous night.

"Do you want to come up and have a look?" Mitch asked.

"I don't know. I want to find out what happened, but not sure if I want to see it."

"Grab a sketchbook, pencil and your camera. You'll be fine. I'm going to be right there."

Nicole was resolute in documenting Mitch's statement. It was something they needed to preserve. She'd had visions from the past appear before her. Perhaps this connected the events. "Okay."

"I'll get everything set up." Mitch turned the corner at the foot of the stairs and disappeared.

Where did she last use her sketchbook? Nicole embarked on a quest, walking through the formal dining room to the small living room at the front of the house. It wasn't on the coffee table. She then worked her way out from there and into the bigger room on the opposite side of the house. The one where she found the marriage certificate in the desk.

Nicole opened the top right-side drawer. Her pad was there. She took it out and leafed through the pages. It was almost entirely full. She'd have to go into

Brighton soon and stock up on supplies. The shop she had always dealt with in Belleville had opened another location in town, making it far more convenient when she needed pencils, sketchbooks, and other art supplies.

She pulled a couple of sharpened pencils from the middle upper drawer and walked to the stairs, ready for the upcoming activity with Mitch. The ladder wasn't lying on the kitchen floor, so Mitch must have come back and retrieved it while she was busy.

As she climbed the stairs, the ladder clanged against the treads on the metal spiral staircase, filling the air. He wasn't far ahead of her.

"Need a hand?" Nicole asked, walking into the room.

Mitch turned on the halogen work lights and aimed them towards the vaulted ceiling in the room directly above the spot where the blood pooled on the floor. There wasn't any discolouration of any kind in the rafters. That made no sense. He positioned the ladder so that it straddled the dark patch on the floor and climbed, ensuring he didn't blind himself in the beams. Even from his lofty perch, there was nothing to show anything had seeped through the roof and into the room. It made no sense at all. The blood had to come from somewhere.

Nicole stood near the foot of the ladder, sketchpad open and pencil in hand. Mitch descended and joined her. "I don't get it. There's nothing on the ceiling here. The blood that dripped through this floor and into our bedroom is right here. Or was." Now the two stood next to a patch of darker floorboards.

He squatted and touched the spot that last night had been wet with blood. Dry. Bone dry, and no sign there had been a pool of anything there. A chill passed through the room. Not an expected draft chill, but something colder, clammier, and unearthly. Mitch shivered. Perhaps restoring and updating this old house as a home wasn't such a good idea. He quickly discounted that thought. He didn't believe in ghosts, the supernatural, or any other phenomena with no logical explanation.

As Nicole's sketch developed, a discoloured section of the floor suddenly emerged, taking on a life of its own. The once-random shape now bore a disturbing resemblance to a sunken, screaming face. The more she sketched, the clearer the image became, until she stared into a pair of hollow eyes and a mouth opened in what seemed to be mid-scream. What had terrified this person?

Startled by the image before her, she dropped her pencil and let out an astonished squeak, her heart pounding in her chest. Mitch was at his wife's side within seconds, concern etched on his face.

"You okay?" he asked.

Nicole shook her head and turned her sketchbook towards him.

"I've seen that face somewhere," he said.

"There is a haunting familiarity to it, but I can't place it," Nicole mused, her hand hesitating over the sketchbook. She attempted to continue working, but an unseen force seemed to restrain her hand. "Mitch," she said slowly, "I can't move my hand. It's like someone is holding it and not letting me work."

"I think it's time we left here," Mitch said, his voice tinged with urgency as he ushered her towards the door.

Chapter Five

MARCH 26, 1832

The boarding house was quiet by the time Whitmore returned, save for the occasional creak of the floorboards overhead and the hiss of Mrs. Cole banking the cookstove. He lit the stub of a candle at his desk and set out his journal. Its blank page almost dared him to make sense of the day.

> *Finally, the enigmatic Mr. Greaves crossed my path.*

He paused, pen hovering. How might he describe the feelings he had while the man watched him? It had not been mere instruction, nor even authority, but something heavier, something that pressed at the edges of thought.

> *The men follow him without question. A single look, a word sets everything in order. Yet, over ale, I had heard something totally different. People mentioned Greaves's name in the same breath as the disaster in Kingston. But how can both things be true? Can such command and ruin spring from the same hands?*

His script grew sharper as he pressed harder on the nib.

> *I saw marks on the ground where he had drawn before I arrived. Not letters, not*

measurements. I know of no mason's chalk or architect's rule I've seen in books. They twisted and turned in ways that defied logic, and yet he traced them as though they held meaning. They were alien and disconcerting.

He leaned back in his chair; the candlelight flickering across the page.

His whispers warn me, yet his presence is undeniably captivating. I must stay vigilant. But what if his influence extends beyond mere stone?

The nib scratched one last line.

For now, I watch and I listen.

Whitmore closed the book and snuffed out the candle. Sleep, when it came, was fitful and thin.

As Elias Greaves descended from his lofty perch, an orange smear of sunset cast the landscape in a watercolour haze. Once on the ground, he stood beneath a crooked maple, his boots sunk into the soft earth, and his hat in his hands.

Behind him, the house rose slowly, almost defiantly, stone by stone, timber by timber. His house and his vision. A vision that had consumed him, that had become a part of him, and yet, a part that he would never truly own.

But it wasn't his. It had never been. There were nights when he doubted. When the lines he'd drawn, carved into paper or etched into beams, blurred, the house's wants became clear. Never needed, but wanted.

"I am but the vessel," he said, his voice almost lost to the breeze. "You gave me the dream. I merely follow it."

Elias pressed a hand to the worn satchel at his side. Inside it, parchment maps, pages of drawings, a journal with entries that dated back a decade, if not more. The history inspired awe because he had shaped this house for so many years before they broke ground.

Still, there were voices. Greaves heard them the clearest when dusk settled. Whispers beneath roots, behind stones. They weren't evil. They were never that, but they were older than he understood, carrying a wisdom that commanded respect. He never knew who uttered these words that came to him.

He'd tried to explain it to Whitmore, his apprentice, but despite being bright, his mind was too bound by rules and logic. The young man, with his sharp intellect and practical nature, would never fully grasp the ethereal essence of Elias's connection to the house.

Greaves lifted his head and looked back. "One day," he said, "they'll understand." He turned then, slowly and carefully, and walked away as the shadows lengthened behind him.

Chapter Six

JUNE 18, 2023

Downstairs, Nicole walked from room to room, inspecting the photographs and paintings on the walls and mantelpieces. Not a single one resembled the face she had drawn. Why did it look so familiar? And not just to her; Mitch had noticed it, too. Still, despite them both recognizing the face in Nicole's sketch, there wasn't a painting or photograph downstairs of the person. So, where had she seen it before?

"You won't find him in any of the paintings or pictures," Mitch said when he caught up with Nicole in the room that had the Freemason's symbol on the ceiling medallion.

"Why do you say that?"

Mitch produced a brittle, yellowed piece of newsprint and spread it out on the desk. "I remembered where we found the stack of pictures and the newspaper clipping of the man who died in the Freemason ritual gone wrong. On a hunch, I went back to that wardrobe, and there was a false bottom in it. This was under it."

Nicole moved closer to inspect the fuzzy image of the man in the paper. She placed her sketchbook next to it. They were definitely the same man. Even the printed page was difficult to read.

"Who is he?" she asked.

"Article says he was the architect."

Nicole swallowed hard, looking between her sketch and the picture of the man in the newspaper clipping. "But why now?"

"I don't know. Do you think he's trying to show us something?"

"By dripping blood on me and our bed? Funny way of going about it."

"Too bad the article is in such poor shape. I'd like to read it. He sounds like my kind of man."

"We might find it online. Most newspapers have historical issues digitized."

Nicole had set her computer up on the desk in the front part of the now double room. Workers removed the pocket doors during the renovation, and they framed the archway with similar wood.

As she typed into the search bar, Mitch scanned the old newspaper clipping. It was impossible to read, as it had faded significantly over the years.

"Here, I found it," Nicole said.

THE BRIGHTON ENSIGN
October 14, 1883

Elias Greaves: The Architect of Shadows

Visionary Designer of the Harrowick Tower Leaves Legacy of Mystery
By J. Thaddeus Crone, Special Correspondent

For over four decades, the Harrowick estate's tower has stood, a monument to the enigma that is Elias Greaves. The architect of this now-infamous stone spiral, Greaves, vanished in the final stages of construction of another project near the city of Cornwall. No obituary. No marked grave. No trace.

Born in 1805 to a family of stonemasons and spiritualists, Greaves was already sketching cathedral spires before he wrote his own name. He trained in Scotand before emigrating to Upper Canada, where he took on commissions few others dared: chapels, crypts, and private homes with unusual specifications.

But Harrowick remains his most curious project. Commissioned by a distant cousin in 1832, the house became Greaves's obsession. Records show he altered the plans repeatedly, especially the tower. It had to be built with a narrow east-facing window to capture the morning light at the summer solstice and one opposite for the sunset at the winter solstice. Stone had to be quarried from a specific ridge near Napanee, where, he claimed, "the minerals sang."

Locals whispered Greaves believed the tower served as a conduit, not merely to the heavens but to something older. Construction stalled repeatedly. Workers quit. Some claimed their tools moved on their own. Others saw a figure watching from the top of the tower when no one had gone up.

In 1870, with the Cornwall area structure nearly finished, Elias Greaves vanished.

The apprentice working on the Brighton project abandoned the job before completing it.

In recent years, the house has changed hands multiple times. The Harrowick family stayed less than a year. The Smiths followed them. The next family, the Grahams, has stayed the longest, still living there today. The tower remains locked. Still, some claim that on moonless nights, a candle flickers behind its narrow window, and that the house breathes with memories not its own.

"So, the Graham mansion isn't this place's original name. That puts a new spin on things," Mitch mused.

"Don't you go disappearing on me like this man did."

The image included in the article in the online edition was clearer than the worn paper and matched the sketch Nicole had created from the discoloured spot on the floor, from where blood had dripped onto their bed.

Nicole was lucky and found a parking spot across the street from the art supply store. She needed personal supplies and those for work, so the transactions would have to be done separately — cash for her personal items, and the company credit card for the work-related ones, which included pastel pencils rather than ordinary ones. She had thought about using them in her personal drawing and sketching, too, but had decided against it. She was vigilant in keeping her work and personal supplies separate.

This location wasn't as big as the store she was used to shopping at in Belleville, but the convenience more than made up for it. She still used the original location if she needed something on days she worked in the office.

As she exited the door, the bell above the door jingled, and a familiar voice stopped her cold.

"Still chasing your little hobby, Nicki?"

Her chest tightened, and she turned slowly. There stood Brad. The same smug grin. The same icy eyes.

"It's not a hobby," she said, her voice low but steady.

He looked her up and down. "Still touchy. Some things never change."

Nicole clutched her bag tighter, her heart hammering in her chest. She refused to give him the satisfaction of knowing how much his appearance affected her. "You're right," she said coolly. "Some things don't. Like the way abusers never think they're the problem."

His grin faltered.

"Goodbye, Brad."

She walked away without looking back, legs shaking, but stronger than she used to be.

Fifteen minutes later, Nicole pulled into the driveway and turned off the engine. She sat behind the wheel, her whole body trembling with the shock of the encounter. This unexpected meeting with Brad had left her more vulnerable than she would acknowledge. She refused to bring this vulnerability into her home. Nicole had to gather her strength quickly. She took a few deep breaths and then stepped out of the car.

She entered the kitchen and closed the door with more force than intended. The echo travelled through the old house like a warning. She leaned against it long enough to take a shaky breath. She hadn't expected to see *him*. Not here, and not after all this time.

With stiff fingers, Nicole pulled off her shoes and padded barefoot to the room housing her computer. Each creak underfoot seemed to pierce the silence. The unease was no longer just about Brad. It was pervasive, as if the house had absorbed her tension and was now reflecting it back to her.

She stopped cold. Her laptop sat open on the desk, the faint hum of life in its power light. Nicole stared at it. She always closed it, always, especially before going out. Nicole crossed the room slowly, keeping her eyes on the device, as if it might spring to life. Nothing else looked out of place, but somehow that made her suspicion even stronger.

She reached out and closed the cover; the click sounded too loud in the still room. Had Mitch used it? Why? After all, he had his own.

Did she get distracted when she left? But Nicole remembered shutting it. She was sure of it. The back of her neck prickled.

"I'm being ridiculous," she said aloud in the empty room, but her words didn't dispel the sense that something, or someone, had been there while she was gone.

Nicole sat in the chair in front of the desk, her hands clasped so tightly that her knuckles had gone white. Only the occasional creak of the old house broke the eerie silence that filled the room. She had shut down her laptop and closed the lid, but her eyes kept drifting back to it, as if it held some ominous secret.

"Hey, you're back. Everything okay?"

She looked up. "Define 'okay.'"

He stepped closer, frowning. "What happened?"

Nicole hesitated and then said, "Brad," her voice barely above a whisper, which sent ice-cold shivers through her — again.

Mitch's expression darkened at once. "Where?"

"Outside the art store. He just appeared as if he knew I'd be there." She rubbed her arms, chilled. "He acted as if nothing had ever happened."

Mitch moved closer to her and put his hand on her shoulder. "Are you all right?"

"I thought I was. But then I came home and ... I can't shake off this sense of being watched." Nicole glanced towards the desk.

He followed her gaze. "What is it?"

"My laptop. It was open when I came in. I know I closed it."

"You're sure?"

"Yes," she said, her voice tight. "I remember pressing the lid down."

He checked the device. "No sign anyone or anything tampered with it. Nothing opened on the screen?"

"No, wait a minute, the article regarding Elias Greaves. I had my browser open, and it was on the current tab." She laughed dryly. "Between what we found upstairs, the blood, the sketch, and now this, maybe the house doesn't want us here."

Mitch turned to face her. "No. If it didn't want us here, I think we'd know. This ... feels different. Like something's trying to get our attention."

Nicole stared at her computer again. "You think it's him, don't you? Elias Greaves."

"I think he's part of it," Mitch said. "And I don't think he's finished."

Nicole stood and crossed to the window. "You, who doesn't believe in ghosts, are thinking we're being haunted by the architect who built this place?"

"What other explanation is there?"

"I'm tired of ghosts. If seeing the past is the gift Mummy mentioned in her letter to me, then it's not a gift but a curse."

Mitch joined her and rested his hand on her back. "Let's find out what they want and why."

Chapter Seven

MARCH 26, 1832

Whitmore lay on the narrow bed, the low ceiling pressing down on him. The rooming house had grown quiet; the usual footsteps and murmured voices swallowed by the night. He laced his fingers behind his head and gazed at the beams overhead, the light from the town's gas lamps flickering over them like restless shadows.

The day replayed itself in stubborn fragments. Greaves on the scaffolding, commanding with that magnetic voice, drawing the men into his orbit as though he were more than just a master builder. The uninhibited laughter, the reassuring pat on the shoulder, yet something colder beneath, something that unsettled Whitmore the longer he watched.

His conscience twisted, a knot of uncertainty tightening in his gut. He should say nothing. Keep to his role, record measurements, note progress, follow orders. That was the safest thing to do. Yet, recalling the men's faces, trusting and unaware, gnawed at him. What if Greaves's confidence masked a flaw? What if the rumours he had overheard the previous day held the truth?

Kingston loomed in his mind. The collapsed building. The whispered accusations that had chased Greaves here. If he sought answers there, he might expose the truth ... or find nothing but dust and hearsay. To confront Greaves directly was reckless. Just by looking, the man could strip away defenses and make doubts sound foolish before someone voiced them.

Do nothing? The thought pricked at his pride, a sharp sting he could not ignore. To do nothing was to be complicit if the whispers proved true. But to act was to risk everything, his job, his reputation, perhaps even his life.

Whitmore shifted restlessly, a stalk of straw from the mattress poking into him. Duty and fear trapped him, as did admiration and suspicion. He closed his eyes, but sleep refused to come.

At last, he whispered to the still room, as if testing the significance of his decision aloud. "Kingston, then. If there are answers to be had, they lie there."

The words hung in the darkness, fragile but binding. And though doubt still tugged at him, a small, cold resolve took root. He would go to Kingston, he decided, his voice firm in the silent room.

Chapter Eight

JUNE 19, 2023

Did Mitch believe in ghosts? He didn't think he did, but what other explanation was there for the things that were happening in the house Nicole had inherited from her aunt? In one of her visions, she'd seen her father witness a Freemason's ritual gone wrong. They had blood dripping from their bedroom ceiling onto them. And Nicole had sketched Elias Greaves, someone whom she'd never met before, but came to her from a dark patch on the floor in the room above their bedroom.

He couldn't believe he was thinking it, but what was this architect from days gone by trying to tell them? What was it about the house? Or was it the current inhabitants that brought him forward? Mitch shook his head. This was unnatural to him. What did he know about the supernatural, ghosts, and other phenomena on a different plane? The secret of the house's history was akin to a puzzle that tugged at him.

Were the Grahams who lived here related to the man? The newspaper article said a distant cousin commissioned Greaves to build the house. Were the two families connected somehow? People always knew the mansion as the Graham mansion, long after Robert Holbrook married June Graham, and they, along with their family and descendants, lived here.

Mitch needed to find out more about Elias Greaves. Then, he could make an informed decision. Nicole had only searched online for a more legible copy of the newspaper article he found under the false bottom of the wardrobe.

The man's name sounded familiar to Mitch. Had he come across it during his post-secondary education? Was he mentioned in his textbooks? He climbed the stairs to the room, which served as his office. Along one wall, close to his drafting table, his textbooks from university filled the shelves.

He ran his fingers along the spines of the well-worn books, many of which he'd bought used because of his financial limitations, and stopped at ***Echoes in Stone***.

Mitch pulled it from the shelf and placed it on the table, then made himself comfortable on the stool. He flipped through the pages slowly, skimming until a name caught him off guard. Elias Greaves. His pulse spiked. "No way. Can't be," he said, his surprise clear in his voice.

His eyes scanned the paragraph, his heart thudding louder with each sentence. Towered estate. Outskirts of Brighton. Hidden passages. A vanished architect.

Mitch read the passage two more times, his mouth agape. "He built this place," he said in the empty room, "and considered it bewitched."

A cold draft brushed the nape of his neck, and he turned sharply, but nothing or no one was there. He glanced at the textbook again; the words blurring before his eyes. Bewitched. Ill-starred.

With his hands tingling, Mitch closed the book. Nicole needed to see what he'd found. When he stood, the sound of the wind rattling a loose windowpane echoed eerily behind him. It sounded to him like a man's laughter, adding to the already suspenseful atmosphere.

Nicole was unpacking her sketchpads and other supplies from her tote bag when Mitch returned to the room carrying a textbook.

"I knew the name sounded familiar. He was one architect we studied." He placed the open book on the desk next to Nicole's laptop. "Have a read."

Nicole paused sorting her work-related shopping

from her personal and sat to read the passage from the book. "What am I looking at?" she asked.

"Last paragraph," he said, pointing.

She did.

Chapter 6 — Gothic Revival and the Rise of the Towered Estate

Among the lesser-known figures of Ontario's architectural heritage, Elias Greaves (b. 1805, disappeared c. 1870) remains a subject of curiosity and speculation. Greaves was a private man with few documented commissions, well known for his intricate floor plans, love of asymmetry, and frequent inclusion of narrow towers or turrets—often to no apparent functional end.

Greaves's most enigmatic work is a sprawling country house on the outskirts of Brighton. An unnamed landowner commissioned the mansion in the early 1830s, and it featured extensive interior woodwork, hidden passages, and a nursery. People said the nursery was in use before they fully completed the structure.

Though praised for its craftsmanship, the house's eccentricities led some to view it as "bewitched" or "ill-starred."

"This is our house. I know it is," Nicole said before going back to the textbook.

Greaves left the area shortly after its completion and locals rumoured him to be building a house near Cornwall, Ontario, from where he vanished without a trace. Authorities never filed a formal death record. Though rumours persist, ranging from accidental death to murder, his fate remains a tantalizing mystery. Some believe he never left the property.

"He was here," she said, her voice barely above a whisper.

Mitch nodded. "I think he came back."

Nicole glanced towards the ceiling and the rooms above her head. The nursery, their bedroom with the dripping blood. "What if this entire house is trying to tell us something? The drawings, the newspaper article, the face in the stain ..."

"This sure puts a different spin on things," Mitch said. "Wonder what else we can find on the man? It's almost certain that our house is the one mentioned in my textbook. And before I left to bring this down to show you, a cold draft brushed the back of my neck, and I heard what sounded like a man laughing."

"Why, Mitchell Kane, are you slowly becoming a believer?" Nicole asked with a note of sarcasm in her voice. "Never thought I'd see the day."

"Funny. Laugh it up. You weren't there. And I have experienced nothing else weird like that since we moved in. Not even when I was working on the restoration and renovations."

Nicole closed the book gently, as though the pages might whisper secrets if left open too long. She wanted to tell her brothers about her encounter with Brad in Brighton, but that would set off an entire chain of events she didn't want. She also wanted to tell them about the blood and the architect whose face had come to her in a vision in the darkened patch on the floor above their bedroom, and now what Mitch had found in his textbook.

"Whatever happened to him, he wants us to see it," Nicole declared with a determined tone, her resolve to uncover the truth unwavering.

Mitch didn't argue.

The wind sighed through the window glass again, soft and low, like a breath against her ear, adding to the eerie atmosphere of the house.

Shivering, Nicole stood and left the room. Once she was in the kitchen, Nicole pulled her phone from her back pocket, looked up her brother, Connor, in the contacts and composed a text message.

Still strange things happening here. Why don't you and Cooper come out for supper tonight? I'm cooking and not just ordering in pizza.

She quickly typed out the message, her fingers trembling slightly, and hit send.

Once she'd sent the message, she set her phone on the counter. When she lived in her Belleville apartment and had her brothers or Mitch over, her go-to was pizza from her favourite pizzeria in town. She had stumbled across a recipe for baked potatoes done in the crock pot, and hers was big enough for four good-sized ones.

Nicole crossed the kitchen to the fridge. Sour cream, check. Bacon bits, check. Cheese Whiz, if anyone wanted it, check. So now for the meat. What could she get thawed in time to eat? Making another trip to Brighton wasn't high on her priorities, especially since she'd run into Brad earlier. Plenty of romaine for a salad, red onion, too. Mushrooms. She'd be happy with carbs and greens, but her brothers and Mitch liked — no, loved — their meat.

About once every eight to ten weeks, Nicole did a big meat shop at Costco. She checked the chest freezer and found two packages of steaks for two. She had sorted out supper. Her phone vibrated from the other side of the room.

What time?

She hadn't thought of a specific time. If they left directly from work ... that gave her some leeway. The steaks would go on when they arrived. It would give everyone a chance to unwind and talk about the goings on in the house and at the office.

Come straight from work. I promise you'll enjoy the meal.

Now to figure out her and Mitch's lunch. Nicole opened the fridge again. Black Forest ham, Swiss cheese, lettuce, tomato, and mayo; the fixings for a good sandwich. A package of kaisers languished in her wooden breadbox. Still fit for human consumption and well before their best-before date. Nicole put together two enormous sandwiches.

"Lunch is on the table, Mitch," she called.

Mitch had been searching for information about Elias Greaves beyond what the newspaper article said about him. He found some information on Wikipedia, so he highlighted and printed it.

When Nicki called him for lunch, he grabbed the paper off the printer and took it with him to the kitchen.

"I did some digging on Elias Greaves. More than just the newspaper article and the paragraph in my textbook. I don't know if he was a genius or crazy." Mitch paused and took a bite of his sandwich and chewed thoughtfully.

"Why do you say that?" Nicole asked, carrying two mugs of Earl Grey tea.

"Might as well give you the whole story. The man was born between 1805 and 1810. His most active period was between the 1830s and the 1870s."

"Okay, but where do you get crazy from that?" Nicole asked.

"Here's where things get weird. People knew him for unusual, almost esoteric architectural flourishes. Hidden rooms, spiral staircases, and towers aligned to celestial events."

"Sounds a lot like this place."

"There's more. Greaves had rumoured links to Freemasonry, spiritualist movements, and maybe even the occult." Mitch took another bite of his sandwich while Nicole processed what he had just told her.

"He allegedly died under mysterious circumstances ..."

Nicole cut him off. "Who hasn't in this house?"

"True, but anyway, his death may have occurred in a house he designed, or he vanished from before completion, leaving a segment of the design undocumented."

Nicole sputtered. "Like the secret passage? Was it supposed to be more?"

"Not sure, babe."

"Where can we get copies of the original plans for this house?"

"Might not get the actual blueprints, but we might find some things out at the local Land Registry Office, or Municipal or County Archives, or even the Provincial Archives. The local historical society might even have documents. Not necessarily the plans, but correspondence between the person who wanted the house built and Greaves."

"That's a lot of legwork."

"Or, we might get lucky and find something here in the mansion that's been hiding in the open all this time."

Mitch was prepared to make sacrifices, even if it meant travelling to Toronto to find out information on the house and the eccentric architect's death.

"Invited my brothers for supper tonight."

"You might have asked me first."

"Sorry. I didn't think you'd mind, and I thought they'd be keen to find out what we'd discovered here. And, no, it has nothing to do with that person with the four-letter name we won't mention."

Chapter Nine

MARCH 27, 1832

The chill of the early hour clung to the air as Elias Greaves arrived at the Brighton site before the men. It was barely light out. He carried a lantern to guide him. A layer of frost covered the grass, and his boots left dark prints on the frozen ground. He liked these moments; the quiet before the shouts and hammering began, the raw timbers waiting for the day's shaping.

He strolled the perimeter, eyes trained on the skeleton of beams that resembled the house in his mind. His fingers brushed a joint, tracing the gap where two timbers didn't quite meet flush. He frowned. Not large enough to compromise. The walls would hold. The men had worked hard, and he had pressed them to keep pace with his plans. To tear out and start over again, to repair a minor flaw would cost weeks.

Still, he stood and gazed at the joint.

The smell of damp wood seemed to thicken, turning acrid in his memory. For a heartbeat, he wasn't in Brighton but in Kingston, the dust, the shouts, the sudden, deafening roar when stone and timber gave way. He heard it even now. The crack like thunder, followed by men's voices, which had turned from laughter to screams.

Greaves gripped the beam until his knuckles whitened, his breath locked in his chest, and his heart pounded in his ears. That day had never left him. The rubble, the silence which followed. The accusing eyes of survivors, looking not at fate, but at him.

He blinked hard, forcing himself back to Brighton and the solid timber beneath his hand. This was not Kingston. This house would stand. He would see to it, his determination a comforting reassurance in the face of his past errors.

And yet, as he straightened and drew in a deep breath, the flaw seemed larger than before.

A crow cawed from a nearby fencepost, its voice raw in the frozen morning. The sudden sound jolted the serene atmosphere. Greaves pulled his coat tighter and told himself it was nothing. Nothing at all.

Mrs. Cole's boarding house stirred with the creaks and signs of waking tenants. Whitmore was already dressed and perched by the narrow window of his room with his journal open on his knees. He had slept little. The dark thoughts that tormented him all night remained long after he had snuffed the candle.

Now, with pale light spreading across the rooftops of Brighton, his pen hovered uselessly over the page. Words refused him.

Greaves's voice lingered in his ears. Firm, commanding, so sure that the men seem to follow without question. Whitmore had seen it often enough in others. Charisma, leadership, the sort that could bend will to its purpose. And yet ...

He had also seen the way Greaves's gaze lingered in the beams, sharp, appraising, then dismissive. Flaws that another man might have paused over, Greaves brushed aside with that same certainty. Whitmore could not shake it from his mind. The timbers were sound enough for now, but was *enough* ever truly enough?

The question needled him like a thorn.

Whitmore tapped his pen against the paper in a restless, staccato rhythm. He thought of Kingston and the voices he had overheard in the tavern, the whispers that would not let him rest. He thought of the men labouring on the site, trusting Greaves with their safety.

The heaviness of his duty bore down on him, a burden he could not shake. What *was* his duty?

The tension between action and inaction was

palpable, a knot in his stomach that refused to unravel. Staying silent was easier. Leaving Brighton and pursuing the trail to Kingston would be costly and fruitless. To confront Greaves outright might be reckless, and yet, could he live with himself if he chose inaction and another calamity followed?

The morning light sharpened, cold and thin through the window. Whitmore shut the journal with a decisive snap. He had written nothing, but the silence of the page seemed answer enough.

He realized with a jolt that something would have to be done, and soon.

Chapter Ten

JUNE 19, 2023

Mitch sat at his drafting table, unable to concentrate on the business of completing the designs to restore another Victorian property. He'd visited the owners, taken plenty of pictures. Things they wanted preserved, and other things that could go. His eyes kept drifting to the bookcases. Was there something more about Elias Greaves in one of them?

He stood and walked to the shelves. He had lucked out and found a snippet in one of his texts, and some limited information on Wikipedia. His fingers traced along the spines of his books. He paused at ***Foundations and Façades: Visionaries of Pre-Confederation Architecture***. Dr. Helen Marchand authored the book and published it in 1987. He pulled it out and scanned the index for the surname Greaves and found it.

> ***Chapter 4. The Forgotten Eccentric: Elias Greaves (1805-1870)***
>
> *While William Thomas shaped the public and ecclesiastical identity of Upper Canada's growing towns, and James Renwick, Jr. brought Gothic Revival to American soil, Elias Greaves toiled in relative obscurity along the St. Lawrence River and Lake Ontario.*
>
> *Contemporaries often dismissed Greaves's work as unnecessarily elaborate and structurally indulgent. His use of hidden passages, deceptive symmetry, and faux ruins*

foreshadowed a taste for the theatrical more commonly associated with stage design than architecture. Some scholars speculate Greaves may have drawn inspiration from John Nash's picturesque country homes or even the darker, cathedral-like grandeur of George Gilbert Scott's later works.

Unlike Thomas or Renwick, Greaves left behind few buildings and few patrons. What remains of his legacy exists in private dwellings, cryptic sketches, and the occasional critique printed in local newspapers. Yet, recent scholarship has begun to re-evaluate his influence, particularly as the public's fascination with 'haunted' houses and romantic ruins has grown.

Mitch sat back. He couldn't believe what he had discovered about the man Nicole sketched from a bloodstain and the newspaper article he had found. The article continued.

The line between genius and madness is narrow, and Greaves tiptoed it in iron-soled boots.

If that wasn't ominous, Mitch didn't know what was. He continued reading.

Letter from Charles Whitmore, apprentice to Elias Greaves, 1835

By all outward appearances, Elias Greaves should have found success equal to that of his peers. Educated in Edinburgh and briefly apprenticed under the renowned Scottish architect, Thomas Rickman, and possessing a fine hand for Gothic detail, Greaves arrived in Upper Canada around 1831 with ambition stitched into every seam of his frock coat.

But Greaves was not content to replicate.

> *He was determined to create "buildings with memory," often designing features that evoke emotional responses rather than serving functional purposes. His private commissions, few as they were, included chimneys built at odd angles to "direct warmth toward the heart of the house," staircases that curved not out of necessity but as a "gesture of welcome." Most famously, a walled-off nursery said to be accessible only by crawling through a child-sized door concealed behind a panel of embossed plaster. His designs were not just structures, but living, breathing entities that resonated with the emotions of their inhabitants.*

Was that the room used as a nursery by Nicole's ancestors?

> *Critics balked. "Whimsy has no place in stone," wrote one editor. Greaves replied in a now-lost pamphlet titled* On the Sentience of Houses, *which he claimed to have been co-authored by his "dearest muse. The house itself."*
>
> *Greaves's drawings, discovered posthumously in trunks and behind false walls in his former residence, are rife with marginalia: notes in verse, sketches of gargoyle-like faces, and annotations in mirror writing. One early floor plan included a room labelled only "for grief."*
>
> *His final commission, an estate west of Cornwall known colloquially as Greaves House, was both his masterpiece and his undoing. Rumours persist he lived in its tower room alone for the last months of his life, claiming he was "consulting the structure" and awaiting an answer. He disappeared in 1870 without a trace, leaving behind a mystery that still haunts the architectural world.*

> *While Greaves never achieved the recognition of his contemporaries in his lifetime, modern scholars of architectural psychology have reexamined his work. Their findings suggest that his focus on emotional resonance and spatial symbolism places him decades ahead of his time, sparking a fresh wave of excitement in the architectural community.*

Mitch needed to share this with Nicole, but there wasn't time for her to read the entire chapter before her brothers arrived. He left the book open, facedown on his architect's table and headed out to his workshop. He still had work to do out there, and it would not do itself.

Even though there was plenty of room at the table in the kitchen to seat four comfortably, Nicole opted to set up the formal dining room for supper. She didn't use the fine china housed in the sideboard, but pulled out the melamine placemats covered with paintings of orange Maine Coon cats. They had to belong to her aunt. The woman had a cat of this breed and colour named Bruiser. The familiar sight of these placemats brought a sense of comfort to the room.

Mitch passed through the kitchen on his way out to his workshop. "We're not entertaining royalty. It's only your brothers," he said, his voice carrying a hint of playful banter.

Nicole rolled her eyes at the comment. "Other than you, they're the only family I have," she said, more abruptly than she intended. "Sorry, just running into you-know-who and the weird things happening here, I'm flustered."

Mitch moved closer and drew her into a hug. "I know. You're not the only one who's questioning their sanity at the moment. I still don't believe in ghosts, but our buddy Elias seems to want to make a believer out of me."

"Buddy? That's a bit much, isn't it?" Nicole suppressed a giggle. "Anyway, back to supper, we use the kitchen all the time. I thought it would be nice to eat in here for a change. It's not like we don't have the space."

"I'll give you that. Headed out to the shop for a bit," Mitch said before leaning down and kissing Nicole on the cheek.

This house, with all its foibles, had grown on Nicole. Now, the enigma of Elias Greaves unveiled another piece of the puzzle. That didn't necessarily mean they'd see them all. They might be thwarted. Like a 1,000-piece jigsaw puzzle, finished save for one piece, the mystery of Elias Greaves loomed, waiting to be solved.

At about six o'clock, the familiar sound of Cooper's SUV increased as he drove up the driveway. Nicole peeked out the kitchen window. They were here. Mitch was still out in his workshop. Another thing they had done since moving in was to get permission from the township to install a driveway off the main road. It circled the house and kept access to the old route off the back.

"Hey, sis. Something smells good," Connor said as he hugged Nicole.

"I can't believe the difference in the place since we explored it and you inherited it. You and Mitch have done a fantastic job," Cooper said, adding his comments to the conversation.

Cooper rarely passed out compliments, but he was even less inclined if it meant mentioning Mitch's name.

Before Nicole and Mitch married in the house, they had completed most of the work, but they did more afterward. A few things she had refused to compromise on, and one was the ornate light on the newel post.

"So, what's up?" Connor asked. "Not like you to invite us for a home-cooked meal with no strings attached. What do you need moved? Your donkeys are here."

"It's nothing like that, but I want to wait for Mitch to come in before I tell you."

"You're not."

"No, I'm not about to make you two uncles any time soon."

"Then what? Can you at least give us a hint?"

"No. I want to wait until we're all here." Nicole heaved a sigh. Sometimes her brothers were pains, and this was one of them.

Mitch heard the car pull up the driveway. Things had been better between him and Cooper, but not great. They used to be inseparable, like two peas in a pod, but life had pulled them apart. He put his tools away, brushed the sawdust off his clothes and strode towards the house.

The sun was setting, casting a warm glow over the countryside. "Hi, guys," he said when he opened the door. "Did Nicki offer you a beer or anything?"

"No, but we're driving, so probably shouldn't," Cooper replied, a hint of a smile playing on his lips.

"I think there's some near beer in the fridge."

Nicole turned away from the salad she was prepping on the table.

"I'm going to grab a quick shower," Mitch said.

"Can you light the barbecue before you head upstairs, please?" Nicole asked.

"Sure thing, babe," he said, a sense of responsibility in his voice.

Mitch turned around and went back onto the porch and lit it. He placed his hand on the side of the propane tank and hoped there was enough left in it to cook whatever his wife planned on for supper. He intended to take an empty tank to Brighton to fill or swap. So far, it hadn't made it to either place. He hoped they wouldn't run out of fuel partway through cooking.

"Barbie's lit," Mitch said when he re-entered the kitchen. He paused long enough to give Nicole a kiss on the cheek before heading upstairs.

Chapter Eleven

MARCH 27, 1832

The morning mist clung low across the fields as Whitmore stepped onto the Brighton site. From a distance, the half-formed skeleton of the house jutted skyward like bony fingers. As he moved closer, the rasp of saws and the strike of hammers became audible. The chorus of the men's labour was quickly becoming familiar.

Men moved with a rhythm that spoke of long practice, hauling timber, mixing lime, setting stone. Whitmore made notes in his pocket journal. The progress on the western wall was steady, but in need of bracing. The quality of the timber was sound. He found himself in awe of their precision, an emotion he struggled to conceal. A stranger still, and an outsider with an ink-stained hand among men with calluses.

One of the younger masons nodded at him as he passed, but most kept their eyes on their work, their concentration obvious. Only when the overseer shouted orders did the clatter break and voices rise like gulls startled from the shore.

Whitmore paused near the frame of the great window that would one day overlook the sprawling front gardens. For a moment, he almost pictured it finished with curtains, firelight and laughter. He closed his journal with a snap, unwilling to dwell on fantasies.

It was the afternoon before Greaves appeared. The man carried himself with an ease that commanded the surrounding ground, a stark contrast to the ruggedness of the building site. His coat, too fine for a construction site, billowed in the wind. His boots, well-polished, stood out against the thick mud of the plot. Men straightened subtly when he paused, some with respect, others with unease, a tension that filled the air.

"Taking notes again, young Whitmore?" Greaves's voice was smooth and bemused.

"For the record," Whitmore said evenly.

Greaves smiled broadly and knowingly. "Then be sure you record shows this house will stand long after we are all gone and reduced to dust."

He gestured towards the rising walls as though he had laid every stone himself. Whitmore shifted under the man's gaze. He sensed there was something concealed behind that polished exterior. The charismatic figure and the tale he had overheard in the tavern fought for the apprentice's attention.

Greaves tipped his hat, eyes glinting. "Write it down, young Whitmore. History has a way of favouring the bold."

Whitmore said nothing, though his pen hand itched. Later alone, he would set it down in his diary. Greaves, charismatic, magnetic, yet curiously alien. The men obey, but do they trust?

The wind rose and rattled the loose boards, and the thought of Greaves's departure lingered with Whitmore long after the man had strode away, leaving a sense of mystery in his wake.

Greaves liked the way the men fell silent when he approached. Not out of respect, that he knew full well, but out of something closer to fear. Fear was serviceable. It kept the mortar mixed and the timbers cut, and it spared him from the tedium of repeating himself.

Whitmore, though. The fellow with his notebook, always scribbling as though ink would steady stone. Greaves had caught the look in his eye, skepticism laced with fascination. He smirked at the thought. Whitmore and the likes of him would never understand what it took to make a thing endure. Not words. Not paper. Will.

Boldness. The audacity to demand permanence of a world built to crumble.

Let them whisper in taverns if they wished. Let them tally the debts that would not be called in while Greaves was still alive. What mattered was the house. His house. His monument. When the walls rose, and the roof crowned them, who would recall a few mutterings over ale? His self-assurance was unshakable.

He poured himself a snifter of brandy and lifted it in a silent toast to the future. Fear, fascination, or slander — he would turn it to his advantage, his cunning strategy always at play, his mouth opening and closing like a fish out of water.

Chapter Twelve

JUNE 19, 2023

"So, what do you think of this place?" Connor pulled out his phone and showed Nicole and Mitch a large Victorian house with a narrow tower with two tall, round-top windows on each of the four sides.

"Interesting."

"Why don't we explore it on the weekend?" Connor said, a glint of excitement in his eyes.

"Where is it?" Mitch asked.

"Well, here's the thing. It's in the middle of a small town west of Cornwall. One of many communities affected when they built the Seaway."

"That's risky, don't you think?" Nicole asked, her tone cautious. "And isn't that an ADT sign along the fence?

"Ah, but here's the beauty of it, sis. The house is up for sale."

"Have you gone completely bonkers, Connor Holbrook? Are you looking to get us all arrested?" Nicole's voice rose with concern, her eyes narrowing at her brother.

Mitch stood, walked to the kitchen, and leaned on the sink. The words that had just left Connor's mouth dumbfounded him. Use a real estate agent to gain access to a property to explore. It was a clever ploy, making it seem legitimate, but was it ethical? The thought of it being a waste of the realtor's time troubled him. He couldn't imagine that he and Nicole would want to buy the place. Yet, the property held a strange allure. Was it the asymmetry that intrigued him? Or was it the fact that Elias Greaves, a name shrouded in mystery, had a hand in its construction? While it wasn't as grand as their house, the design was of the same era. So, possibly he was.

He and Nicole hadn't told her brothers about their latest findings here. Mitch heaved a sigh and came back into the room.

Nicole sighed as Connor scrolled on his phone, the room fraught with tension. Mitch sat across from her, arms folded, his expression tight with unease.

"I found the listing," her brother said, turning the phone so she could see the Victorian home on the corner lot. Connor leaned back and smiled. "You book a showing, saying you're interested and pose as prospective buyers to the real estate agent. Technically, you're not doing anything wrong. Then, after you arrive, you tell him or her that your brothers are meeting you there. You're planning on a home office kind of thing, and we're there to check Internet speed, Wi-Fi viability or even wired connections."

Nicole frowned. "It's still dishonest."

"I'll give you that. But it's legal. And it gets us inside without hopping fences or dodging security cameras."

Mitch rubbed the back of his neck. "It feels off. If we're pretending we might buy it, doesn't that cross a line?"

"We're not stealing anything," Connor countered.

Nicole remained silent. Her gaze drifted towards the foot of the stairs, where the low creak of the old house settling made the hairs on her arms stand on end. "This house is giving us more than enough to dig into at the moment."

Cooper raised an eyebrow. "You mean ghostly sketches and bloodstained secret passages?"

Mitch snorted. "Actually ... yeah."

Nicole picked the worn textbook from the sideboard and opened it to the page she'd carefully marked without dog-earing the place. She set it on the table in front of her brother. "Mitch found this in one of his old architecture books. There's a paragraph about Elias Greaves. He designed this house."

"This is when it gets creepy. The other night, blood dripped from the ceiling in our bedroom. Mitch went up the next day with his big ladder and bright work lights. The blood up there was dry. It hadn't flaked or anything, just a dark spot on the floor. I sketched it, and it wasn't until I had almost finished that I realized what it was."

Mitch looked at his wife. "It was a face. I recognized it from somewhere, but couldn't place it. Then I found a brittle, yellowed newspaper article under a false bottom in our wardrobe. Nicole's sketch matched the man in the photo — Elias Greaves. It was further confirmed with the textbook entry."

Cooper looked from one to the other, visibly unsettled. "So you're saying ... Greaves is haunting the place?"

Nicole didn't even blink. "I'm saying something happened here. Something that no one has ever explained. And I think Greaves is trying to show us what it was."

A silence settled over the room, the kind that hummed with possibility and dread.

Her brother exhaled. "Okay, well ... that's a twist. Like there already hadn't been enough of them related to this place."

Mitch leaned forward, elbows resting on the table. "If we check out this other place, we need to be smart. It might connect back to this. No doubt, Greaves worked on more than one house."

Nicole met Connor's eyes, since it was his idea to visit this other Victorian mansion. "We'll go. But no games with the realtor. We ask questions. We look for clues. And if something feels wrong, we leave," she declared with determination in her voice.

After a brief pause, her brother nodded. "Deal," he agreed, his voice firm.

Later that night, when the house had fallen into the still routine that came when darkness fell, Nicole headed upstairs. The light was on in Mitch's office, and the door was slightly ajar. She peered in, her curiosity piqued, but her husband wasn't there. A book lay face down on his drafting table. She frowned. Mitch had never been one to leave a book that way.

Gently, she lifted it and smoothed the spine. ***Foundations and Façades: Visionaries of Pre-Confederation Architecture.*** The book was open to Chapter 4. She gasped when she read the title. *The Forgotten Eccentric: Elias Greaves (1805-1870).*

Nicole sank into his chair and pulled the book closer. "Of course."

The author painted Greaves as brilliant but secretive. Further in the chapter, Greaves described his designs not as eccentricities, but as deliberate concealments, hidden chambers, narrow stairways, and passages designed as though the walls themselves had something to remember.

Nicole traced a finger down the margin until she came to an account by one of his apprentices. A line in this section made her pause.

> *Some believed his greatest works carried messages meant for a future he would never see, but hoped would one day understand.*

Her chest tightened. She leaned back and stared out the office window towards Mitch's dark workshop.

Quietly, she said in the empty room, "We understand, Elias."

Nicole left the book open to the page, the words lingering in her mind. She retrieved her sketchbook, flipping to the image she had sketched of their home in Brighton long before it became theirs. Back when they first explored it with her brothers. On the sheet, she wrote *meant for a future he would never see.*

She set the pencil down and studied the two objects side by side. Mitch's textbook and her sketchpad. Scholarship and imagination, fact and interpretation.

Closing his book gently, she placed it exactly where Mitch had left it, but left the image of the house angled on top. A quiet answer, waiting for him to notice.

With one last glance through the window at the darkened workshop, Nicole said, "Now it belongs to both of us."

She turned off the light and slipped out into the corridor, leaving the conversation open for Mitch to discover.

Mitch pushed the door open, expecting to find the drafting table as he'd left it. Instead, his eyes caught the difference. His textbook wasn't alone anymore.

Her sketchbook rested on top, angled deliberately. He smiled as the image of their house was where she had left her book open. One of the very first sketches she had made of this property. In the margin, next to her careful lines, was his favourite sentence from the textbook: *meant for a future he would never see.* The sight of their personal items together on the table filled him with a sense of warmth and connection, a tangible representation of their shared past and future.

For a moment, he just stood there, the silence of the room holding him. Still, Mitch could almost perceive the talk between the two tomes, a muted exchange that reflected their own. His precise diagrams and footnotes; her fluid sketches and instinct. Scholarship and art. His world and hers, meeting on the pages the way they had in life.

He thought back to when they first explored this mansion. It was old, abandoned, and dusty, with a vertical secret passage that led off from the tower room. Tall, cobweb-infested, and creepy. But in the middle of it all, Nicole's eyes shone. She had seen something there that he had missed. Her inheriting the mansion and land from her aunt was a total surprise, even more than discovering his wife's Holbrook family had owned the property.

He traced her pencil strokes with his fingertip, then closed the sketchbook carefully, placing his hand over both. "Yeah," he said to the empty room. "Ours now."

Then he left the light on, as though keeping watch, and went to find her.

Chapter Thirteen

MARCH 28, 1832

The sun hovered low behind the trees. Charles stood at the clearing, shovel at the ready, watching Mr. Greaves crouch beside the foundation trench, his fingers stained with lime and dirt.

Elias had not spoken to him for well over an hour. He muttered now and then, but not specifically to Charles. To the stones? Or to the house he claimed was already here? It was invisible to everyone else until someone or something could persuade it into the world.

Charles cleared his throat. "Sir?"

Greaves didn't look up. "The angle must be precise, young Whitmore. The sun, the land, the slope of that elm. We must respect the lines that already exist."

Charles stepped closer and peered at the markings scratched into a slate board propped up beside the trench. "This isn't the layout you showed me last week."

"No. The house shifted." Greaves stood and dusted off his coat. His dark eyes were bright with something Charles couldn't name. "It will not be bound by my first intentions. She ..." He paused, tapping his chin with his bony right index finger. "Required adjustment."

"She, sir?"

"The house. She speaks if you learn to listen." He looked at his apprentice, and his expression softened. "Perhaps you're still too rooted in squares and rules."

Charles bristled. It wasn't the first time his employer had ridiculed his education. Somehow, like the other times, he held his tongue.

Greaves turned towards the woods."We build for the living, yet. But we also build for the silence between their footsteps."

"I don't follow," Charles said, furrowing his brow.

Greaves smiled, as if he didn't expect him to understand. "You will."

The older man walked off, his boots crunching over gravel and roots. Charles remained, staring at the half-finished trench and the misaligned foundation markers. The house was not square. Not symmetrical either. Not anything like he'd learned in his apprenticeship back in Toronto. But people respected Greaves, mad as he might seem. Feared, especially when the man spoke of buildings that whispered long after the mortar dried.

Charles exhaled and returned to the trench, but his thoughts lingered on the way Greaves had said *she*. It was as if the house was waiting for something or someone.

Elias stood alone at the rim of the clearing as he watched the half-formed foundation gleam in the fading light. The air was thick, smelling of pine and wet earth, but his thoughts were elsewhere. He tethered his mind to the shape that hovered just beyond sight, the spirit of the house he sought to summon.

He ran a hand over the rough stone hewn for the tower's base, his fingers tracing patterns no one else saw. The world called him mad. His peers dismissed his designs as eccentric at best and heresy at worst, but Elias knew the truth. The house was not just alive; it was a mystery, a vessel for something older than timber and mortar.

"She is waiting," he said, his voice barely louder than a breath. "For the right moment and for the one who can hear her call."

He strengthened his resolve. The foundations might shift and the walls might twist, but he would see his vision through to completion. No matter the cost.

The distant bark of a hound came from the woods

behind him. Elias turned; a faint shadow crossed his face. It was a flicker of doubt buried beneath the unwavering commitment to his obsession.

Yet, even as night fell, the house seemed to pulse with a hidden life, and Elias Greaves was its unwilling, anxious servant.

Beneath a canvas stretched between trees, Elias hunched over his table. By now, the moon had risen high over the clearing. The candlelight flickered across the scattered parchment and sketches, casting a warm glow that fell through the long shadows. Still, none reached the corners of his restless mind, a mind haunted by the ponderousness of his task and the fear of failure.

His quill scratched feverishly, drawing intricate lines that twisted and spiralled, akin to a secret language. The designs were more than mere architecture. They were an invocation, a blueprint to unlock something buried deep beneath the earth, a secret only he could decipher.

He paused; his fingers trembled as he retraced the shape of the tower. "She demands it," he said with urgency. "Not just stone and wood, but a passage. A gateway."

The wind rustled the leaves above his head, and the canvas flapped, its ropes loosening and tightening with the sway of the trees. Elias didn't flinch. He was not just a resident of this house, but a part of its story, bound to it by purpose and madness.

As the candle guttered low, he leaned back, exhaustion clawing at his limbs. Sleep was a stranger to him now because the house was waiting. And so was he, his weariness confirmation of his unwavering dedication.

Charles remained in the foundation trench near the makeshift canvas shelter. The scratch of Elias's quill reached his ears like a steady heartbeat. Each night, the architect worked later. The fever in his eyes burned brighter than the flickering candle.

He watched as Elias leaned close to the drawings. The man's lips moved in whispered incantations no one else would understand. The lines on the parchment seemed to twist and writhe, shifting from blueprints to something else. Something alive. The mystery of Elias's work deepened with each passing moment.

"Mister Greaves," Charles finally said, "you must rest. This work consumes you."

Elias didn't look up. "Rest is for those who only build with stone and timber. I am crafting a doorway, young Whitmore. A passage to things beyond our world."

Charles swallowed hard; his unease settled like a rock in his gut. He had seen the man change. Once Elias Greaves, driven by pride and vision, was now haunted by shadows that only he saw. His once bright eyes were now sunken and rimmed with dark circles; his once vibrant spirit was now consumed by a dark obsession.

"I fear this patch may lead us into darkness," Charles said, his voice tinged with concern, stepping closer.

Elias's eyes flashed, fierce and unyielding. "Dark and light are two sides of the same coin. I will see this through no matter the cost." His resolute tone echoed in the night.

Charles nodded. His warning would go unheeded. The house was already claiming its master.

After a filling meal of potatoes, beef, and carrots, followed by a slice of Mrs. Cole's infamous apple pies, Charles returned to his room. There were so many things that seemed strange about this house outside of Brighton that his employer was building; he needed to get them committed to paper before they vanished from his mind.

> *As I write this by candlelight, the flame flickers far more than usual. Is it a draft? It shouldn't be because I closed and latched the window, and my door is well closed.*
>
> *Mortar dust still cakes my hands. Will I*

ever get it off completely? Somehow, I doubt it. My knuckles split and bruised when I pried loose those damn floorboards on the third level. Mister Greaves insists it is necessary. The angles must be reset, but he can never explain to me what he means. It's always 'to align with the flow' or 'to let the house breathe properly.' Whatever that means. I just know it's maddening.

The man speaks as if the house were a person, or worse, something more ancient and listening. What does that mean? He said to me one day as I was leaving, 'This place does not take kindly to the inattentive, young Whitmore.' Even from his perch on the scaffolding of the tower, I could see his eyes. They weren't angry, but sharp. Too sharp.

I tried to sketch the new layout from memory, but the rooms don't fit together. The nursery adjoins the tower stair, but no stairwell exists on that side of the house. Will they install it in time? With Master Greaves, it's hard to say. The measurements of this house defy the geometry we rely upon, and I fear I've made a mistake in accepting this apprenticeship.

It's as if the house noticed me, and a part of me remains tied to it now. Worse than that. It welcomed me.

I mustn't dwell on this. It will drive me insane if I do. I'll write no more tonight. My candle is low, and I hear tapping from the floorboards. No doubt it's Mrs. Cole telling me to snuff my candle and go to bed, for tomorrow is another early start.

Charles closed his journal, dried off the nib of his pen, and closed the inkwell. He'd try one more time to get the grime from the day's work washed off before he retired. Not that it would do any good. The grime was embedded in his skin.

The last thing he did before climbing into his bed was pinch the candle wick between his wet thumb and forefinger to douse the flame.

Chapter Fourteen

JUNE 24, 2023

Mitch pulled his truck to a stop just past the cracked sidewalk. Nicole leaned forward in the passenger seat, squinting through the windshield at the house. It looked even more tired than in the photos Connor had shared on his phone. The second-floor shutters hung crooked, and a gap in the fascia made the roofline appear as if it were sneering.

"This is the one?" Nicole asked, unzipping her backpack and pulling out her sketchpad and pencil case. She began sketching the house from this angle while they waited for the realtor to arrive.

Mitch nodded. "Hard to believe it's for sale."

"And not condemned," she said.

"That's what makes it interesting. And what vibes you pick up from previous lives lived in it."

A rusted number plaque clung to the wall as if it were afraid to fall. The house loomed behind it, brick mottled with lichen, and the lace curtains inside the bay window were yellowed and torn.

A sleek black car pulled up behind them, much newer than Nicole's hatchback and Mitch's truck. The realtor, a blonde woman, maybe in her mid-thirties, wearing a navy blue pantsuit and a white blouse, stepped out, holding a clipboard and a planner under one arm.

"You must be Mitch and Nicole," she said as she approached them. "Lovely day for a showing."

Nicole kept her smile locked in place. "It is. Thanks for meeting us."

"No trouble at all. This is a bit of a hidden gem. Needs TLC, but you won't find craftsmanship like this anymore."

Now that they had exchanged pleasantries, Nicole returned to eyeing the house. It had a watching quality. Almost as if it knew who she was.

Inside, the air shifted. Cooler, heavier, and a mustiness lingered. Dust motes hung in slanted beams of sunlight that slipped through the holes in the curtains.

Mitch trailed a hand along the banister. "Original railing?"

"I believe so," the realtor said. "The house builders constructed it in the mid to late 1860s, but parts of it might predate that. There was talk of an addition or a rebuild over a foundation from an earlier structure."

"Do you know who designed the house?" Nicole asked.

The woman flipped through her notes. "The listing mentions a man named Elias Greaves. He was an architect in this region in the mid-1800s. Apparently, this was his last project."

Mitch glanced at Nicole. She kept her expression neutral, but her fingers tightened on her sketchpad and pencil.

They moved through the rooms. Someone redid the kitchen in the 90s. Ugly linoleum, fluorescent lights, and boring beige. Walls, cabinets, everything. The upstairs was another story. This was the way the house would have been when it was first built – ornate plaster mouldings and patterned floorboards.

In one of the back bedrooms, there was a narrow, warped door barely three feet high.

"What's in there?" Mitch asked, his curiosity piqued.

"Storage, I think. Some old linens and such."

"I'll take a look," he said, his determination unwavering as he crouched to open it.

Nicole stood in the middle of the room. Something

pulled at her peripheral vision. A flicker. The ornate border of a picture frame. She turned.

A faded portrait hung on the hallway wall outside the room, partly obscured by shadow. Nicole walked towards it. Through the dust-covered glass, a face peered out at her. A man with piercing eyes, a sombre face, gaunt and severe. Nicole leaned closer. Elias Greaves. Despite their agreement, go ask questions and leave, she flipped to a new page in her sketchbook and captured the face within the frame.

The face was no stranger to her. She'd sketched it from the blot on the floorboards back in the mansion she and Mitch called home.

"Nicole?"

She jumped, startled by the sudden interruption. Mitch stood beside her, equally surprised.

"That's him. From the patch on the floor in the room above ours," Nicole said, pointing.

"Yeah, that's him all right."

The realtor appeared behind them. "That's the original owner, I believe. Or one of the early ones at least. Funny thing, they say he disappeared. The house sat vacant for years afterwards, but I wouldn't put much stock in old ghost tales."

Nicole didn't reply. Her gaze remained locked on the man in the frame. She experienced it again. That faint static hum in the air. Something or someone was trying to speak. And they were listening now.

"May I ask what your interest in this property is?"

Nicole and Mitch looked at each other. "We're looking into heritage homes for the possibility of converting them to holiday rentals. I'm a graphic artist, and my husband, Mitch, is an architect with a background in restoration."

"Interesting."

"My brothers will be meeting us here. They're coming to check how difficult it's going to be to upgrade the house for wired or wireless Internet, as that's part of our business plan."

"I'd like to check the wiring in the basement,"

Mitch said, his conscience pricking at the deception. "Can you show me where the entrance is?" He didn't like it, but it allowed them to explore.

The realtor's smile faltered for a moment, a flicker of unease crossing her face. She pointed to the door leading to the cellar, just as her phone rang. "Excuse me, I'll just step outside to take this."

The narrow steps creaked with every step Mitch took. The air, thick with mildew, grew cooler as he descended. The walls were damp. Bare, cobweb-infested lightbulbs hung from pigtails, creating strange shadows. His phone's flashlight barely cut through the gloom, but it was enough to detect the hulking silhouette in the middle of the room. The tension in the air was unmistakable, adding to the suspense of the moment.

"Damn."

A cast-iron furnace loomed like an enormous beast, its rusted ducts stretched outward like limbs. He took a step closer, instinctively ducking as one of the ancient pipes dipped low over his head. The thing was a relic and took up most of the floor space. Industrial-sized and original to the house, or close to it, and filled about half the room. This part of the basement didn't seem as large as the upstairs. Had someone divided the space into different rooms, and he hadn't found the access to the others yet? The furnace, with its ominous presence, added a sense of dread to the scene.

Mitch swept the light across its side, where the manufacturer's plate had almost corroded away. Only a few etched letters remained, barely readable under the oxidation. "GREA ..." followed by a smear of rust.

"Greaves?" he asked. It couldn't be that. He leaned in closer. There was more writing, but it was hard to make out. He decided to take a picture of the mysterious nameplate. Nicole might be able to bring it out more. She had done that with other photos taken at previous sites.

His flashlight beam jittered as he adjusted his grip, sending shadows dancing across the foundation walls. Something that resembled a doorway, or a brick-arched opening. He edged around the monstrous heating system, careful not to brush against the low-hanging pipes, which were likely covered in asbestos, a popular insulation material.

In this part of the cellar, the floor was uneven. Not even concrete, but packed dirt in places, and old brick in others. The house had clearly shifted over time. Mitch crouched next to the brick section. It didn't match the rest of the wall. Different mortar.

He reached out and ran his hand across the bricks. A faint draft curled through a tiny gap in the mortar, cool against his skin.

"Mitch?"

Nicole's voice echoed from above, faint and distorted.

He stood and brushed the dust from his jeans. "Down here," he replied.

"What's taking so long?"

Mitch hesitated. Something in this space didn't want to be disturbed. But, he couldn't ignore it either. "You wouldn't believe the size of this furnace," he called.

His gaze remained on the strange wall. Someone had sealed off whatever had once been here — and not with the same care or material used elsewhere. It was as if they had done it in a hurry, leaving a residual mystery in the air.

He took a photo with his phone, but paused in front of this abnormality in the wall. The furnace groaned behind him as the house settled, a long metallic creak that sounded too much like breathing.

Nicole stood in what once would have been the parlour. The room where elegant Victorian ladies had tea and cucumber sandwiches and chatted over embroidering. She crossed her arms as she took in the room's unusual dimensions. The wallpaper had long since yellowed and peeled at the corners. Still, the bones of the house were elegant with graceful archways, elaborate crown moulding, and even the remnants of a once-grand chandelier hung from a decorative ceiling medallion. A creak on the floorboards behind her made her turn.

"Nicole."

She looked up just as Cooper stepped inside, followed by Connor, who wiped his feet on the mat outside the front door.

"You made it." She smiled at her siblings, relieved to see them. "The realtor left the door open for us. She'll be back in half an hour."

Connor whistled as he scanned the room. "This place looks as though nobody has lived in it for years."

"Decades, more like," Cooper said. "It's like a museum in here."

"Kind of like mine and Mitch's place when we first explored it."

"Yeah, but empty longer."

Nicole tucked a strand of hair behind her ear. "It's been on the market forever. Big place, big problems and small town."

Connor grinned. "So, naturally, we're here to investigate. Where's Mitch?"

"In the basement," she said. "He found an ancient furnace. Said it looked like something out of a horror movie."

Cooper let out a chuckle. "Hope he doesn't get eaten by it."

Nicole half-smiled but didn't laugh. Something about the house had already gotten under her skin. The quiet, and the way the rooms seemed to breathe when you weren't looking. Her encounter with Brad earlier in the week, which she had yet to tell her brothers about, lingered in the back of her mind, along with the eerie vision in the mansion.

Connor nudged her shoulder. "You okay?"

She nodded. "Yeah, just ... places like this, you know? Too many stories in the walls."

"More for us to wire," Cooper said, pulling a small flashlight from his pocket. "Let's look around, figure out where the easiest cable runs might go."

Her brothers were playing their parts in this exploration well. Nicole opened her mouth to reply, and the floor creaked overhead. All three turned towards the sound.

"Was that Mitch?"

"No," she said. "He's still downstairs ..."

The siblings exchanged glances.

Connor forced a smile. He had experienced sudden chills in rooms and heard unexplained noises when they explored Kembleford Manor. "Old houses make noises."

"Yeah," Cooper said. "Sometimes, they also watch you back."

Nicole let out a breath she didn't realize she'd been holding and headed to the base of the stairs. "Let's find Mitch."

Cooper was the first of the siblings to descend the steps into the basement. Stone foundation. He pressed his palm against the wall. Damp. Dampness and mildew filled the air, making him sneeze. The furnace was as enormous and evil-looking as Mitch had told Nicole earlier.

He turned his flashlight towards the ceiling. Totally unfinished. The bare floor joists and underside of the subfloor above were all that was there. Some plumbing pipes and electrical wires threaded their way through, creating a web of galvanized pipe and plastic-coated wire. Cooper made his way to the panel. A previous owner updated the electrical service at some point. He searched for the approval date of the job, but he couldn't find it.

Connor navigated towards him, dodging the ductwork as he went. "Don't much fancy setting this up for wired Internet. I think Wi-Fi is the way to go with repeaters added to boost the signal where it weakens."

"I agree," Cooper said, taking off his ball cap and wiping his forehead with his upper arm. "Where did Nicki go? She was with us a few minutes ago."

"Still on the other side of the furnace sketching and ..."

Connor didn't get the chance to say anything more because the flash from Nicole's camera lit up the dark, dingy space in a brilliant flash of light.

Cooper spotted Mitch and worked his way to

where the man stood. "What've you found?"

"Check it out. It appears someone bricked this in at some point. I've been through this entire part of the cellar, and this differs from the rest."

Cooper ran his hand over the rough surface of the old brickwork, then paused. "Is there another basement in the other section of the house? There's a draft here. It just blew on my neck."

"I felt it, too. I thought I imagined it since it was so faint. But if you experienced it, as well ..."

"Want to check and see what's behind it?"

By now, Connor had joined them. The men discussed how best to remove just one brick so they could look beyond the wall. There was one weak spot where the mortar had fallen away partway around a single block.

"Nicki, you might want to come watch and be ready with your camera and sketchpad," Cooper called.

Nicole found her way to her two brothers and husband. She arrived just as Mitch was pulling his jackknife out of his pocket. As he worked the blade into the crack and wiggled it to remove more mortar, she sketched him working. The camera flash was too bright at this proximity and would blind him. She didn't need him to injure himself again after the episode when he cut his finger on broken glass.

She flipped to a clean sheet in her sketchpad, ready to capture the next stage. Just then, a waft of what looked like smoke but didn't smell like it curled into the air. She furiously sketched this. "Close your eyes, guys. I'm going to take a picture and don't want to blind you."

When they assured her they were ready, she snapped several photos in quick succession. The motor-drive for her DSLR was a godsend. It would continue to shoot as long as she held her finger on the shutter button. Newer cameras had the feature built into them, but she loved this model and never saw the need to upgrade.

"Okay, I'm done," she said, lowering the camera.

The blade of Mitch's knife scraped against the mortar, but the progress was slow. When he finally had it removed, he gripped the brick and wiggled it out of position. It dropped to the dirt floor with a hollow thud.

"What's behind the wall?" Nicole asked, trying to peer through the small hole over her husband's shoulder.

"Dunno." Mitch aimed his flashlight through the opening. "Damn. That's strange."

Nicole pushed forward and shoved the lens of her camera through the hole and shot another burst of images. She backed up, and while Mitch held the light for her, she looked into the space they had found. It was narrow, barely the size of an old elevator shaft. At first, she thought it was a damp and claustrophobic space. Shadows and dust, nothing else. But then Mitch's light caught something.

Someone had set a narrow bench or built-in seat into the back wall. Was this a priest hole? Presumably, the same person had carved the wood panelling. Not a decorative design but precise, architectural lines etched into the surface.

Something rested on the seat. It appeared to be a small, square, leather-bound book; its cover warped from the moisture. Next to it, a rusted lantern and an ancient boot? Not a pair, just the one, ancient and brittle with age.

The air in this small, confined space smelled of old iron and damp cloth with an underlying cloy of something metallic, almost like blood.

"We need to get in there," Nicole said. She relayed to everyone what she'd seen. "It might have been a priest hole, but with this side bricked over, how did a body hide in it? The back wall appears solid, too. Do we know what's directly above? Think there's a trapdoor in the floor above?"

"I think we're just in front of the bay windows. If there's access to this hidden room, it's likely to be there," Mitch said, his architectural knowledge showing.

"Are we going to put the brick back in place?"

Nicole asked.

"We don't know if the realtor has visited this chamber of horrors yet. If she has and sees the brick missing, she'll know it was us," Connor said, wiping his palms on his thighs.

Cooper picked up the block of fired clay and set it in the opening. "If anyone doesn't look closely, it won't look like we disturbed it," he said.

Mitch wrapped his arm around Nicole's shoulders, and they started towards the stairs. Something was on her mind. He knew her well enough to recognize that thoughtful expression. She wanted to retrieve the contents of that room, if only to photograph the pages in the old book, and return it. His removal of the mortar in the wall pushed their "take nothing, leave only footprints" mantra.

Once upstairs in the corridor, he led the way to the place where he figured the access to the sealed room was located. A dusty area rug covered the floor with a heavy, sheet-covered sofa set in the centre. Mitch was about to move the couch when the front door opening and closing stopped him dead.

"Hello again. Seen everything you need to see?" the realtor said, entering the room where they stood.

"We've got a plan for the Internet now, so we'll be on our way," Connor said, nudging his identical twin.

"We're good," Cooper agreed, and the two shuffled to the other side of the room.

Nicole adjusted her bag. "My husband and I would like to come back for another viewing. There arc still some things we need to work out."

Chapter Fifteen

MARCH 29, 1832

The thaw had left the ground slick and treacherous, a stark contrast to the sharp scent of pine that clung to the air. Mud sucked at boots with every step across the site. Whitmore picked his way along the rutted track where wagons had hauled in fresh-cut timber that morning.

Greaves stood at the centre of it all, his coat unbuttoned despite the chill, voice raised above the clatter of axes and the rasp of saws. He moved effortlessly between crews, sharing a jest with the carpenters shaping beams, offering a firm word to the men laying stone for the foundation. Everywhere he turned, men seemed to straighten, respond, and even smile.

Charles Whitmore held his notebook open, recording the event. *Timber delivered, foundation progressing, local men employed at good wages.* Factual, neat, and precise. Yet, his pencil slowed as he watched Greaves. That magnetic quality unsettled him. A man whispered about in the tavern, accused of the building's collapse, yet here, nothing but confidence and charm.

The clang of a hammer on iron pins rang out, startling Whitmore with its suddenness. He shut his notebook a little too sharply. He had lost the sound because of the din from the building site, but it still echoed in his ears. He could not reconcile the man before him with the shadow hinted at in hushed voices.

Greaves's laugh, warm, commanding, and untroubled, carried across the site. Whitmore adjusted his grip on the book, its leather cover slick beneath his damp glove. Perhaps, he told himself; it was best to keep to facts, but unease clung to him as stubbornly as the mud on his boots.

The mud was no hindrance to Greaves's authority. He strode through it as though the mire was a mere inconvenience, just as the Red Sea had parted for Moses. His shoulders were square; his steps deliberate. Men looked to him instinctively, others with wariness, but all with a deference he relished.

"Keep those beams steady, lads. You'll thank me when the walls stand straight," he called, his voice loud enough to carry over the scrape of the saws. The air was thick, smelling of sawdust and the sound of hammers on nails. A ripple of laughter answered him when he said, "And when you aren't sleeping under a crooked roof."

It cost him little to jest, less still to nod his approval when a young carpenter drove home a peg true and clean. Praise was a coin men never tired of, and he spent it freely when it served his purpose.

Greaves paused at the edge of the site, surveying the rising skeleton of the structure. Not much to look at yet, but he saw it as clear as day. The shape. The promise. Brighton was young, raw, and ready to be impressed. This mansion, his brainchild, would make its mark, confirmation of his vision and ambition. And so would he.

He caught sight of his apprentice hovering at the margins, notebook in hand, lips pressed tight in that way of his. The young man was useful, diligent, though too keen-eyed for his liking. Greaves let his smile linger as he met Charles's gaze, warm and unbothered, until Whitmore, sensing the severity of his stare, looked away.

Confidence won men as surely as money. And both he intended to have in abundance.

The boarding house was quiet except for the faint creak of timbers settling as the night air cooled. Whitmore sat before the small desk in his room, a candle burning low, its flame illuminating the notebook open before him. His pencil hovered over the page above his earlier entry from the site.

Timber delivered. Foundation progressing, local men employed at good wages.

Charles tapped the pencil against the margin, his mind wrestling with the decision. He could leave it there, only reporting what was observable and nothing more. Yet his hand strayed towards the back pages of his book, where he sometimes tucked personal notes between official accounts. A place for thoughts not meant for other eyes.

He paused, pencil poised, his inner turmoil clear. To write his doubts would be to give them shape, perhaps even life. Better to let them drift unspoken, as uncertain as the spring fog still clinging to the village streets.

With a sharp motion, he closed the book. The decision sat uneasily with him, a heavy weight on his chest. He extinguished the candle, lay back on the narrow bed and stared into the dark. The echo of Greaves's laugh still lodged in his ears.

Chapter Sixteen

JUNE 24, 2023

Nicole and Mitch walked to the front door ahead of the realtor. They stood on the porch while they waited for the woman to lock the house.

"Next Saturday?" Nicole asked, anticipation filling her voice. "We work during the week, so it has to be a weekend viewing."

The realtor brushed her hair back from her face and opened her planner. "Next Saturday is Canada Day. What about the following Saturday at two o'clock? Does that suit?"

"Perfect," Nicole said, with a smile. She was disappointed to have to wait an extra week before their next viewing.

She and Mitch returned to his truck, which he had parked on the northwest corner of the intersection.

"Another showing?" Mitch asked, arching his eyebrow.

Nicole nodded. "Absolutely. There's something about this place. Too many secrets in too little space."

"I don't know if I need another viewing, but I'd love to get my hands on the blueprints for this place," Mitch said as he opened the truck door for Nicole.

"Do you think that room in the cellar would be on them?"

"Possibly," he said, climbing in behind the wheel. "Although if that was an afterthought, maybe not. All we know is that Elias Greaves had something to do with this house and ours."

"I'm going to text the guys and see if they want to

come back with us next time. If we're going to get into that room, it's going to take more than just one person."

"You won't be helping?" Mitch asked in a tone of mock-surprise.

"I'll be documenting your progress." She left the conversation at that and pulled out her phone.

Mitch & I are returning to the M'burg house on July 8 for a 2:00 viewing. Want to meet us there, or we can pick you up?

"I suggested we could pick them up. I mean, your truck is big enough for all of us. Or they can meet us here, like today."

Mitch shook his head but remained silent. Five hours — two and a half each way — with Cooper in the same vehicle? Sure, things had been better between them since his and Nicole's engagement, but they were still far from perfect. The tension between Mitch and Cooper lingered, and then there would be the time they'd be in the house, too. He hoped they'd prefer to meet at the location.

Today, they hadn't seen the entire house. There was still the third floor, mainly in the eaves. And the tower above that? If indeed it was a tower. It could be an elaborate way of letting more light into the upper level of that section of the house. Without seeing it, he couldn't hazard a guess. The basement and the bricked-in room took up most of their time. Elias Greaves's photograph hung on one wall on the second floor.

Greaves had designed his and Nicole's house as well. So, that there were oddities in both didn't surprise him. But what happened to the man? Did he go insane? Hang himself from one of his towers? The newspaper article said Greaves vanished in 1870, before completing the work on this house. Who finished it? He knew he didn't enjoy having to come in and finish a job that someone else had started. Did his apprentice complete the job? So far, all they were getting were more questions. The lack of answers was becoming increasingly frustrating.

"I didn't tell you about the manufacturer's plaque

on the furnace," Mitch said, glancing towards Nicole. "The letters GREA were all that remained. Corrosion destroyed the rest of it."

"I'll search online and see if I can come up with anything while you're driving."

"I took a picture. I'll send it to you when we get home. Think you can work your magic and make it clear?"

A ping sounded in the truck's cab before she had a chance to answer. Nicole picked up her phone. "Connor says they'll meet us. Save you getting off the highway at Belleville and driving to their place."

"Tell him thanks." Mitch sighed with relief. He hoped it was low enough that his wife didn't hear him. Nicole wasn't dumb. She knew things weren't good between him and Cooper, better but still far from ideal. It was possible Cooper was as uncomfortable around Mitch as he was around him.

Nicole jumped out of the truck before Mitch shut off the engine. "I need to check my pictures. I'll start supper after that." She dashed into the house, sat at her desk, removed the SD card from her camera and plugged it into the slot on her laptop. While she waited, she drummed her fingers on the desk. It seemed to take forever. But then it always did when she was anxious to discover what the camera captured. Finally, the screen filled with thumbnail images of the photographs she had taken in the parts of the house they had been in during the viewing.

The ones she was most interested in were the ones shot through the opening in the wall into the concealed room and the mist that wafted out from behind the barrier. She scrolled down until she found the image. Whatever that was turned up in the photo. So, it wasn't anything supernatural, or not likely to be.

Nicole zoomed in on the first image she had taken through the opening. The lantern sat off-centre with the warped book propped against the wall. But just behind it ...

Her stomach flipped. It was a shadow. Nothing

more, nothing less. But it was a figure. Lean and tall, with blurred edges like fog trapped on film, or when light got into the camera. No one stood behind her. She would have sensed it. Mitch stood to her right, and her brothers on her left.

Nicole scribbled down the image number of that one so she could show Mitch later and send it to her brothers. She continued flipping through her burst shots of the carvings on the wall. One frame near the end included something that wasn't in the previous ones. She scrolled backwards to double-check them, and nothing else appeared. It was faint. It almost looked like it was bleeding through from behind the wooden wall. A single word. RETURN followed by the initials E.G.

The screen door slammed shut behind Mitch when he entered through the kitchen. He knew he'd find Nicole in front of her computer looking at the pictures she'd taken. He stopped at the fridge and peered inside. A cold beer would wash away the dust and grime on his insides, but there wasn't any in it. Instead, he grabbed a glass from the cupboard, filled it with cold water from the cooler, and gulped it down. They were on a well out here, and the water was hard. The softener worked well for laundry, showering and cooking, but not drinking. Without going through the device, the water tasted of iron and other minerals, and through it, it was salty.

Before Mitch went upstairs to shower, he stopped to see what Nicole had discovered from her pictures.

"I think I found the name of the furnace manufacturer," she said, minimizing her photo screen and bringing up the browser with several images on it. "I think this is our best bet."

GREATON IRONWORKS LTD.
HOT WATER Heating Works
Est. 1836
Patent No. CA2438791
Toronto, U.C.

Mitch took his phone out of his pocket and pulled up the image. It might be the company. He forwarded the photo to Nicole. "Just sent you the picture of what remains of the plaque. I'm going to shower."

"Wait a minute. I have to show you these," Nicole said, excitement filling her voice. "Look. The mist that curled out of that sealed-off room. I really wasn't expecting the camera to capture it, but it did. And this, this shadow on the back wall. It's as if Elias Greaves were standing behind me. And I know that's impossible because it was only you, my brothers and me down there."

Strange things had occurred when the four explored Kembleford Manor. Things Mitch couldn't explain, but Nicole saw. They even happened here in this house. Before she inherited it and afterwards. So, it wasn't beyond the realm of possibility that they happened in that house, too.

Chapter Seventeen

JUNE 28, 2023

Once Nicole had cleared everything away from their supper, and she had tidied the kitchen, she went back to the sketches she had started earlier. She sat cross-legged on the floor of the room where she kept her laptop. It was on the floor with the folder of all the photos she'd taken through the gap in the wall where Mitch had removed the brick.

Pencil in hand, she traced the symbols that were carved in the wall at the back of the sealed room inside the Morrisburg property. Nicole spread the other sketches she had made of the house among them. She tried to recall every angle, every curve. The evening sun slanted across the room but barely reached the far corners, where shadows lurked.

Mitch leaned against the doorframe, arms folded. "Still at it?" he asked.

She glanced up, eyes focused. "I can't stop thinking about them. Every time I look, there's another detail that doesn't fit. It's like he's left pieces of a puzzle I can't fully see yet."

He stepped closer. A simple unlit beeswax taper in an iron holder with a finger ring sat on the desk. "Think a little light will help you think?"

"It might, not that it will solve the puzzle for me."

Nicole lifted the candle to the slash of light coming through the window. The object glowed as if someone had put a match to its wick. For a moment, the room seemed to breathe along with her thoughts. She shivered, not from cold, but from remembering what she had seen in that house, in that small room, in every corner she had glimpsed.

Mitch squatted beside her. "Whatever it is you're chasing," he said, "you're closer than you think. You've already seen more than most people ever will."

The candle flickered in the draft, and both of them glanced towards it. It remained unlit, and yet the shadow it cast seemed to stretch with intention, almost like a silent sentinel waiting.

Mitch exhaled. "Okay, that's enough eerie ambiance for one day," he said, though his eyes lingered a moment longer on the candle. "We'll figure it out, Nicki. Piece by piece."

She nodded, set her pencil down, and leaned back. The quiet of the room pressed in, broken only by the sounds of country living. A dog barked somewhere in the distance, followed by terrible screams.

"Sounds like a coyote caught himself a rabbit," Mitch said.

Nicole only half heard him; her focus remained on the unlit candle, which reminded her that the past was never far away.

Mitch crossed the room and stooped over to examine the candle. The wick swayed, though the flame wasn't even lit. It was almost imperceptible, a movement at the edges of his vision that made his stomach tighten.

"Did you see that?" he asked, his voice barely above a whisper.

Nicole glanced up from the array of sketches around her. "See what?"

He shook his head and forced a smile that didn't reach his eyes. "Never mind. Probably just my imagination. This place has ... character." Not just character, but characters. Nicole's father had witnessed a Freemason ritual gone wrong. The ghosts of the Grahams and Holbrooks, from whom she descended, were previous owners of the property.

Even as he spoke, his gaze drifted back to the candle. The shadow it cast on the floor appeared to ripple, as if it were breathing. He rubbed his neck, trying to shake his unease. Rationally, he knew it was impossible. The candle was unlit. The draft in the room wouldn't do that.

Still, the sense of someone watching, of someone lingering just beyond perception, washed over him. A thread of instinct whispered at the back of his mind. *Pay attention.*

Nicole reached out and laid a hand on his arm. "Mitch," she said, "it's just shadows. This house has crazy angles, so there will be some weird-shaped patches of light and dark."

He nodded, drew in a steadying breath, letting her calm anchor him. Yet, as he looked at the candle once more, the flicker returned — faint and teasing. It wasn't malicious, but it carried a weight, a quiet insistence that made his skin prickle.

He leaned back, shook off the lingering dread and smiled at Nicole. "Okay," he said, trying to sound lighthearted. "Maybe it's just a stubborn draft. Or maybe we've got a ghostly apprentice watching us work."

Nicole laughed, but he saw the same flicker of apprehension in her eyes. They shared a glance that was equal parts thrill and caution.

Mitch straightened and raked his fingers through his hair. Whatever the candle wanted, whatever the past was nudging them towards, they'd face it together. For now, though, he'd keep one eye on the shadows and the other on Nicole.

Chapter Eighteen

APRIL 1, 1832

The village was quiet this Sunday morning, more so than usual. The indistinct murmur of livestock drifted across the fields, and the faint clatter of distant work from neighbouring farms. Elias moved through the half-built Brighton house with the ease of a man intimately familiar with every timber and joint. No labourers today, so no curious eyes to question his actions. Today, it was only him and the empty beams waiting for their story.

He crouched by a corner post, chisel in hand, and traced a subtle notch into the wood. Preserve. Protect. Endure. Each mark was deliberate, yet almost invisible to the casual glance. His fingers stayed on the grain, sensing the echoes of those who might pass through here decades later.

A hollow board creaked beneath his knee. He paused and listened. Nothing but the wind teasing the half-open windows. His secret would remain just that. His silent dialogue with the future.

Greaves moved through the rooms methodically, leaving faint marks in shadowed corners, along unseen beams, and under floorboards that would eventually cover them. Each notch and tiny cut was a message from a guardian embedded in wood. He imagined that one day people would uncover them, eyes widening in recognition. They wouldn't know him, but they would know his care, his foresight, and his insistence that some things should survive, unseen but present.

Finally, he stood in the centre of the hall and let

his hands brush the surrounding beams. The house would rise around these marks, shelter them, and carry them forward. Satisfied, he packed away his tools and stepped outside. The sun glinted off the snowmelt in the yard.

No one would know he'd been here today, so no one would see the delicate symbols hidden in plain sight. But he did, and that was enough.

Chapter Nineteen

JUNE 28, 2023

The candle flickered again, casting long, trembling shadows across the room. Mitch shifted in his chair, eyeing the tiny flame as if it held secrets he hadn't yet earned.

He tried to shake it off. The draft? Probably, but the movement of the shadows was wrong. It was too deliberate for a simple gust of air. His gaze drifted along the archway, which divided this room from the one at the front of the house. The spot where the candlelight kissed the wood seemed … different. Subtle notches, almost imperceptible, caught the glow strangely. Impossible. When the subcontractor removed the pocket doors and the opening reframed and finished, there were no exposed beams.

He ran a finger along the grain, and the irregularity under his palm was rough. Goosebumps prickled his skin.

"It's nothing," he said, muttering to himself. But even as he said it, the feeling of presence, of intent of someone, or something, had left a message for him to find centuries ago stayed with him.

Across the room, Nicole's pencil scratched against her sketchbook; the sound grounded him in the present. Yet, he kept glancing back at the flickering candle. Each shadow it threw seemed like a whisper of the past, echoing the carefully hidden markers that Greaves left behind, waiting for eyes that could read them.

Mitch exhaled slowly, a mixture of dread and awe curling within him. He didn't understand yet. Perhaps he never fully would. But he could feel the connection, the invisible thread stretching across time. And somehow, that thread carried a warning and a promise.

Nicole leaned over her sketchbook, pencil hovering above the page, tracing the curve in the newel post from the Morrisburg house's main staircase. The candle beside her trembled in its holder, casting a light that danced over the graphite lines.

Her eyes flicked towards the ceiling. Shadows pooled along the walls, stretching and shrinking as the flame danced. She tilted her head and frowned. "It's just a draft," she said with a whisper, though her voice sounded too small in the high-ceilinged room.

She returned to her sketch, but her pencil faltered, as if it, too, sensed something. The line drawing seemed to catch the light differently, to suggest a depth she hadn't intended. Nicole glanced towards Mitch, who was watching the flame with a tense, unreadable expression.

"Do you feel it?"

Mitch's jaw tightened. "Yeah ... like it's not just a candle. Like it's pointing out something."

Nicole looked back at her sketches, eyes narrowing. The marks, the subtle notches in the beams, the curves that only someone paying attention could read. They weren't just decoration. Someone intentionally left them, knowing that one day others would notice them.

The candle flickered again, sending the shadows into brief, unnerving shapes. Nicole swallowed. She didn't need to understand it fully. She just needed to *see*, and trust that the past had left them a map, if they were careful enough to follow it.

Mitch watched Nicole's hand move over the sketchpad, her pencil scratching against the page. The soft glow from the candle on the table cast long shadows across the room. Shadows that seemed to lean closer to the corners than they should.

He frowned. The flame flickered, small but

insistent, as if someone, or something, were nudging it. A draft? No. The windows were closed and the house still. He shifted, unsettled by the way the shadows danced across the tabletop.

Nicole paused mid-sketch, eyes narrowing at the candle. “Did you see that?”

Mitch shook his head. “See what?”

She tilted the candle; the light catching a tiny groove along the edge of the table. It was almost imperceptible, but enough to make the flame wobble. Nicole traced it with her finger; a quiet hum escaped her lips. “It’s ... like someone wanted me to notice it.”

He leaned closer, heart beating a fraction faster. “Or maybe it’s just the candle,” he said, though his voice lacked conviction.

Nicole didn’t answer. Her gaze lingered on the flicker, on the subtle indentation in the wood. Deep inside, Mitch sensed a similar odd draw as she did, as if a breath of time was touching them.

The shadows shifted again, almost knowingly, as if carrying a message only meant for those paying attention.

He exhaled slowly, forcing himself to relax. “Well, if it’s a message, at least it’s polite enough to wait for the right eyes.” He tried for lightness, though his chest remained tight.

Nicole smiled faintly, but her eyes stayed on the table. The candlelight danced, and for a moment, Mitch sensed the past leaning close, curious, patient, and watching.

Chapter Twenty

JULY 8, 2023

Nicole had risen early, her heart pounding with excitement, eager to get back to the house and that warped book in the concealed room in the cellar. While the coffee brewed, she put together a picnic lunch for herself and Mitch. She cooked breakfast and put it in the oven at a low temperature to keep it warm.

She'd like to come home along the river. They had built the seaway long before she was born. Before her parents, too. It wasn't until Connor mentioned it in relation to the house they'd quasi-explored two weeks ago that she had developed an interest. They might stop along the Long Sault Parkway on their way home.

How were they going to get inside that small room? They couldn't remove all the bricks that closed it off. That would be too obvious. Did the owner of the book hide away down in the bowels of the house and draw plans? Keep a diary? There had to be another way in there. The mystery of the sealed room was like a puzzle waiting to be solved. Perhaps the next occupant of the property sealed it off after the owner of the book died. That made sense. Then there were the strange carvings on the wall.

If they went straight to the room on the side of the house where the bay window was located, and they moved the heavy sofa, folded back the area rug, they might find a trap door in the floor.

Someone needed to keep the realtor occupied while this took place. If Nicole had anything to say about it, she wouldn't be the one. She was determined to keep her investigation a secret, to uncover the truth on her own. She needed to get down there, sketch and photograph the space in situ. There might be things that revealed themselves only to her.

"You're up early."

Nicole turned in the voice's direction. Mitch stood in the doorway separating the front hall from the kitchen.

"Coffee's almost ready. I made us a picnic lunch. Although it might be more apt to be an early supper depending on how things go at the house. Can we drive home along the river? At least part of the way? Eat somewhere on the Long Sault Parkway?"

Nicole's eyes sparkled when she was excited. This house exploration and a drive along the river were the cause of it. He grabbed his mug from the tree. Every time he used it, it made him smile. Nicki had picked it up somewhere. Someone had emblazoned the words *REAL men marry graphic artists* on the side. Knowing his wife, she designed it and had a company print it. He'd have to come up with one for her. Something better than *#1 wife.*

"I can't see why not. We definitely won't have time before the appointment, so we'd best eat a big breakfast."

"Sausages, eggs and mushrooms suit?" Nicole asked.

"Sure."

"Sit down, then." Nicole bent over and pulled two plates of breakfast out of the oven. "Here you go," she said, placing one plate in front of her husband. "Over hard, just the way you like."

"How long have you been up?" Mitch never smelled the aroma of cooking sausages wafting up from downstairs. During the week, they never had big breakfasts. A muffin, croissant, or something fast since they both worked.

"An hour or so. Too excited about today. Couldn't sleep. I hope there's a way into that small room in the cellar from above. I need to get in there to see everything. Sketch and photograph the entire space."

Mitch put his hand over hers. "Slow down. I'm only guessing there's a way from above into that room. Maybe the only way in is the bricked-up passage in the basement."

"If that's the case, we'll never be able to get a look inside that book."

"Even if we do, there's no guarantee we'll get anything useful from it. After all, it looks to be in terrible shape. Mould and mildew might have ruined or destroyed it." Mitch hoped his words reassured her, but he didn't want to dampen her spirits too much.

Nicole mulled over Mitch's words as she chewed on a sausage. She'd seen the mist. Even her camera picked it up. The carvings on the wall, too. Sometimes, he was too practical for his own good. Yes, there might not be an alternate way into the sealed room, but if there was even a sliver of hope, she'd follow it. That one picture ,with the single word 'RETURN' followed by the initials 'E.G.' had piqued her curiosity. She needed to find out what E.G. was trying to tell her. It was a message from beyond.

It wasn't the first time she'd experienced strange phenomena in a house. Kembleford Manor was the weirdest. The ghosts of Albert Kembleford, his daughter Ophelia and grandchild, Anna, all appeared to her, not to mention the tragic death of little Grace Birkhoefer there.

This house had ghosts, too, but so far, they were closer to Nicole and her brothers than those in the mansion at Pike Falls. These were her direct ancestors. Her father, aunt, grandfather, grandmother and back through time. She discovered that her mother descended from the Kemblefords several generations ago. Not quite the same.

Whoever Elias Greaves was, he designed and built this house, as well as who knows how many others. Why else would the blood that dripped onto her from the room above reveal his face when she sketched the dried stain on the bare wooden floor? The man had a hand in building the house that she, Mitch, and her brothers would return to later today.

Chapter Twenty-One

APRIL 2, 1832

Charles Whitmore bent over the drawing board, the scratch of his pencil the only sound in the dimming light. Greaves had already left for the day and had left him to finish the elevation for the parlour wall.

It was almost complete. Only the finishing lines for the moulding, but something about the upper corner made him pause. There it was again. That enigmatic diamond with a loop motif, a symbol that seemed to hold a secret waiting to be unveiled.

At first, he'd assumed it was just one of Greaves's flourishes. Ornament for the sake of ornaments, but the more drawings he finished for the man, the more Charles saw it. Not always the same size. Sometimes the design stretched into a border. Other times inverted, but always hidden, never part of the official client presentation sheets. It was as if the symbol held significance beyond its mere appearance.

Why?

He leaned back and rubbed his eyes. In the low light, the symbol seemed to shift. For an instant, he thought it was coiling inward like a seashell. He blinked, and it was a mere drawing again.

Greaves never explained these things. When Charles had once asked, the older man had fixed him with that sharp stare and said, "Some details are best left to the master's hand." His secretive nature heightened the intrigue.

But what details and why repeat them? Charles

shook his head and decided not to finish the corner. He'd wait until morning and Greaves. Better for him to fill in his own secrets.

Still, he made a quick copy of the motif on a scrap of paper and tucked it into his notebook.

Just in case.

Elias Greaves closed the door to his hotel room behind him, the latch clicking softly. He was a man of secrets, preferring to work in silence, away from the clatter of tools and the curses of apprentices who lacked his patience for precision. Charles, a talented boy, had been staying up late, as his curiosity easily distracted him.

Greaves settled at the desk and unrolled a set of plans. His next commission, to be built in Kingston, spread out before him. The inked lines seemed to breathe in the lamplight. Geometry and proportion were married to something older and more profound, a mystery that only he could unravel. He traced a long, thin fingertip over one of the hidden marks woven into the design. Most people would see only a flourish of ornamentation, but to those who knew, it was a key.

He thought of Charles's endless questions, his sidelong glances at the older blueprints. It would not do for the young man to notice the repetitions. The way certain angles aligned with the points of the compass, or how each of his grand houses hid the same faintly inscribed motif.

The house in Brighton was nearly complete. By the time it stood in all its splendour, it would hum with the same timbre as the others.

He dipped his pen in ink and began to annotate the draft, his motions smooth and deliberate. Each line, each mark, was more than design. It was an invocation.

Outside, the wind grew stronger, and dry branches scraped against the window. Greaves didn't look up. He had work to finish before the night was done.

And young Whitmore ... well, he would have to be kept at a distance.

The day's labour clung to Whitmore. Dust in his cuffs, the ache of sun and wind across his face. He climbed the narrow stairs to his room at Mrs. Cole's boarding house, boots heavy on the worn treads, and thinking of the simple but filling supper below.

As he turned the key in the lock, a folded letter caught his eye, resting on the floor of his room. The landlady, it seemed, had slipped it under his door in his absence. The seal, now bathed in the last rays of daylight, added to the mystery.

He stooped, picked it up, and a faint unease swept over him as soon as his fingers touched the paper. The crest was one he knew from Toronto, a city he had left behind years ago. An old acquaintance, whose handwriting had always carried a kind of precision. Cautious.

Inside the words were cordial. Reports of timber shipments slowed because of the spring flooding. The mention of a mutual colleague now employed near York, a man Charles had once trusted with his life. Harmless at a glance, but a line in the middle of the page gave him pause.

The warehouse still casts a long shadow here. Some wounds are slow to close.

He read it once, then reread it. The edges of the paper dug into his fingertips as if the words pressed back against him.

The room was hushed except for the faint creak of timbers. Somewhere below, the muffled clatter of crockery marked the first serving of supper. Whitmore remained rooted in place, staring at the letter as though it contained a cipher he could not break, fooling the walls of the room closing in on him.

When he folded it again and slid it into his breast pocket, he found no answer in himself. Only the heaviness of the memory. In the tavern, he overheard a hushed exchange about a past they should have buried. Unease stirred slowly, and he thought perhaps Kingston had not finished with him.

Supper had been plain but hearty, a warm respite from

the chill of the evening. Mutton stew, bread that leaned towards stale, and strong black tea. Mrs. Cole had baked pies during the day, and he enjoyed a slice of her apple pie. The chatter around the table had been a welcome distraction. When the landlady cleared the plates and the tenants drifted away, the familiar solitude returned to wrap itself around Whitmore's shoulders, a cold shroud in contrast to the warmth of the meal.

In his room, the air was close, almost suffocating. It carried the mingled scents of wood smoke and damp plaster, a stark reminder of the harshness of his surroundings. He lit the stub of a candle and sat at the narrow desk, his journal open before him. The letter lay beside it, the broken seal like a wound that refused to close.

He dipped his pen, poised over the page. Words should have come easily. Observations on the day's work, the slight miscalculation he had noticed in the masonry. The manner in which Greaves commanded the site with confidence that might yet shade into arrogance. All of it begged recording, if only to make sense of the unease coiled within him.

His hand hovered; the nib caught the faint tremor of indecision. Writing would give shape to what troubled him. To set it down would be to admit his doubts had teeth, sharp and biting, tearing at the fabric of his resolve.

Instead, he leaned back, pen suspended, eyes unfocused on the flickering candlelight. The room seemed filled with a deafening silence, the house settling, footsteps receding on the street outside, and his conscience pressing hard against him, all magnified in the absence of any other sound.

In the end, he closed the journal without a word written, the blotter unused, and the ink still fresh in the well. He slid the letter into the drawer, as if burying it would bury the thoughts it stirred.

But when he stretched out on the narrow bed, the darkness offered no relief. *The warehouse still casts a long shadow.* Some wounds are slow to close, and his unease, like a persistent ache, refused to be ignored.

Whitmore turned and faced the wall. He set his jaw, and he knew he could not leave it unwritten forever.

Chapter Twenty-Two

JULY 8, 2023

Nicole nudged Mitch as they stepped into the parlour above the sealed basement room. She gazed at the antique sheet-covered sofa and the equally old, patterned rug beneath it. "This is it. We're directly above the hidden room in the basement, if your calculations were correct."

Connor and Cooper had already split off on their quest to distract the realtor. "Five minutes," Connor mouthed from the hallway, as he steered the realtor towards the kitchen.

The couple sprang into action, their shared goal uniting them. Mitch took one end of the heavy sofa while she grabbed the other. It groaned as they tried to move it. Even he couldn't get it more than a couple of inches off the floor. She couldn't lift her end at all. The rug beneath it bunched as they shifted it.

Nicole dropped to her knees, her fingers scrabbling at the corner to pull the carpet back. "Please let this be the place."

The rug peeled back, and there it was. A square outline, slightly darker than the rest of the floor. A tarnished iron ring sat flush with the boards, invisible if you weren't looking for it.

Nicole tugged on the ring with determination. Mitch dropped beside her, his eyes reflecting their shared curiosity. The hatch popped open with a jerk and a puff of stale, earthen air. Beneath it, a narrow wooden ladder led into the darkness, a challenge they were both eager to accept.

Muffled voices and footsteps sounded from above. "Quick. We'll go down and look. I'll get some pictures. If we hear anything, we close the hatch and pretend we were admiring the floorboards." Nicole said, her voice low and urgent. The plan was to investigate the sealed room without raising suspicion.

Mitch grinned. "Classic urban explorer logic," he said, referring to the strategy of blending in and appearing innocent when caught in a potentially compromising situation.

He went first, and they disappeared into the shadows, the rug folded back beside the open hatch.

Nicole paused about halfway down the ladder, her hands clutching the rungs. When she exhaled, her breath misted in front of her. The air grew colder the moment Nicole's foot touched the dirt floor. She swallowed. It was colder down here than it should have been.

Mitch's phone light cut a harsh beam through the gloom, casting eerie shadows. The small room was barely larger than a closet, with crude brick walls that were not entirely even. The only wooden wall stood behind the bench. The warped book remained propped against the wall behind the lantern. Today, before she pulled out her camera, the space seemed ... different, in a way that sent shivers down her spine.

The shadows pulsed. Nicole turned slowly. The carved lines in the wood seemed more jagged today. It seemed someone had cut them in haste or rage. Her eyes traced the pattern, and then she saw it, not with her eyes, but through them.

A flicker of movement. A tall, thin man in a long coat stood with his back to her. His hands, fingers splayed, pressed against the wall as if he was searching for something. A murmur, a word she couldn't make out, bubbled in the air before it vanished.

Nicole blinked. In an instant, the figure was gone, leaving behind only the bench, the lantern, the book, and the walls. She hadn't pulled out her sketchbook and drawn what she'd seen, let alone photographed it. The sudden emptiness of the room was jarring.

She inhaled a slow, shuddering breath.

Mitch turned. "You okay?"

Nicole nodded too quickly. "Yeah, just ... feels weird in here."

"And what kind of weird do you mean? Cursed-book-and-brick-room-weird, or your usual ghost-sense weird?"

She stepped forward and crouched by the book, her hand hovering just inches from it. "Both."

A faint vibration rolled up through the soles of her boots, like something deep below the house had stirred in response. She looked up at the ceiling, the walls, at the places the light didn't quite reach. "We shouldn't stay long. But I'll sketch and photograph everything. I think someone sealed this room for a reason." The urgency of the situation was evident.

Mitch arched an eyebrow. "You mean besides aesthetics?"

She forced a smile. "Something or someone's been waiting."

Behind her, a whisper broke the stillness. One word.

RETURN.

Nicole's spine snapped straight. Her phone flashlight swept the darkness as she turned. No one was there. Only her and Mitch.

But scratched into the wood beside the lantern, fresh and unmistakable, were the letters E.G., the initials of Elias Greaves, the architect of the house and the man who had supposedly cursed the book.

Was Elias Greaves trying to communicate with her? If so, what was he trying to tell her? She didn't understand. Nicole pulled out her sketchbook and furiously captured the scene. Then she repeated the process with her camera. They had little time left. Her brothers were good, but not that good that they could keep the realtor busy indefinitely.

Despite it going against their motto, take nothing, leave only footprints, Nicole scooped up the warped book and shoved it in her backpack.

Back upstairs, Mitch had no sooner spread the area rug back over the trap door than the realtor and Nicole's brothers arrived. The real estate agent looked at the two of them with a puzzled expression.

"Admiring the pattern on the carpet. Are the furnishings included in the sale price?" Nicole asked.

The woman flipped through her notebook. "I have nothing here stating that. I'll have to check when I get back to the office."

"Please do."

Mitch couldn't help but marvel at Nicole's quick-thinking. The ease with which she effortlessly came up with an excuse for the sofa being moved was confirmation of her intelligence. He knew she was special and had been for a long time.

"If there's nothing more here you need to see today, shall we?" The woman gestured towards the front of the house.

"I'm good," Cooper said.

Connor agreed with his twin's statement.

"I'd like to look around upstairs some more before we leave," Nicole expressed her curiosity. "Is that okay with you, Mitch?"

"Sure."

The realtor, clearly growing impatient, rolled her eyes and escorted them to the main staircase.

They had toured this part of the second floor the first time they were here, but not the one above. "How do you get to the next floor?" Nicole asked.

They stood before the portrait of Elias Greaves. His eyes seemed to follow them. Almost gleam with interest.

"If there's no way to the floor above us, then why go to the bother of the elaborate dormer windows and the cupola?" she asked.

No sooner had the words escaped her lips, and the expression on Elias's face in the portrait changed from interested to angry. She couldn't apologize to the painting, at least not with a third person in the room who didn't know of Nicole's unique gift.

"The house we live in outside of Brighton is one of Elias Greaves's creations, too." Mitch paused for a moment. "If I remember from the piece in my architecture text, the man was fond of spiral staircases."

"So?" the realtor said.

"Then, one of these closed-off rooms houses a spiral staircase. The weird angles of the roofline, the ..."

Nicole nudged him before he said any more, afraid he might let slip the secret room they found in the cellar.

The door to the bedroom was open, so she entered and looked out the window. "We're directly below where the cupola is. I think the staircase will be on this side of the house. But if not, then I don't know." She rejoined her husband and the real estate agent in the corridor.

Nicole trailed her fingers along the faded wallpaper, seeking seams, panels, anything that might give.

"We've checked every door up here," Mitch said. "Except for the closet."

She ignored him and stepped closer to the end of the hall where the 'closet' Mitch mentioned stood. She opened the door and ducked her head inside. Yes, it was narrow, but deeper than on their first visit. A wooden rod ran across the top without a shelf above. But, stranger still, there was no back.

Nicole pressed her fingers along the right wall. The wood gave under her touch. A section of the panel popped open with a creak, revealing the tight curve of a wooden staircase spiralling up into the darkness.

Mitch let out a low whistle. "Damn. There it is."

The air that wafted from the stairwell was colder than it should have been and carried a faint whiff of stale air. Nicole reached into the hidden gap and grasped the railing. The wood was smooth and warm beneath her hand, like someone had used it recently, but dust lay thick and undisturbed on every stair tread. Her stomach tightened with a flicker of something she couldn't name.

It wasn't fear. Not really. Anticipation perhaps? Or memory? She turned to Mitch. "Let's go."

He raised an eyebrow but remained silent. A faint creak echoed upward from somewhere in the tower, too far away to be their weight.

A shiver prickled its way up Nicole's spine. She tightened her grip on the warm handrail. As if planned, the warmth entered her fingers.

"After you," Mitch said.

Nicole swallowed. The house seemed to hold its breath.

She put her foot on the first step.

About halfway up, the air seemed to thicken. Nicole slowed her pace as her pulse pounded in her ears. A faint scent of old wood smoke drifted past her nose, gone before she could inhale it again.

Even the railing pulsed with heat, like a hand clasped hers from the other side. She froze and glanced down. Mitch stood at the bottom, his hand nowhere near the handrail.

Something up above her whispered, but it was too faint for words, but urgent enough to make the hair on her arms stand on end.

Nicole forced herself to keep moving, each step defying the cold pressing in on her from all sides. Above, the tower landing loomed, shadowed and waiting for her.

Her breath formed a pale cloud in the dimness as she reached the last turn. The whispering from before had stopped, now replaced by an absolute stillness that pressed on her ears. She stepped onto the wooden landing, the warped boards creaking under her weight.

The tower room stretched before her, square and narrow, its tall windows weeping trails of condensation despite the unearthly cold. A single chair sat in the centre of the room, turned facing the glass as if someone had recently occupied it. On the seat's faded cushion, a shallow impression lingered, shaped unmistakably like a human form.

Behind her, the spiral stair groaned, but not with the sharp snap of a settling house. This was the slow, deliberate weight of footsteps climbing towards her.

Nicole's pulse spiked, and she spun towards the stairs, clutching the warm railing in a death grip. Another groan rose from below.

"Mitch?" she called, her voice caught in the cold air.

Silence.

The next step creaked. Whoever or whatever moved too slow for it to be Mitch rushing up to her. Every instinct screamed for her to back away, but her feet refused to move. Her gaze flicked back to the chair and the hollow in the cushion. Had the chair's occupant risen and was now coming for her?

The sound came again, but this time accompanied by a faint wet breath that ghosted up the stairwell.

Her grip on the railing burned now, as if the heat from it leeched into her bones. The cold air thickened, clinging to her lungs, making each breath harder to take.

"Mitch," she said again, but it came out only a little more than a whisper.

The step right below her creaked.

Something shifted in the darkness. Not so much a shape as a disturbance, a ripple in the air like heat on a hot summer day radiating from the hot asphalt, except this was ice. Despite everything, she held her camera up, pressed the shutter button and continued to shoot bursts of pictures in the small room.

Nicole's vision wavered, and for a split second, she saw it. Half-formed and indistinct, but the outline of a man in a long coat leaning forward, one hand reaching towards the railing where her other one rested. He traced lines in the air — sharp, angular, and deliberate — like the carvings in the priest hole.

The warmth beneath her palm surged to near scald. Nicole yanked her hand back with a gasp, stumbling against the wall.

The figure's head lifted, and in a voice as thin and brittle as frost on glass, it whispered one word.

"Return."

Then it vanished.

Footsteps pounded, real, solid and familiar. Mitch burst up from below, his flashlight slicing through the dust. "You okay? You look like you've seen a ghost."

Nicole swallowed hard, her throat tight. "I think I have."

Chapter Twenty-Three

APRIL 3, 1832

Elias Greaves stood at the edge of the property, his coat collar turned up against the morning chill. Fog had formed overnight and shrouded the half-finished mansion. The mist made the house look older than it was, almost as if it had already stood here for centuries.

Workers dedicated to their craft moved like shadows, their hammers muffled, and their voices low. He watched them without speaking, noting each measured strike, each board laid according to his plans. Even from this distance, he could tell when a measurement was off.

He stepped forward, and his boots crunched on the frost-hardened earth. One man glanced up, fear flickering in his eyes, and looked away. Good. Their performance improved under observation.

Greaves's gaze settled on the highest point of the roofline, where the final stonework would be a flourish invisible to most. When the last piece slid into place, the design would be whole.

He smiled faintly. No one here understood what they were building. Not yet.

The wind shifted, carrying with it the scent of wet earth and wood shavings. Greaves turned and walked back towards the road, his cane tapping in a slow, deliberate rhythm. The house would stand for generations, as would what he'd put into it.

Mrs. Cole's was quieter this evening, the murmur

of conversation from downstairs subdued, as if the day had drained the life from its tenants. Whitmore climbed the stairs, and each step echoed in his mind like the toll of a clock counting down.

His room greeted him with the same closeness as before. Candlelight flickered against the cracked plaster. The journal lay on the desk where he had abandoned it when he returned from the job site. The cover closed as though the object sulked at his neglect.

He sat, pulled the book towards him, and opened it to the empty page. The blotter waited, as did his pen. His hesitation clung like a weight around his wrist.

Charles kept his entry simple. No speculation, no judgement. Only the facts.

He dipped the nib and touched it to the paper.

> *April 3, 1832*
>
> *The site progresses at a pace, yet my mind lingers on its foundation. Specific courses of stone seem ill-set. Minor flaws, but troubling when considered collectively. Mr. Greaves dismisses such concerns, and no one dares contradict him.*

The words flowed haltingly and unevenly, but they were words nonetheless. Whitmore paused and listened to the scratch of the pen fade into silence. After a moment, he added more, almost against his will.

> *There is something in his manner. Assurance so complete, it borders on concealment. I cannot name the cause, only that it unsettles me.*

The line darkened on the page. Ink pooled where he had pressed too hard. He laid the pen aside, his breath slow, but his pulse quickened. Writing had not eased the weight. It had merely fixed it more firmly in place.

He closed the journal, but not with finality this time. Instead, he left it on the desk, candle flickering beside it.

As he lay down, he knew he had crossed a threshold. Whatever unease stirred within him was now recorded, anchored. There would be no unthinking return to silence.

Chapter Twenty-Four

JULY 8, 2023

Nicole sat propped up with pillows in bed with her laptop open beside her with her camera's SD card plugged into the port. The motor-drive bursts clicked like a flip-book. Wide angles of the rooms, close-ups of the cracked plaster, and dust-coated furniture. She had flipped through the photos from earlier twice already, lingering on the ones from the priest hole, zooming in on the carved lines and the warped book, many times.

She went back to the same image, where a shadow was near the far wall. Elongated, human-shaped, and blurred at the edges, as if it were moving. Nicole hadn't seen it when she took the photo, and Mitch hadn't mentioned it. A chill and a sense of unease crept over her.

She scrolled to the staircase sequence. The first few images were clear. Mitch stood at the base, looking up. The next showed her hand on the railing then she froze.

A faint shimmer bled along the banister, similar to a heat haze distortion. In the next frame, it condensed into something darker. It appeared as a shadow with edges just sharp enough to hint at a human form. The hand closest to her was pale, almost translucent, and its fingers curved in mid-gesture, tracing a pattern in the air.

Nicole leaned closer, her heart in her throat. The motion blur resolved enough to make out the shape. Angular lines intersected at odd angles. Greaves had carved the same pattern into the wall of the concealed room.

She stared until her eyes burned before she scrolled again. The figure was gone now, but in the grainy dust above the step where she'd stood, a word had taken shape, like someone had written it with their fingertip. RETURN. E.G.

Her throat constricted. The surrounding room, quiet as it was, seemed full of energy. Like someone was standing just out of view, waiting for her to acknowledge them. She closed the laptop and pushed it onto the floor, the heaviness of her aloneness clear. Her fingers were ice cold.

Sleep didn't come easily, and when it finally did, she dreamed of brick walls pressing in on her, suffocating her. Of the man, she couldn't see murmuring her name like a memory, not a warning, but a premonition of something sinister.

When she woke, a single word rang clear in her mind, spoken in a voice she'd never heard before.

"Soon."

Nicole rolled onto her other side and stared at the closed laptop on the floor. The ghost image on the screen reflected her uneasy expression. If she told Mitch, he'd want to go back, and that was the problem. She wasn't sure whether she wanted to return.

She pushed herself off the bed and paced, her arms wrapped tightly around her. He hadn't come to bed yet. When they got home, he went straight to the room he used as his home office. If he were involved in sketching the property in Morrisburg, he'd be there all night. Did she check on him? Make sure everything was all right?

He wouldn't mock her. He might not believe in the supernatural, but he believed in her photos and sketches. She couldn't make those things up, especially when both agreed.

Nicole knew she'd experienced something on those stairs. The sudden chill, the way the air pressed against her like a held breath. And now, the impossible shadow, the pattern, and that damn single word. She rubbed her arms, still chilled. For the time being, she would keep her observations and experiences private until she comprehended their significance.

Her phone buzzed, making her jump. Was it one of her brothers? She picked up the device. The text was from Mitch.

Ready for round three? We can make a reasonable excuse for a third viewing.

She typed and deleted three different responses before settling on one she hoped sounded casual enough.

We'll see.

She set the phone face down on the nightstand. The word from the photo lingered in her mind, whispering with a weight she couldn't shake.

RETURN.

Mitch stopped in the kitchen and made a mug of coffee. Nicole had been unusually quiet on their drive home from Morrisburg. Even though he'd gone out of their way to take a trip along the Long Sault Parkway before making the final head west, along Highway 2, along the river until they reached Long Beach. He got on the 401 there because, from that point, unless you drove along the 1000 Islands Parkway, there wasn't much to see. With the time they spent in the house and the stop on the way home, it was too dark to appreciate the view.

Despite his exhaustion, Mitch's mind was consumed with the house. He couldn't shake the image of the stairs, the tower, and the hidden room in the basement. His determination to uncover the house's secrets was unwavering.

Nicole's behaviour was unusual. Normally, her curiosity led her into situations without a second thought, but tonight, she seemed to contemplate every step. Mitch knew she had a unique perspective, often seeing things he couldn't. She could look at an old doorknob and see a century's worth of history, while he saw only brass and rust.

Still, she had a knack for noticing things he didn't. Things no one else did, for that matter. Perhaps her visions could help him piece together the missing bits, and he could bring the plans for the old house built by Elias Greaves to life.

Mitch sent a text to Nicole, eagerly awaiting her response. When it finally came, it wasn't the excited *hell yes* he had hoped for. Disappointment crept into his expression as he frowned at the screen.

Mitch set the phone on his drafting table, picked up his mug and drained the cold dregs from the bottom.

Chapter Twenty-Five

APRIL 4, 1832

Charles Whitmore settled at the small desk in his room. The morning light coming through the single window was pale and watery. His letter from the night before lay folded on the boards. The seal was still soft from where he had pressed it shut.

He had slept little. The words he had scrawled returned to him in fragments, phrases that seemed bolder in candlelight than they did now by day. Reckless perhaps, but dangerous if delivered into the wrong hands.

With a sigh, he opened the journal to his entry from the previous night. His handwriting was sharp and hurried, each line carrying a burden he had tried to ignore. Mentions of Greaves, uneasy choices, and shadows that seemed to cling to the stones they raised in Brighton.

Whitmore pressed his palm to the page as if to still the words. A part of him wished to tear it into scraps and feed them into the wood stove. Another part, the stubborn and relentless one, insisted that the truth, once seen, demanded record. The conflict within him was unequivocal. If he silenced it here, would it not fester more?

He set it aside without deciding. The ink was his confession, his burden, and whether it ever found a reader was a question for another day, a day filled with uncertainty.

He closed the window against the chill. The sound of hammers already echoed from the site. Greaves would be there by now, surveying with that unshakable air of command, his piercing gaze and authoritative voice. He clenched his jaw. Brighton's walls would rise, but at what cost?

Chapter Twenty-Six

JULY 17, 2023

Shortly after four o'clock, Nicole, a talented graphic designer at CNC IT Solutions, logged out for the day. She focused on creating a new set of graphics for a potential client. Tomorrow, she had a meeting at their Belleville location, but she was used to the weekly drive and looked forward to returning home afterwards.

This house had been quiet since the night the blood dripped from the ceiling onto her arm. Even after they determined the face Nicole sketched from the dried stain on the floorboards above was Elias Greaves, the mystery surrounding him only deepened. She got more vibes from him when they visited the house he designed in Morrisburg. What was he trying to tell her with his cryptic one-word messages — RETURN. Once, he included the word soon in a message. Regardless, the man's initials, E.G., followed

After they put in a driveway from the main road, they moved their mailbox next to it. Mitch's construction business used the back entry.

Nicole walked to the back door. The lights were on in her husband's workshop. He'd be there for another hour at least. That was where he built things and stored lumber, windows, and other materials. He dedicated the upstairs bedroom to design.

She walked through to the front of the house. The flag on their rural mailbox showed that the mail carrier had already delivered the day's mail.

Nicole pulled the small padded envelope from the

stack of mail. The printed label read *To the Occupant* followed by their Brighton address. No return information. The postmark wasn't local. The smudged ink made it hard to read.

She carried it inside and laid the rest of the mail on the kitchen counter. There was weight to this package. Something inside that shifted slightly when she tilted it. Nicole grabbed a paring knife, slid it under the flap, and sliced it open. The faint smell of old paper escaped.

Inside was a book with a worn and scuffed leather cover, its spine softened by age. She traced the embossed border with her index finger before flipping it open. A bookplate bore a name written in careful, spidery strokes: Charles Whitmore. Who was he?

The entry bore the date March 25, 1832. The handwriting was slightly backhand, but neat. The occasional ink blot made her think the writer had been hurried or distracted. He mentioned a ruin in Kingston and people rumoured Greaves caused it.

The following entry showed the date March 26, 1832.

> *Today, I begin my service under Mister Greaves. He is a man of considerable talent, though reserved to the point of severity. The commission is to build a fine home for Mr. Harrowick on the outskirts of Brighton. The work promises to be challenging, and I must prove myself equal to it. The tower design intrigues me.*

Nicole turned the page, her pulse quickening. Sketches filled the margins. The curve of a staircase, the outline of a tower window, even a section of the floor plan that looked unsettlingly familiar. She glanced towards the front of the house, where the same set of stairs now rose into shadow. The eerie familiarity of the sketches sent a shiver through her body. Another entry caught her eye.

The employer speaks little, but I sense in him a restlessness, as though his mind builds far more than his hands ever could. Sometimes he pauses mid-construction and looks, not at the work, but as though listening for something that no one else can hear.

Nicole closed the journal slowly, the hairs on her arms prickling as she broke out in goosebumps. She double-checked the envelope. Whoever had sent this hadn't included a note, hadn't explained how it found its way there. The mystery of its origin hung in the air, thick and palpable.

Now, as she pondered over the journal's contents, a sudden realization dawned on her. This journal appeared less a gift and more like a summons, a call to unravel its secrets.

Chapter Twenty-Seven

APRIL 5, 1891

The attic smelled of cedar and dust. Charles Whitmore's wife, Mary, stood in the narrow space holding a lantern while he rummaged through an old trunk. After all these years since he'd walked away from his apprenticeship with Elias Greaves, he had decided to clear out the remnants of his past life. Plans, sketches, his journals, and memories he wanted to banish.

Greaves's name still lingered like a sour taste. The Brighton commission had finished without him, and he'd heard the man had started another project in Kingston. He didn't care, so he told himself, but in truth, he did.

He pulled out a stack of rolled vellum and set it aside to be burnt. When his fingers brushed the small leather-bound notebook, he hesitated. This notebook, a repository of his past, held years of sketches, some his own, others secretly copied from Greaves's work, including that strange motif that still haunted him.

His wife leaned closer. "You aren't keeping it?"

Charles shook his head. "I've no use for it now. Let it go with the rest." His voice carried his decision, one that lifted the heavy burden from his shoulders.

He slipped the notebook into a crate already half-filled with discarded books from their parlour shelves, a volume of poetry, a gardening manual, and even an outdated almanac. Whitmore would send the box to the parish auction the following week. A farmer would buy it for pennies, not knowing the value or the burden hidden inside.

Charles closed the trunk, dusted off his hands and took the lantern from his wife. As he left the attic, he told himself it was better this way. His decision was final, and he was resolved to move forward.

Someone else could be the keeper of the secrets.

Chapter Twenty-Eight

JULY 17, 2023

Mitch leaned over the desk, tapped his pencil against the sketch he'd been working on of the Morrisburg house's tower. The angles refused to cooperate. The spiral staircase they discovered in the back of a closet never quite fit where it should. He and Nicole had searched for it and found it, but to draw the plans and have them work out? He had been at this for at least an hour. It was as if he were an angler following a shadow in murky water.

The workshop door banged open, and cold air rushed in. Nicole stood in the opening, her hair windblown, cheeks flushed. In one hand, she gripped a battered leather book; in the other, a crumpled padded envelope.

"You won't believe this," she said, breathless.

Mitch straightened. "I'm not sure I like the tone. It sure isn't a good 'you won't believe this'."

"You're right. This is way better," Nicole said, crossing the room in a few strides. She slapped the envelope down on the desk and placed the book beside it with care. "This just showed up. No return name or address. Addressed to 'The Occupant' with our full mailing address."

He pulled the envelope towards him and scanned the postmark. Smudged, but he could make out M****lle, SK. That, in itself, was weird because neither one of them knew anyone in the province of Saskatchewan.

When he opened the book, the smell of old leather

and dust drifted up, and he sneezed. The first page bore a name in fading ink — Charles Whitmore.

The hair on the back of Mitch's neck prickled. "You're kidding me."

Nicole shook her head. "Read the second entry."

He did, eyes narrowing. The date, March 26, 1832. The mention of a Mister Greaves. Might this be Elias Greaves? The Brighton house.

"This is ... crazy," he mumbled. His mind was running through possibilities. Architectural archives, old apprenticeship records, the chance it could be a fake, but his gut said otherwise. The pen strokes had the same confidence and ink spread he'd seen in other period documents.

Nicole hovered next to him, still jazzed from what she'd read earlier. "It's like someone knew we'd need it."

He closed the journal gently and rested his fingers on the cover. "Or like it needed to get here, no matter how."

Mitch pondered how someone from so far away could find their house. The sender used their Brighton address, so perhaps they took a chance and used Google Maps and street view to find it. There couldn't be any other Brightons with a mansion like this in or near them.

Mitch eased the journal open again. This time, the spine creaked in protest. Neat handwriting, periodically interrupted by an ink sketch, filled the pages. A window frame here, the curve of a banister there, a tower silhouette that looked exactly like his and Nicole's house. The journal, a treasure trove of secrets, held the key to a long-buried mystery.

About halfway through the book, an ink blot marred the margin, as if the writer had hesitated. The entry beside it was terse.

> *April 2, 1832*
>
> *I cannot smooth over my disagreement with Mister G. His methods ... they no longer align with my conscience. Will finish my*

commitments to the Brighton commission only insofar as I must.

Mitch sat back and stared at the words. “Well, it looks like Whitmore walked out on Greaves.”

Nicole leaned closer and read over his shoulder. “What do you think happened?” Uncertainty filled her voice, mirroring the suspense that hung in the air.

He flipped to the next page. Another drawing, not of the house, but of a small, intricate carving that resembled an emblem or crest. Symbols spiralled outward from it; Mitch did not recognize them, but their precision in arrangement made them seem intentional, like a code. The mystery of the symbol hung in the air, piquing their curiosity.

“I don’t know,” Mitch said, tracing the shape with his finger. “But whatever it was, it mattered enough for him to record it.”

“Do you think that symbol is the same as in the book we found in Morrisburg?” Nicole asked, unease filling her voice.

“Possible,” he said. “And if it is, Whitmore’s the first actual link between the two houses we’ve had. Whoever sent this,” he said, tapping the envelope, “they’ve just handed us the missing piece. Or … perhaps, the next breadcrumb.”

Mitch closed the journal gently, as if the brittle paper might crumble from too much pressure. The emblem lingered in his mind, every curve and spiral burned into his memory.

“Let me lock up, and we’ll see what I have in my textbooks in the house.”

Mitch walked around the table and straight to the tall bookcase in the corner. The one he had looked at the day before, ***Echoes in Stone: Symbolism and Secrets in Architecture***, still lay open on the table’s surface. No, he had another textbook in mind this time. One that might unlock the secrets hidden in the very architecture he studied.

His fingers traced over the spines until he found

the one he wanted. ***Sacred Geometry: Patterns of the Past.*** He pulled it down and flipped through diagrams of interlocking circles, pentagrams, and ancient sigils. Nothing was quite the same, but certain elements matched. A curve here. A repeating arc there.

Nicole stepped closer. "Anything?"

"Not exact," he said, "but it's ... related. The proportions are deliberate, mathematical. It's like the Fibonacci sequence meets a family crest."

"A Fibo ... what?"

"Fibonacci was an Italian mathematician. His sequence is a series of numbers. Flower petals, pinecones and the like. But here's the neat thing. It's also used in math. Suppose you divide a larger Fibonacci number by the one just before it. In that case, the result is about 1.618, the golden ratio, which is considered aesthetically pleasing and artists and architects use it in their work. Here, I'll show you."

Mitch grabbed a sheet of paper and started the calculations in the sequence.

0+1=1
1+1=2
1+2=3
2+3=5

"Make sense now?"

"And you know this, how?" Nicole asked.

"Studied the man in one of my university classes."

She tilted her head, and Mitch shot her a quick smile.

"You've read *The Da Vinci Code*, haven't you? Well, Brown had a knack for making you believe this stuff could unravel the entire world."

Nicole folded her arms. "So you're saying that Whitmore and Greaves — we now have both journals — have left us a code to crack?" Her eyes sparkled with the thrill of the unknown.

"No. What I'm saying is, if Brown's characters had been stuck with this thing, they'd be halfway to Paris by now." He tapped the page. "We're starting in Brighton." The gravity of the situation was thick with the potential for danger.

Chapter Twenty-Nine

APRIL 5, 1832

The morning had been steady work until it came to raising the north frame. The men strained at the ropes, their boots grinding into the earth as the timber lifted.

"Hold. Steady there!" someone cried.

The hemp rope snapped, the sharp report like a pistol. The beam lurched and swayed wildly. Men scattered, their faces a mix of fear and determination. One stumbled and went down hard, and for an instant, Whitmore thought the timber would crush him. He darted forward, his heart in his throat.

The beam caught against a brace and stopped with a shudder that shook the entire frame. Dust rained down. The pale and shaken worker scrambled free.

For a breathless moment, no one moved.

Then, like a beacon of calm in the storm, Greaves strode into the silence. His presence was commanding; his demeanour unruffled. He barked for new ropes, for hands to right the timber, his tone brisk but reassuring. He crouched beside the fallen man, checked him quickly, and clapped him on the back with a laugh, his reassurance a balm to the shaken crew.

"No bones broken. A scare's all it was. Back to it, lads. We'll have her upright before the day's done."

As the tension eased, a collective sigh seemed to escape the crew. Nervous chuckles, like a gentle breeze, spread among them. By the time men hoisted the beam again, the near-disaster seemed almost forgotten, replaced by a renewed focus on the task at hand.

Charles stood with his notebook pressed against his chest, and could not forget the look in the fallen man's eyes, or the sight of the frayed hemp dangling uselessly in the dirt. The incident had left a mark, a reminder of the dangers they faced every day.

Chapter Thirty

JULY 18, 2023

Nicole's keys jingled in her left hand as she slid her laptop into her backpack with her right. She was due in the office in a little over an hour and still had to stop for coffee. The driving time would take about thirty-five minutes or longer, depending on traffic and the whims of the red-light gods. Her sketchbook was nowhere in sight.

She frowned and scanned the desk's surface. Not there. Opened each drawer systematically. Not in any of them either. The kitchen was next on her search list, not on the counter, not on the table. The same held true for the dining room. Not on the table, nor in the sideboard or anywhere.

Next, Nicole checked the living room. Some nights she sat on the couch with it, working on designs. Not on the coffee nor end tables. She got down on her hands and knees and peered under the sofa. A few dust bunnies, her missing slipper, but still no sketchbook.

Her stomach tightened. That book went everywhere with her. Coffee shops, client meetings and road trips. It held weeks of work and ideas she couldn't afford to lose. The more she searched, the more her anxiety grew, and a knot tightened in her abdomen.

"Mitch?" she called up the stairs. "Have you seen my sketchbook?"

"Which one?" His muffled voice drifted down.

"The one I use for work. I have a meeting this morning, and my designs are in it. It should be on my desk, but it isn't."

After a brief pause, Mitch appeared at the top of the stairs. "Want a hand looking?"

Ten minutes later, they both searched through the house. Again, Nicole retraced her steps from the night before, and still found nothing.

She climbed the stairs and searched their bedroom, since some nights she worked on designs in bed. Nothing on or under the bed, nor either nightstand.

Her gaze caught on the stairs to the third floor. She hadn't been on that level and in that room since she had sketched the floor stain. The room above their bedroom.

She ascended the staircase slowly. Partway up, Mitch called out from the kitchen to tell her the book wasn't in her backpack. Nicole knew that. It was the first place she looked.

The door to the upstairs room was ajar. A faint smell of old wood and something metallic met her as she stepped over the threshold.

Her sketchbook lay in the middle of the floor — open. The sight sent a shiver down her spine; the eerie atmosphere was palpable in the room.

Nicole froze. She hadn't left it here. She had used it after she drew the stain, and it morphed into a face.

She crouched, picked it up, and then fanned through the pages. The air was still, and the only sound was the soft rustle of the pages as she turned them. Her breath caught. This page was familiar. It held her sketch of the dark stain on the unfinished floorboards. The shading was still rough, especially the lines where she'd thought she saw a man's face. Elias Greaves. But now, it was different. The face was sharper. The eyes were deeper set, the expression darker, almost as if someone had drawn over her work. The shock of the alteration left her speechless.

Nicole flipped to the next page. Symbols. Dozens of them, along with interlocking lines, geometric flourishes, some repeated as if for emphasis. She didn't recognize a single one, and she *hadn't drawn them.*

Her hands trembled as she turned another page, then another. More of the same. Some had faint architectural features like arches, vaulted ceilings, and intricate details that she had never sketched in her life.

Behind her, the floorboards creaked, and she turned around. Mitch leaned against the doorframe, watching her flip through the book. “You found it, I see,” he said.

Nicole swallowed hard, staring at the symbols. The pencil strokes were darker and heavier than hers, as if pressed into the paper.

“These aren’t mine. These are his. Elias Greaves.”

Mitch took the sketchbook from her hands carefully, as if the pages might crumble. They didn’t. They were just paper, but what was on them was another matter.

The lines were deliberate and precise. Not idle doodles. Whoever made them knew exactly what they were doing.

He flipped back to the stained floor sketch. Nicole’s rough work was underneath, but someone had sharpened the lines into the face of Elias Greaves. The eyes seemed to meet his directly.

“Hell of a likeness,” he mumbled to himself, but it came out louder than expected.

Nicole crossed her arms. “That’s not what I drew.”

“I believe you.” Mitch turned the page. Symbols repeated in strange patterns. He’d seen them before. Not these exact drawings, but fragments, marginal scribbles. Greaves’s journal, they found in Morrisburg, plus faint notations in the Brighton house blueprints. Back then, he’d thought they were a draftsman’s shorthand or decorative flourishes. Now, they looked … intentional

“This one,” he said, tapping the diamond shape surrounded by loops, “is in the margin of the Brighton parlour elevation. And here,” he turned the page and pointed to a fan of curved lines, “this is in the Morrisburg entry hall sketch.”

Nicole leaned closer. “You mean Greaves was putting the same designs into both houses?”

“Not just that.” He traced one of the odd patterns of a spiral inside an angular frame. “This isn’t what you add for pretty. This means something. Whitmore mentioned in his diary that he didn't know what it was. Said Greaves was being secretive, not letting him near certain parts of the drawings."

Nicole shivered. "Why draw them in my sketchbook then?"

Mitch didn't want to answer that question. If he said it aloud, it would make it real. That somewhere in this house, someone or *something*, was trying to make sure they saw what Greaves had hidden.

He closed the sketchbook gently. "I think we just got the key to the whole thing. Now we have to figure out what lock it opens."

Chapter Thirty-One

APRIL 8, 1832

Whitmore wrote the word *frayed* three times in his ledger, each stroke of the pencil imbuing it with a weight that seemed to tear the page. He had measured the rope ends himself. Weakened, stretched past their service. Yet Greaves had brushed it away with charm, as if danger were an inconvenience best laughed at.

He set the pencil down with trembling fingers. The image of the timber swaying, the man pinned beneath its shadow, replayed with merciless clarity. It had been chance alone that spared them tragedy.

The whispers in the tavern returned to him. *Greaves leaves ruin in his wake.* He had dismissed them at first, wary of putting stock in rumours. Now, they clung to him like burrs.

If Brighton was to escape worse, he needed more than whispers and his own uneasy suspicions. He needed proof.

His gaze drifted east, as though Kingston lay beyond the thin walls of his room. The collapsed building, the one they say Greaves had raised. The community's trust in him had collapsed along with it. The answer waited there.

Whitmore closed his ledger, his resolve sharpening with each passing moment. He knew he had to act, and act fast. He would go.

Chapter Thirty-Two

JULY 18, 2023

Now that Nicole had found her missing sketchbook, Mitch walked her to her car so she could drive to Belleville for the meeting with her brothers and their client. When she returned at the end of her workday, they would discuss the implications of its contents.

The restored façade of the house gleamed in the morning sun. Every line and detail was sharp now that the months of work had stripped away the years.

He let his gaze wander over the roofline like he always did, not because he expected to find something new but because he couldn't get used to how good it looked. The sight of the restored house filled him with a sense of pride and accomplishment. Then his eyes caught on a curve of stone just under the peak.

Mitch froze.

It wasn't the first time he's seen it, but for whatever reason, in this light, it registered differently. Or was it because they had found Elias Greaves's notebook in Morrisburg and had come into possession of Charles Whitmore's journal? This was more subtle than a carving, but more deliberate than a quirk of the mason's hand.

Nicole opened the hatch of her car. "You're staring like the house is about to sprout wings and fly."

"That flourish up there. It's not just decoration," Mitch said, pointing to the strange symbol, a unique design that seemed to be several ancient symbols combined into one.

She tilted her head and followed his line of sight. "Looks decorative to me."

"It's supposed to look that way," he said, setting his insulated mug on the roof of Nicole's car. "Be right back." He disappeared through the back door, returned with a rolled copy of the Morrisburg blueprints he had recreated from their visits, and spread them across the hood of Nicole's car, then tapped on a spot on the plans. "Greaves used the same curve in the Morrisburg house. Same size. Same placement."

Mitch's gaze returned to the roof's peak, and his jaw tightened. He narrowed his eyes as if the stone itself might answer. "I've got a hunch it wasn't just for looks."

Nicole pulled her coat tighter against the morning's chill, placed her backpack in the hatch and closed it. "I'm going to be late," she said, but she didn't move from Mitch's side. Her eyes remained fixed on the roofline where he'd pointed to the curious flourish, a strange symbol etched in the ancient stone.

"You're sure it's the same?" she asked.

"I'd bet my truck on it." Mitch's tone was steady, but she knew his mind was racing ahead, filing this away with everything else they had uncovered about the eccentric architect, known for his enigmatic designs and reclusive nature.

Nicole took a slow breath and forced herself to look away. "Whatever it means, it'll have to wait until tonight. I've got a meeting I have to be at in less than half an hour. I'm going to be late." Her professional responsibilities clashed with her burning curiosity, creating a palpable tension.

Mitch gave her a sidelong look, rolled up the plans and grabbed his mug from the roof of Nicole's car. "Right. Because it's so easy to focus on office work when you've just found out your house might be sporting some kind of Greaves signature."

She gave him a thin smile. "I'll manage. You don't start climbing up there without me."

"Promise," he said, his determination shining through, though she knew to him that was more like a loose guideline.

Nicole climbed into her car, started the engine and headed for the main road. At the end of the driveway, she glanced in the rearview mirror. Mitch still stood staring at the roofline, his insulated mug in one hand and the plans rolled up under his arm.

The image stayed with her as she drove off. Her husband rooted the spot, alone in his confrontation with a century-old mystery that seemed to stare right back at him.

“Sorry, I’m late, guys,” Nicole said as she dashed into the office, sliding her backpack off her shoulder and onto her desk. “More weird stuff happening at home.”

Both her brothers looked up from their monitors.

“I told you about drawing the face of a man in the blood stain, and we discovered he was Elias Greaves. Well, since then, we’ve found his journal.” She didn’t mention she’d taken it from the house they explored in Morrisburg. “And someone sent us his apprentice’s diary from a place in Saskatchewan. The sender wrote our address on the envelope, but only addressed it to the occupant.”

“Okay, I’ll give you that that’s weird, but there’s more to it. I can tell,” Cooper said.

Nicole pulled her sketchbook from her backpack and walked around her desk, stopping between her brothers. She flipped to the image of Greaves. “I made the initial drawing, but someone came along after me and added to it.”

After a brief pause, she flipped to the next page. “This morning, when I was packing up to come in, I couldn’t find my designs. I know I normally keep work and personal stuff in different pads, but this was the first one I grabbed that day. I found it on the third floor, in the room above ours. This is what I found.”

She waited for her brothers to examine the page before she flipped to the next one. “This is not my work. I have no idea what these symbols and other things mean. A few lines in his apprentice’s journal suggested the man didn’t have all his faculties.”

"A nut bar," Connor said, snickering.

"Yes."

"Anyway, when I was getting ready to leave this morning, Mitch found one of these decorations up near the roofline of the house."

"So?"

"The same design is in the plans we got for the Morrisburg property."

"The architect designed two houses. That's not strange," said Cooper.

"Not in itself. It would take too long to tell you everything, but from what we've read in his apprentice's diary, it appears the man was building a portal to another dimension, or possibly a hidden passage between the two houses. It's creepy."

"What's next?"

"I don't know. Let's just get this meeting over with."

The office door opened, and Nicole looked up to see two people step in, carrying themselves with a casual confidence.

"Hi, I'm Simon Kessler," the taller of the two said, extending his hand. Warm, approachable, with a faint trace of hops in his cologne, or maybe Nicole imagined it. "And this is Fiona Reyes. We're with Ironwood Brewery."

Fiona's handshake was firm, and her smile was friendly. "Thanks for having us. We're excited to see what you've done with the brand."

Nicole gestured to the conference table. "Right this way. I've got the mock-ups and photography queued up on the screen." Despite having digitized her designs so she could show them in a PowerPoint presentation, she insisted on having the actual artwork on hand. You never knew when a technical glitch would hit and the electronic version would be useless.

As everyone settled, Nicole experienced the familiar mix of nerves and focus. Between the morning's discoveries at home and her racing thoughts about the meaning of Greaves's symbols, she had to concentrate hard to keep everything on track.

She tapped the side of her laptop, bringing the screen to light and casting a soft glow over the table. “So, this is what we've been working on for Ironwood Brewery,” she began, clicking the mouse and bringing the first mock-up onto the wall-mounted screen.

Simon’s eyes were bright with curiosity. “Looks good from here, but show us the details.”

Nicole clicked to the next slide, which contained high-resolution photos of the brewery. Each shot had been carefully lit to highlight the warm tones of the wood, the copper tanks, and the amber gleam of freshly poured beer. “We wanted to capture the atmosphere of the brewery itself. The story behind each batch. These images will translate directly to the website, social media and packaging.”

She clicked through to the next slide, expecting the fresh images to fill the screen, but froze. “Oh no,” she muttered under her breath. The slide showed the current Ironwood labels, the outdated website screenshots, and a few blurry photos she hadn’t meant to include.

Great. Just what I needed. Elias Greaves’s face floating in my sketchbook, missing pages, and now this. The universe wants me to look like a total amateur today; she thought.

Fiona raised an eyebrow.”Is that ... isn’t that the current branding?”

Nicole’s cheeks warmed, but she forced a calm smile. “Yes. That’s actually perfect for comparison. Shows you where we are now versus where we’re going.”

Focus, Nicole. Breathe. Pretend the creepy house and mysterious symbols don’t exist for just thirty seconds, she reminded herself.

She quickly swiped to the correct slide. The crisp new can designs gleamed under professional lighting, the brewery’s warm interior captured in rich, inviting tones. “And here’s the refreshed look,” she said as she let the new images fill the screen.

Nicole clicked to the next set of slides. It showed a series of redesigned beer cans, each with bold, modern typography and updated colour palettes. "We've kept Ironwood's signature rustic charm, but refreshed the visuals so they stand out on shelves. Seasonal beers get a unique accent colour to differentiate them, while the flagship cans maintain continuity with the overall brand."

Another voice echoed in her mind. Brad's comments about her art being no good and no one would ever buy it. She tried to push it away. Her chest tightened until she saw their smiles.

The clients exchanged impressed looks. "We love it," said Simon. "It feels alive, fresh, but still us."

Nicole allowed herself a small smile. Her designs were something precious, real and wanted. Until that encounter outside the art supply store, it had been the first time in a long time that her ex's words threatened to destroy her. She had moved on. "That's the goal. We want your customers to see the brewery in every element, online, in-store and in their hands."

She exhaled quietly, her heart still racing from her mini scare. Between her missing sketchbook, Greaves's symbols, and the ongoing mysteries at home, it was no wonder her mind wandered during her presentation. But seeing her clients' reactions, she knew it had all worked out in the end.

Nicole loaded the last of their supper dishes into the dishwasher, and the kitchen settled into that after-supper hush Mitch liked. Warm light pooled on the table, the tick of the old clock on the wall. Nicole sat opposite him, her sketchbook open with the strange curling symbols staring up at them like they, too, had waited for this moment.

He set down his coffee and slid his ***Echoes in Stone: Symbolism and Secrets in Architecture*** textbook across the table, open at the chapter entitled ***Cryptic Marks and Hidden Codes***. Years of use had cracked the book's spine. "I swear I've seen something like these symbols before. Not exactly, but close enough that it's been bugging me all day."

Nicole tilted the sketchbook towards him, her

pencil hovering over the page. "They were everywhere in that section of the tower. Almost like a code of some kind."

"Or instructions," Mitch said, running a finger down an old diagram of stonemason marks. Triangles, spirals, and intersecting lines. "See this? Master masons left these symbols to tell the next guy what to do. Placement, angles, even which tools to use."

Nicole's brow furrowed. "So you think Greaves left them as ... work notes?"

"Not just notes." He pushed the book closer. "Some of these are protection marks. Builders in the 1800s used them to 'guard' a place against fire or evil spirits. If you overlay them onto those sketches ..."

She pulled the pad back and began tracing, her pencil moving quickly. Gradually, patterns emerged. Lines intersected to form what could have been a key or a map.

A shiver ran down Mitch's spine. "Nicki ... I think these marks aren't random. They connect different parts of the house. Maybe even the tower passage."

She looked up, eyes wide. "Shadows through time."

He didn't know exactly what she meant, but the phrase seemed to settle into the air between them, heavy and certain. Whatever Greaves had been doing, it had been deliberate ... and unfinished.

At about 7:30, the phone rang. Nicole set her sketchbook down and took the call. She listened, nodding more than speaking, her expression shifting from surprise to disbelief.

When she finally hung up, she stared at the phone as if it might ring again and retract what she had just heard. "An art show? They actually want to hang my stuff on the wall?"

Mitch looked up from where he was sorting through invoices. "Of course, they do."

She shook her head, a mixture of laughter and daze in her eyes. "But I'm not ... I mean, I'm not really an artist-artist. These are just sketches, designs. Why would they want them?"

"Because they're good," Mitch said, his voice firm with conviction. He came closer and rested a hand on the back of her chair. "Because *you're* good."

Nicole pressed her palms to her cheeks, her nerves and the giddy flutter in her chest waging a silent war. "Oh God, what if nobody likes them?"

Mitch only smiled, but Nicole continued staring at the phone, her heart thudding. She wasn't sure if she was brave enough to say yes. She gazed at the blank space on the wall across from her, as though the answer might appear there, sketched in shadow and light.

Chapter Thirty-Three

APRIL 9, 1832

Now that Whitmore was resolved to go to Kingston by train, he spent his evening packing a few belongings into a small valise.

I have packed little, just what I can carry without notice. It would be too easy to make a show of leaving, to slam the door or speak harsh words in farewell, but I have no desire for such endings. Perhaps the men will think me a coward for slipping away, though none will say so aloud.

Greaves. What shall I make of him? Even now, as I put pen to paper, I perceive the pull of his voice in my memory, that conviction could make stone bend to his will. I also consider whether I am a fool, giving up the chance to work with a man whose influence people might remember long after his structures vanish.

But those marks. I cannot look at them without unease, nor forget the tale whispered in the tavern. They cling to me like smoke. Today, I again asked what they meant, though softly, almost in jest. He did not answer. Only smiled in that way of his that made the other men forget their grumbling. But when his gaze met mine, there was something in it I could not name. It was as though he saw through me, and in that moment, I knew I could not stay.

Tomorrow, when the other labourers head to the Brighton site, I will take a different path. I will not bid them farewell. It's better they think I've wandered off or lost my appetite for work than to admit I'm afraid of what I can't comprehend.

Perhaps in the years to come, I will rue this decision. I might hear Greaves's name spoken with reverence and curse myself for walking away. Or I might hear it in darker circles and be grateful. Only time will reveal the truth.

For now, I leave quietly, carrying both relief and doubt in equal measure. The relief of escaping the unease and the doubt of the unknown future intertwine, creating a bittersweet departure.

Chapter Thirty-Four

JULY 18, 2023

Later that night, long after Nicole had gone to bed, Mitch found himself back at the kitchen table. Moonlight filtered through the window, bathing the room in a soft, eerie glow.

Her sketchbook still lay open; her pencil rested diagonally across the page as if it were guarding the answer.

The overlay they'd created stared back at him. Symbols layered into lines. Lines into shapes. It should have made sense, but something didn't fit.

He retraced the pattern with the tip of his index finger and stopped where a jagged spiral met the edge of the page. The mark seemed incomplete, like a sentence cut short.

Mitch grabbed his textbook and flipped through the stonemason's marks again, landing on a sketch of a spiral with a short slash cutting through its centre. That slash — a symbol of disruption — wasn't in Nicole's version. It was a crucial detail, a clue that could unravel the mystery.

He sat back, a tight unease curling in his chest. The missing piece wasn't just missing from the sketch. It wasn't anywhere they had looked, which meant ... it might still be concealed in the house. Or, someone had already found it. The suspicion gnawed at him like a persistent itch he couldn't scratch.

The thought lodged deep in his mind, colder than a January wind. His heart raced, and a shiver ran down his spine.

Mitch closed the book softly, careful not to let the thud carry upstairs. He wasn't ready to tell Nicole yet, at least not until he was sure. No sense in worrying her over a theory that could be nothing.

He slipped the sketchbook under his arm and padded into the hallway. The old boards groaned under his weight. The air had that faint chill the house collected after sundown, which carried a whisper of damp stone and something older he couldn't name.

The spiral with the missing slash gnawed at him. If someone cut the mark into wood or stone, it was possible that same person erased it on purpose.

He drifted towards the utility room, where boxes of their earlier finds sat waiting to be sorted. The light from the ceiling fixture caught on the corner of an old beam propped against one wall in the far corner. One of the salvaged pieces from the house's original construction that hadn't made it out to Mitch's workshop yet.

Mitch crouched and ran his hand along the grain. His thumb snagged on a faint groove, nearly worn smooth. It wasn't a spiral, but the curve could have been part of one, long ago. He straightened suddenly, the hairs on his neck prickling. A floorboard creaked above.

Their bedroom.

He waited and listened. Nothing followed. No footsteps, no door opening, but the sensation of being watched stayed with him until he pulled his hand away from the beam.

If the missing symbol were here, he'd find it. As long as someone else hadn't already done so. That was a problem he'd deal with when it found him first.

Chapter Thirty-Five

APRIL 10, 1832

Greaves arrived early, as always, his boots sinking into the damp earth. Mist curled around the scaffolding and stacks of timber. The damp chill of the morning seeped through his coat. The site was alive with sound. Hammering, shouts, but one presence was missing. His apprentice.

He frowned and checked the ledger on the table under the canvas. No note. No message. No explanation. Whitmore had never missed a morning without word. A low unease settled in Greaves's gut.

The foremen noticed, too. Some muttered excuses, illness, a late-night errand, but their uncertainty was palpable, mirroring his own. Greaves walked the length of the site, stopping at points where the young man would typically oversee the masons. Each space seemed hollow, a strange emptiness in a place usually bustling with energy.

By midday, concern had grown into something sharper. Greaves questioned the overseers methodically, but they offered little more than guesses. There was no trace, no hint of where Whitmore might be. Something in the site's silence pressed against him, urging caution, making him notice details he usually ignored. The stray coat left on a bench, tools laid out unusually neat, the faint echo of footsteps that led nowhere. Greaves's search was meticulous, every detail scrutinized, every possibility considered.

Greaves stood for a moment near the scaffolding, scanning the area with careful eyes. He didn't understand why Whitmore was gone, but he knew the absence mattered. And although the explanation might be simple, Greaves couldn't shake the sense that something subtle and unseen had shifted.

Greaves lingered near the scaffolding, thumbs hooked on his coat pockets, eyes scanning every angle of the site. The men moved around him, but he barely noticed them now. Their chatter faded into the background, replaced by the distant clinks of metal and the muffled thuds of construction. The apprentice's absence had broken the rhythm of the morning, leaving a palpable sense of unease in the air.

He weighed his options, his mind racing with apprehension. Raising an alarm would draw attention, invite questions he wasn't ready to answer. Yet waiting seemed every bit as wrong. Whitmore was reliable, too reliable to vanish without cause. The knot in Greaves's stomach tightened, his suspicion growing like a storm on the horizon.

He started methodically, his every move deliberate and precise. He checked the area set up under the canvas he used as his office. He searched the labourers' huts, even the tool storage. Nothing. Not a scrap of paper, not a coat, not a discarded boot. It seemed as if the young man had vanished completely from the morning, but Greaves did not give up easily.

Finally, Greaves stepped back and studied the site from a distance, letting his instincts guide him. There was no panic, only calculation. If his apprentice had left of his own accord, Greaves would notice. If something had happened ... he would see that, too, eventually. For now, all he could do was remain alert, watch the patterns of men and materials and trust that the truth would surface.

He turned to the nearest overseer, his voice calm but firm. "Keep me informed of any signs of him," he said. "Nothing is too small."

The man nodded, and a flicker of concern crossed his face. Greaves walked away, unease settling deeper into his chest. Whitmore's absence had changed the site, casting a shadow of uncertainty over the once-familiar surroundings, even if no one yet understood how.

And somewhere in the quiet hum of construction, Greaves experienced the first stirrings of doubt. An instinctive knowledge that the day would not end normally.

The day had drawn long shadows across the site; the sun dipping behind the scaffolding and timber piles. Most of the men had left, their voices and footsteps fading into the distance, leaving behind an eerie silence broken only by the creak of boards and the occasional call of a bird.

Greaves lingered, hands clasped behind his back, eyes tracing the outlines of empty spaces where Whitmore would usually have moved. He had rechecked the ledger. Still nothing. No note, no explanation. The quiet pressed in, heavy and unfamiliar, and his apprentice's absence became larger than a mere missing person.

He ambled through the site, scanning corners, touching tools that seemed untouched, and noting footprints that led nowhere. Every detail screamed normalcy, yet the overall impression was uncanny; a place that should have been alive with labour and energy was now oddly hollow in the absence of the young man..

Greaves stopped at the edge of the scaffolding and let the chill wind cut through his coat. He inhaled, steadying himself. He didn't panic, not yet, but the gnawing knot in his stomach had grown. Simple forgetfulness or a late errand explained Whitmore's disappearance.

He would not leave the site tonight without a plan. First thing in the morning, he'd follow up, check every avenue, question every man again if necessary. His determination was unwavering. For now, all he could do was watch, wait and trust that the truth, whatever it was, would reveal itself.

As Greaves finally turned away and headed

towards his hotel, the wind carried a whisper through the scaffolding, a sound almost like a sigh. He paused as his heart skipped, though he saw nothing. The day concluded, yet the sense of a start remained, similar to vapour in the dimming light, enhanced by the mysterious whisper.

Chapter Thirty-Six

JULY 19, 2023

Nicole settled into the antique armchair by the bay window in the room that once had the Freemason ceiling medallion. Soft summer light filtered through the sheer curtains on each of the bay windows. She had raised the lower sashes, and a gentle breeze wafted into the room. She reached into her backpack and extracted the warped, leather-bound book she'd grabbed from the priest hole in Morrisburg.

The pages were brittle with age, and the edges were curled and stained. Faded ink spilled across them in neat lines of dense script and strange symbols Nicole couldn't decipher. Amongst these were detailed architectural sketches, tower designs, spiral staircases, and cryptic markings which mirrored the carvings she'd photographed. This was no ordinary book; it was a unique blend of art and mystery.

Her fingers trembled as she traced the odd shapes. The script was unlike anything Nicole had seen before. Part was technical jargon, part something different, as if the author encoded messages only meant for certain eyes. It was as if she were uncovering a secret world, one page at a time.

A shiver ran down her spine. This wasn't a builder's notebook; it was more like a ledger of secrets.

Nicole glanced around the quiet room. The stillness pressed in. Hers and Mitch's home was something special, which they and her brothers didn't realize when they first explored it the year before. This house was a mystery waiting to be solved, alive with stories waiting to be unearthed, and she held the key.

The soft creak of the floorboards drew Nicole's attention before Mitch spoke. He stepped through the archway separating the two rooms, wiping his hands on a rag.

"Is that what I think it is?" he asked, nodding towards the open book she held.

Nicole looked up, her eyes betraying the weight of the book's significance. "Yes, it's the book from the hidden room in the basement. I'm still trying to decipher its secrets."

Mitch crossed the room and sat on the arm of her chair. His eyes flicked to the yellowed pages filled with strange symbols and sketches. "Looks intense."

She bit her lip, the weight of the book's enigma pressing down on her. "It is. There's something about this book. It's like it's hiding a message or maybe a warning."

He reached out and brushed a stray lock of hair behind her ear, a gesture of comfort and reassurance. "Whatever it is, we'll figure it out together. Our bond is stronger than any mystery."

Nicole managed a small smile, but inside, the unease was a palpable presence. The house's secrets were more profound than she'd ever imagined, and with every page she turned, the past seemed to reach closer, casting a shadow over her present.

Mitch settled into his chair after dinner. If Nicole continued cooking meals this delicious, he'd have to go on a diet. Still, the weight of the day pressed on him. Nicole's unease about the book lingered in his mind, especially the strange symbols she'd shown him. She had taken the old book from the sealed basement room in the Morrisburg house.

He raked his fingers through his hair, envisioning the faded pages, the angular lines, and the cryptic markings that didn't look like any architectural notes he'd ever seen. The symbols, a series of sharp, angular lines and overlapping shapes, seemed to leap off the page, demanding his attention. Something about them seemed deliberate. Like a code, almost.

He remembered his old university textbooks tucked away in his office upstairs. Volumes on architectural history, symbolism in design, and even obscure references to Masonic influences and hidden meanings embedded in 19th-century buildings.

Might one of them have held a clue? Maybe Elias Greaves wasn't just building a house. Perhaps he was embedding messages or warnings in the very fabric of the design.

Mitch took the stairs two at a time to his study. He ran his fingers over the books as he searched the titles on the spines. There it was. ***Echoes in Stone: Symbolism and Secrets in Architecture.*** He scanned through the index and stopped at a chapter titled ***Cryptic Marks and Hidden Codes***.

Were the symbols Nicole found linked? He flipped through the pages to the chapter. Even the heading sent shivers down his spine.

The text described how architects of the 18th and 19th centuries sometimes embedded symbolic carvings and coded designs into their buildings. These marks weren't always decorative, but served as messages to select groups or warnings to outsiders. These notions weren't folklore. They were real, deliberate practices. One passage caught his eye.

> *Sometimes, these symbols correspond to ancient alphabets or cipher systems, disguising names, dates or secrets within the architecture itself. This was true of homes commissioned by secret societies or influenced by esoteric beliefs. The hidden codes could reveal much about the owner's true intentions or fears.*

The markings on the back wall of the hidden room in Morrisburg, the ones Nicole photographed. Those sharp, angular lines and overlapping shapes. They could be in the form of a cipher.

The chapter mentioned specific repeated patterns could be *keys* to unlocking these codes and often tied to geometric principles or historical alphabets like the Theban or Ogham script.

As he read about the ancient alphabets and ciphers, his mind wandered to Dan Brown's *Da Vinci Code* series. The way symbols and secret codes led to hidden truths in that book echoed the mystery unfolding before him.

"Except this isn't fiction," Mitch said, his eyes narrowing, at the text on the pages before him.

He pictured Elias Greaves, obsessed and secretive, weaving these codes into the bones of the house in Morrisburg and the one in question. If the man was anything like the conspirators in Brown's novels, then the house itself could be a puzzle waiting to be solved.

Mitch grabbed a sheet of paper and jotted down notes furiously, already itching to show his discovery to Nicole. The stakes were higher now. This wasn't just about old walls and forgotten rooms. It was about uncovering a secret that someone long ago desperately tried to hide. He began to formulate a plan to cross-reference the symbols from the book with these ancient systems.

Mitch found Nicole curled up in the armchair with the old book resting on her lap. He took a breath and settled on the one across from her and flipped open his notebook.

"Okay, I was going through one of my old textbooks. The one about symbolism in architecture. Well, I found something interesting."

Nicole looked up; her curiosity piqued despite the tension in her expression.

"It talks about how architects back in the 18th and 19th centuries sometimes hid secret codes in their designs. Not just decorations, but actual messages, sometimes even using ancient alphabets or ciphers."

She raised an eyebrow.

"Like a real-life Da Vinci Code," Mitch said,

grinning.

Nicole smiled, the first genuine smile in a while. "So you're saying Elias Greaves might have been leaving us clues?"

"Exactly. And those strange carvings you photographed? They could be part of a cipher. A puzzle that he wanted only certain people to understand."

Nicole leaned forward, her determination shining through. "Then we have to figure out what he's trying to tell us. We can't let this mystery go unsolved."

Mitch nodded. "I'm going to cross-reference those symbols with the ancient alphabets mentioned in the book. It's going to take some work, but if anyone can crack this, it's us."

Chapter Thirty-Seven

APRIL 10, 1832

The carriage swayed as the train journeyed eastward in the early-morning sunlight. Whitmore gazed out the window, his mind consumed by the tale from the tavern. The sudden collapse of a building, the whispers of shoddy construction, the quiet panic of those who'd been there, and of the men who died buried by the stone. It all seemed so improbable, yet it held a mysterious allure that he couldn't shake off. He had to see for himself.

Each mile brought a mix of excitement and tension. Charles was used to following plans, orders, and blueprints, but this was different. He had no official purpose, no authority to demand answers. Only curiosity and a stubborn need to know.

Arriving in Kingston, he walked the streets with deliberate casualness, noting the signs of recent disturbance: the dust on the cobblestones, the faint smell of mortar, a hastily patched doorway here, a crowd lingering there. Each detail spoke, though no one seemed willing to answer his questions directly.

He made a mental map, memorizing where to return, where to inquire quietly, and where a wrong question might raise suspicion. The tavern story had been vague, but Whitmore's instincts told him there was truth buried in the chaos. And if the collapse had really happened, he would find it.

The young man halted a short distance from a half-boarded building. Something had indeed gone awry here. Small signs, barely discernible from the street. He meticulously jotted down notes in the pocket journal he always carried, ensuring not to attract any unwanted attention. He was determined to follow the trail, quietly and with utmost caution, heightening the suspense of his investigation.

Whatever awaited him in Kingston, Whitmore had made a firm decision. He would not depart until he had unearthed the truth. No one, not even Greaves, could deter him from this relentless pursuit.

Whitmore moved deliberately through the narrow streets, careful to blend in with the locals. He had been under the impression that the collapse, a tragic event that had shaken the town, had occurred well over a month ago, but it still drew a small crowd even now. Most seemed more curious than concerned. Someone had nailed boards across the damaged structure.

He approached a nearby shopkeeper sweeping the sidewalk, casually observing the debris. "Pardon me," Charles said, keeping his tone light, "Do you know what happened here?"

The man glanced at the ruins, shrugging. "Wall came down, they say. Not much more."

He nodded, not pushing. He had learned long ago that people spoke freely only when they believed he wasn't prying. So he walked on, eyes scanning for any hint the collapse had more profound consequences, structural faults, hurried repairs, or worse, corners cut by someone eager to make a profit.

A group of labourers huddled near the edge of the street, arguing over measurements and boards. Charles lingered at a distance, jotting more notes in his journal. Everything told him this was real. Something had gone badly wrong, and it wasn't mere rumour.

As he circled the building, he noticed a subtle detail. A thin crack ran along the far wall, partially concealed by a makeshift plank. It was minor, but to Whitmore's trained eye, it spoke of haste and inattention. He crouched to inspect further, being careful not to draw attention.

A faint sound, a hesitant footstep, made him

glance over his shoulder. No one was there. Yet the hairs on his neck prickled. Kingston was quiet, but the collapse had left traces, not just in stone and wood, but in whispers. He knew the truth wasn't just in what people said. It was in what they avoided saying. The spaces they left empty. And in those empty spaces, danger lurked, waiting to pounce.

And he would find it. No matter the obstacles, no matter the risks, Whitmore was determined to uncover the truth behind the collapse.

Whitmore stood and brushed the dust from his hands. The faint echo of footsteps still lingered in his ears, though the alley behind him was empty. He frowned and made a note in his journal. The collapse was genuine enough. The evidence lay in the mortar, the repairs, but no one was speaking about it. It was a collapse that shook the very foundation of Kingston, a collapse that left more questions than answers.

He circled to the front of the building again. A woman in dark clothing, wearing a matching coloured shawl, her face etched with worry stood at a distance. Her hand clutched a basket to her chest. She seemed to hesitate, then fixed her eyes on the rubble-strewn ground.

Charles approached gently. "Excuse me," he said, keeping his voice even and polite. "Were you here when it happened?"

Her eyes flicked up, filled with wary fear. She shook her head, then, after a pause, whispered. "My brother was."

He leaned closer. "Is he all right?"

The woman pressed her lips together. "Alive, but ... changed." She glanced at the ruined building again. "He will not walk that street anymore. Says he hears the wall still groaning. At night, he wakes, swearing he feels the dust in his throat again."

Whitmore's pulse quickened. This was no mere accident, no passing mishap. He lowered his voice. "Would he speak to me?"

She hesitated, then gestured towards a row of

narrow houses. “If you catch him sober, but he'll not thank you for stirring it up. None of them will.” Her reluctance was palpable.

He nodded and offered his thanks, then turned in the direction she had indicated, his mind racing. First, a crack in the stone, then a whisper of footsteps, now a witness who lived through the collapse but could not escape it. Each clue tugged him deeper, and though he knew he risked drawing unwanted attention, he could not turn back.

Not until he uncovered what had truly happened in Kingston.

Chapter Thirty-Eight

JULY 19, 2023

The last thing Mitch did the previous night was return Nicole's sketchbook to the kitchen table. Despite the late hour, he finally gave up on deciphering the symbols, but he was still up and downstairs before her. He'd made a pot of coffee, and his textbook sat open on the table beside her pad. He couldn't wait to share his theory with her, but by the same token, he didn't want to wake her. They had built their relationship on mutual respect and trust, and Mitch didn't want to disrupt that.

About an hour later, footsteps padded on the staircase, and Nicole entered the kitchen wearing one of his T-shirts, sweatpants, and a severe case of bedhead. The aroma of freshly brewed coffee filled the air, mixing with the faint scent of Nicole's perfume. She yawned and moved to the coffeemaker and poured herself a cup.

"You been up long?" she asked groggily.

"Not *that* long," he said, pausing their conversation long enough to kiss her on the cheek and get himself a brew. "I think I've got it," he whispered, as though he didn't want the walls to hear in case they might be eavesdropping.

Nicole leaned over the table and rested her elbows on it. "Got what?"

Mitch tapped the open page. "This one. See? It's not just a random shape. It's a date. Or at least part of one."

She frowned. "Part of one?"

"Yeah. Your sketch shows this," he pointed, "but in the textbook, there's an extra mark here. Like a slash. Without it, the meaning's incomplete."

Nicole's brows knit. "How?"

He hesitated and ran his thumb along the page's edge. "Let's just say, if the rest is what I think it is, we're talking about a *when* and a *where*. And both matter."

"So, what? A clue?"

"More than," Mitch said, closing the textbook. "It's a warning, and someone made sure it stayed buried."

Her face paled. The kitchen was silent except for the hum of the fridge and the ticking of the clock. Then Nicole leaned back and crossed her arms. "You'd better be sure about this, Mitch. Because if you're right, it changes everything."

Chapter Thirty-Nine

APRIL 11, 1832

Meeting with the woman's brother was unsettling, to say the least. Whitmore sat at the small desk and began to write in his journal.

April 10, 1832

The woman led me to her brother, though she warned he would not thank me. She was right. He received me in a dim kitchen, half-empty bottle on the table, eyes darting to the door as though the collapse might come for him again.

At first, he said little, only that the wall failed and that he had been 'lucky.' Yet, when I pressed him gently, his manner shifted. He spoke of a sound, not the ordinary groan of timber, but something sharper, like a crack that carried through the stone before the wall gave way. He swore that the ground shuddered beneath his feet.

Most curious of all, he claimed he had sensed it coming, not in the way of a man of experience who knows weak mortar, but in some other way. 'It was like a warning in my bones,' he told me. A chill crept up his spine and a heaviness in his chest, but he wouldn't elaborate. He grew agitated, muttering that the building still breathes, that its ruin is not complete. His sister hushed him then and begged me not to encourage him further.

I left with little more than fragments, yet enough to convince me the tavern story was no idle tale. The collapse, a thunderous roar as the walls crumbled and the ceiling caved in, occurred. The evidence lies in stone and dust. But what lingers in the minds of those who saw it ... that is harder to measure.

Whitmore's pen trailed a moment as he gathered his thoughts once again. He knew he must tread carefully. Curiosity is one thing, but some would rather people forgot the matter. He perceived the weight of their caution, the need for vigilance in his every word.

He paused, blotting the ink and closing the leather-bound book with care. He set the journal on the small table in his lodging, the candle guttering low beside it. For a moment, the room was still; the only sound was the faint scratch of mice in the walls.

Then it came again. That tread, soft and deliberate as if someone crossed the floorboards behind him.

He turned, but the chamber was empty.

Charles drew a steady breath and convinced himself it was the house settling, nothing more. Yet, when he reached to snuff the candle, his hand lingered, hesitating. He had an unsettling impression that if he listened too closely, he might hear more than footsteps. He might hear the echo of the walls groaning, stone remembering its fall. The suspense hung heavy in the air, the eerie atmosphere pressing in on him.

He extinguished the flame, feeling a wave of relief wash over him. The calm after the storm, the release of tension in the quiet room.

Chapter Forty

JULY 24, 2023

The electronic doorbell rang when Nicole pushed open the door to the art supply store. The familiar scent of paper, graphite, paint and linseed oil settled around her. She told herself she only needed more sketchpads and a few new pencils, and another package of pastel pens. Practical items, nothing more.

Still, her pulse quickened when she noticed the flyer taped to the counter. Brighton Art Collective — Annual Show & Sale. The same show they had invited her to take part in.

She busied herself with the products on the shelves, a brave attempt to distract her mind from the phone call. What if people laughed at her work? What if the only reason they asked was because they were desperate for filler pieces? These thoughts, like unwelcome guests, kept intruding, but Nicole was determined not to let them win.

"Restocking already?" the clerk asked as she rang up Nicole's purchases, her tone filled with encouragement. "That's a good sign. You're doing great, Nicole."

Nicole smiled, a little distracted, and her gaze drifted again to the flyer. She could almost see her sketches on those gallery walls. Her pen/pencil strokes, her shadows, and her captured moments exposed to strangers' eyes.

She took a deep breath and, in a steady but trembling voice, said, "Yes, I'd like to confirm my participation." When the words were out of her mouth, her knees went weak, but her chest was lighter. She tucked the receipt and fresh supplies into her tote, and for the first time since the invitation, she let herself smile. The weight of self-doubt lifted, replaced by the excitement of the opportunity ahead.

Mitch heard the crunch of tires in the driveway and glanced up from the stack of books he'd been leafing through for more references to Elias Greaves. Nicole came through the door with a tote from the art store in one hand and her keys in the other. She said nothing at first, just set the bag down on the hall table as if it weighed a hundred pounds.

He waited.

Finally, she said, "I told them yes."

Mitch raised an eyebrow. "To what?"

"The art show. I ... I said I'd do it." Her voice was quiet, almost apologetic, as if she had admitted a reckless mistake.

He let a slow grin spread. "Well, it's about damn time."

That earned him a glare, but her arms tightened across her chest, betraying the uncertainty still twisting within her. "What if no one likes my stuff? What if they only asked me because they needed to fill space on the walls?"

He crossed the room and leaned one shoulder against the doorframe. "Nicki, people don't ask just anybody to hang work in a show. They saw something in what you do. Hell, *I* see every time you pick up a pencil. The only one doubting you here is you."

Her gaze dropped to the floor, and she chewed her lip. Mitch stepped closer and kept his voice steady. "You've kept it hidden long enough. Now you get to let the world in on it. Scary? Sure. Worth it? Absolutely."

Nicole didn't answer, but Mitch caught the faintest flicker of resolve in her eyes. He reached past her for the bag and gave it a light pat before setting it back down.

She said yes, and a surge of pride coursed through him. That was the hardest part. The rest, she'd handle just fine.

He softened his voice and added. “I’ll be right with you, Nicki. Your marker, keeping you steady no matter what.”

Chapter Forty-One

AUGUST 5, 2023

Nicole's stomach had tied itself in knots ever since she agreed to showcase her work at Barratt's Office Pro. The discovery of a gallery room next to the supplies section had only added to her anxiety.

It was one thing to sit in a quiet corner and sketch or fill a book with designs meant for anonymous clients. It was quite another to see her drawings, matted and framed, hung on pale walls under stark track lighting.

Mitch had come with her, and his careful handling of her artworks, as if they were precious heirlooms, was a comforting sight for Nicole. His reassuring words, 'They belong here,' were like a warm embrace during her nervousness.

She wasn't so sure, but managed a grateful smile.

Nicole had been unsure what to wear for the event. Anytime she had seen art gallery showings on TV, the artists always dressed to the nines. Black tie and tails, long sequinned gowns. With Mitch's help, she decided on a black, sleeveless, ruched, fitted midi-length dress, and left her hair down. A pair of silver sandals and a matching shoulder clutch finished the look.

For a change, she saw him in footwear that wasn't a pair of work boots, which, given his trade, were required. He looked handsome in a pair of jeans, a pale blue polo shirt and a black leather blazer. His boots were black and highly polished.

Nicole had invited her brothers personally. The art store had advertised online, in their windows, and on local media. She had no idea what kind of turnout the show would garner.

The store's staff had arranged the displays in neat groupings: a series of architectural sketches from their trip to Kembleford Manor in Pike Falls; several of her home in Brighton, including its brooding tower at dusk. Someone mounted a few of Nicole's commercial pieces on a side wall beneath a sign that read *For Display Only.*

As the crowd filtered in, Nicole kept to the edges. Her heart pounded with nervousness. A couple paused at her sketch of the manor's ruined greenhouse.

"Look at the detail in the glasswork," the woman said.

Her companion leaned closer. "It feels like it's still breathing, doesn't it?"

Nicole swallowed hard. Praise — genuine and unsolicited — left her lightheaded.

Just then, the door swung open, and the familiar voices of her brothers reached her. They slid inside, joking and teasing, each with broad smiles. "We wouldn't miss this," Cooper said as his eyes darted from the artwork to Nicole. "You actually made it." He leaned in and kissed her cheek. "Way to go, sis."

Connor hugged her, too. "Cooper always has to be first," he joked. "He was even ahead of me when we were born."

Nicole laughed, relief flooding her. The nervous tightness in her chest eased, replaced with warmth as she saw them. They lingered near the Kembleford Manor sketches with Mitch.

Connor paused in front of the Brighton Tower sketch. "Wow ... this one's different. Almost like it's ... watching over the house," he said, tilting his head.

Nicole traced the lines lightly with her eyes, a shiver of recognition running through her. "Perhaps it is," she said, thinking of the protective markers she and Mitch had been uncovering.

As Nicole drifted towards another grouping, she was taken aback. There, standing in front of the Brighton tower sketch, was Brad.

Mitch, Connor, and Cooper lingered near the Kembleford artwork, aware that it was Nicole's night to shine. Mitch spotted Brad's entrance and nodded to Nicole's brothers. "Bogie, eleven o'clock," he said, a hint of tension in his voice.

The three men started towards Nicole. Mitch, with a protective air, stopped and picked up a glass of wine. When he reached his wife's side, he put a firm arm around her shoulder, kissed her cheek, and handed her the drink. "You okay, babe?" he asked, his concern palpable.

By now, her brothers stood on her other side. They would protect her. And surely, Brad wouldn't be stupid enough to take on all of them. Not here. But then, if it meant ruining Nicole's night, Mitch wouldn't put anything past the man. The tension in the air was palpable, the potential conflict with Brad added a layer of suspense to the evening.

He hadn't changed since the last time she had bumped into him outside this very store. Sharp suit, carefully trimmed stubble, the faint cologne that once made her swoon but now clung too heavily. He tilted his head, lips quirking, as if he had been caught in some private joke.

"Well," he said when he spotted her, "looks like you've finally found your muse." His gaze flicked towards Mitch, standing at her side with his arm around her. Mitch, her supportive partner, had been the one to encourage her to pursue her art, a fact that Brad, her former boyfriend, had always resented.

Nicole's lips tightened. "No," she said firmly. "I found my vision. There's a difference."

Brad arched an eyebrow and leaned closer. "Vision, sure. But funny, I remember when your big dreams didn't get you far. Guess some people needed a little ... guidance, huh?"

Nicole held his gaze, a quiet fire behind her calm. "I've had plenty of guidance," she said confidently. "The difference now? I decide whose advice I follow. Oh, and by the way, when you try to take on one of us, you get all of us. We Holbrooks and Kanes are a family."

Brad's smirk faltered. He opened his mouth, but closed it and turned back to the sketch. "Interesting work," he said before slipping away into the crowd.

Nicole released a breath she hadn't realized she'd been holding.

"You've got people hovering around your greenhouse series," Mitch said proudly. He glanced towards the space where Brad had been but made no comment. "They see what I've always seen."

Warmth spread through her chest, steady and sure. The knot in her stomach loosened, and she was no longer an imposter.

By the end of the evening, several red dots marked her frames. Collectors had offered more money than she'd ever imagined for pieces she'd drawn on urban exploration trips, at the kitchen table or on a window seat. Her artistic success was truly inspiring.

Driving home, she sensed the journals waiting, the mystery still calling from Brighton and Morrisburg. These were some of the places where she had discovered her love for art and where she had left a part of herself. Yet tonight, for the first time, she seemed to be more than just a person stuck in the shadows of history. She seemed herself.

The engine hummed steadily as they drove back towards their house, the evening sky fading to deep indigo. Nicole's hands rested gently on her lap, still warm from the small victories of the night. Mitch stole glances at her, trying to read the unspoken currents in her expression.

She had been radiant tonight, not just for the applause or the red dots marking sold sketches, but in the quiet confidence that settled over her. Mitch sensed it, too, in the way she moved, the way she laughed at her brothers' teasing. She had grown into herself, and part of him wanted to both celebrate it and shield it from anyone like Brad who would try to diminish it.

He gripped the steering wheel a little tighter, a protective instinct he couldn't entirely shrug off. There had been that moment with Brad, and he didn't like the smug satisfaction on the man's face, even if the dig had been harmless. Nicole handled it brilliantly, but he still carried the low, lingering tension that came from knowing someone like Brad would always lurk on the edges.

Mitch glanced at her again. She was now staring out the window, as if replaying the show in her mind. He wondered if she was thinking about the Brighton tower sketch, the protective markers they had been tracing through Elias Greaves's and Whitmore's journals. Or maybe she was just letting herself revel in a night where she wasn't chasing deadlines or expectations. She was being seen, finally.

He exhaled slowly, letting some of his worry ease. "You know, you were amazing tonight."

Nicole's lips curved into a smile. "Thanks. It feels ... different, somehow."

"Good different, I hope," he said, watching her relax into the seat beside him.

She nodded and turned to glance at him. "The best kind of different."

Mitch let himself smile then; a quiet pride bloomed in his chest. She was fearless when it came to the past, to the mysteries of these houses, to the puzzles she and he were unravelling together, but tonight he saw her fearlessness in a new light. She wasn't just confronting history anymore. She was claiming her present.

And he'd be there to ensure no one dimmed it.

As the headlights cut through the darkness along the winding road, a sudden shadow flickered in the periphery for a second. Mitch couldn't tell if it was a trick of the trees or something else. A chill prickled down his spine, subtle but insistent. A reminder that some mysteries didn't end when the sun went down.

The road stretched ahead in quiet ribbons of asphalt, flanked by darkened trees and the occasional flicker of a passing street lamp. Nicole let her fingers brush the edge of her sketchbook on her lap, still warm from her hands earlier in the shop.

Mitch was quiet beside her, the hum of the engine filling the space, allowing her mind to wander back to the journals. The faded ink, the careful sketches, the symbols they had painstakingly tried to decode. The marks weren't just lines on paper; they were reminders, warnings, gestures of care across decades.

She glanced at Mitch, noticing the way he stared ahead, jaw tight, hands gripping the wheel. Protective, always protective. Tonight, it had been different, though. He hadn't hovered over her sketches, hadn't tried to redirect her attention. He had let her shine. That was trust. And that was partnership, a bond that made her feel secure and reassured.

A flicker of movement outside caught her eye on the darkened shoulder of the road. Probably a deer. Perhaps nothing. Still, a shiver traced her spine. The markers, the journals, they weren't just history. They were alive in a way she couldn't yet explain, lingering in the shadows, in corners, in the spaces between past and present.

She turned her gaze back to her sketchbook, imagining the tower on their house in Brighton, the one on the house in Morrisburg, both spaces Elias Greaves had touched.

Nicole exhaled slowly and steadily, experiencing both the excitement of finding and a calm worry.The excitement of unravelling the mystery kept her engaged even in the car's comfort, on a familiar road. The past had a way of reaching forward.

But for tonight, for now, it was enough. She had Mitch beside her. The journals, the sketches, and the markers had guided her this far. Whatever came next, she was ready to face it, a sense of courage and determination filling her.

Nicole shifted her sketchbook one last time. She glanced at Mitch, who drove with a quiet focus, jaw set in that familiar way.

"You know," she said, "I think the houses have more to tell us."

Mitch's eyes flicked to hers. "Yeah," he admitted.

"And we'll be ready."

Another shadow passed across the road ahead, fleeting and uncertain. A subtle prickle at the edge of Nicole's awareness. The markers, the journals, the past. They hadn't finished speaking.

But for now, the drive was theirs. The night held its quiet mysteries, and for the first time in a long while, they were ready to face them together.

The back door clicked shut behind them, and the quiet of their house enveloped them in a comforting embrace. Nicole kicked off her shoes, the familiar creak of the floorboards grounding her after the excitement of the evening. The cool ceramic tiles soothed her tired, sore feet after having stood in heels for most of the evening.

She set her sketchbook on the kitchen table and brushed a hair from her face. The sold pieces. The dots of red and green marking her success still lingered in her mind. She hadn't just survived the show. She had flourished, and the achievement gave her pride and pleasure.

Mitch hung up his jacket and leaned against the doorway, watching her with that half-smile that made her feel seen in a way he always could. "You were brilliant tonight," he said in a low, steady voice.

Nicole returned the smile, heart still buzzing. "I couldn't have done it without you," she said. "Even when ..." She stopped, thinking of Brad. Not worth the energy. Not tonight.

She wandered into the living room and sank onto the sofa. Another copy of her sketch of their home hung on the wall. The house with the tower gleaming in the early morning sun. The faint echoes of the symbols hidden in the shadows of the tower. Somehow, they were alive here, too. She traced them with her eyes, the edges of her mind tugged by the past.

Mitch joined her and handed her a mug of tea. He sipped slowly as his eyes scanned the sketch. "Looks like someone's keeping an eye on the house," he said, almost joking, but Nicole heard the edge of concern in his tone.

"Maybe they are," She remained focused on the picture. The lines, the symbols, the journals — they still had more to say.

For tonight, it was enough to be home. But she knew, deep down, the past had another story to tell, and they were beginning to hear it.

Chapter Forty-Two

APRIL 12, 1832

Dawn broke grey, and the morning mist, thick and ethereal, rolled over the scaffolding like smoke. Greaves arrived early, as always, expecting, half-hoping, to see his apprentice waiting with his usual energy. But the place was unchanged from yesterday. The ledger still bare, the foremen already shifting uneasily.

He did not show his irritation. Instead, Greaves, the seasoned overseer, moved among the men, offering clipped instructions and keeping order. Everywhere he looked, Whitmore's absence stared back at him. The mortar lines left unchecked, the masons muttered over measurements. Small inefficiencies that Whitmore had smoothed as though they were second nature.

By mid-morning, one of the younger men approached, hat in hand. "No sign of him, sir?"

Greaves studied the boy for a long moment before answering. "No, but the work continues with or without him. That is all you need to concern yourself with."

The boy nodded and retreated, but the question lingered. They all sensed it. Charles had not taken ill or overslept. Something else, something mysterious, kept him away.

Greaves climbed partway up the scaffolding and surveyed the site from above. His jaw tightened. He wouldn't speculate out loud, not yet. In his mind, a thought pressed with unwelcome weight, a thought that carried the gravity of the situation. A man so constant does not vanish without reason.

He inhaled slowly, letting the fresh morning air fill his lungs. If Whitmore did not return today, he would need to decide whether to act or let the matter lie and see what truths surfaced on their own.

As the men paused for their midday meal, Greaves found himself unable to shake off the mystery of the apprentice's absence. He'd investigate, careful not to appear too eager. He entrusted the site to the overseer and made his way to Brighton, where his apprentice was staying at the boarding house.

When Greaves knocked on the door, the stout landlady greeted him with a suspicious gaze. Her sharp eyes missed nothing, a fact that was not lost on Greaves.

"Mr. Whitmore?" she repeated when Greaves inquired. "I thought he might have gone off to visit friends."

"Friends?" Greaves asked, though he doubted the young man had many acquaintances outside the site.

She shrugged and folded her arms. "He kept to himself. Polite, but private. Paid his rent without fuss. Left after breakfast two days ago, and said he'd be back late. Never returned."

The landlady's words took Greaves aback. Whitmore disappeared from more than just the worksite. He thanked the woman, left a coin on the hall table out of habit, and stepped back into the street, his mind racing with questions.

The fog had dissipated, but in his mind it lingered. Men disappeared for many reasons, primarily drink, debts and scandal. Yet Charles did not strike him as the sort to drift. There was a steadiness in the young man, a moral ballast.

As Greaves turned back towards the building site, he thought of the ledger, the mortar lines, the unease in the younger men's eyes. The work should proceed without Whitmore, but Greaves's instincts whispered otherwise.

Something had unsettled him, and whatever it was strong enough to draw him away.

Whitmore lingered in the shadow of the fractured wall, his fingers brushing the faint line in the stone. It was small, hair-thin, yet to his trained eye it whispered of a strain carried too long. He glanced back over his shoulder, pulse quickening at the memory of those phantom footsteps. The alley was empty. Only the echo of his breath accompanied him.

Later at a corner tavern, thick with pipe smoke and damp wool, he found the witness he had been hoping for. An older man, bent at the shoulders, sat nursing a tankard by the hearth. The barman called him MacCready, and when Whitmore offered to pay for the next round, the man's tongue loosened.

"Aye, I saw it come down," MacCready muttered, his eyes distant. "That old wall looked sturdy enough until it weren't. Whole side buckled. Screaming. Dust so thick you couldn't breathe. They said the mortar was poor. Rushed work. Corners cut." He spat into the fire, as if even the memory tasted foul.

"Do you recall who oversaw the construction?"

MacCready's gaze slid towards him, wary. "Names don't matter much when stone buries men." He paused. "He was an odd sort. Talked about singing stones and other nonsense. Promised a building that would stand the ages. Didn't stand five months."

Charles experienced a chill deeper than the spring air. The conversation he had overheard in the Brighton tavern was not a rumour. And who else talked about singing stones? It had to be Greaves. The man he currently worked under. He left MacCready with coin enough for another drink and returned to his lodgings, head pounding with the weight of this newfound knowledge, a sense of impending danger creeping over him.

That night, by the light of a single candle, Whitmore opened his journal and wrote.

The crack in the wall may be but a scar, but the story behind it runs deeper. People whisper Greaves's name, though they never speak it outright. If what I have heard is true, then the work at Brighton carried the shadow of Kingston's ruin. And I … I stand in the midst of it.

Should I confront him on my return? Reason tells me caution. Greaves is measured and careful, and you shouldn't provoke him lightly. Yet, I cannot ignore what I have seen. If someone takes risks, if lives are endangered, silence is not an option. The weight of this decision presses heavily on me.

I imagine the conversation already. Measured words, pointed questions, watchful eyes. Greaves will deflect, minimize, perhaps even deny. But my conscience will not permit half-truths. Leaving the matter unchecked is an invitation to disaster.

Still, there is hesitation. Something in the man's presence commands a kind of respect, even wariness. I have no proof beyond the witnesses and my own observations. Would accusations without certainty serve justice, or only sow discord?

I will return to Brighton and observe first. Measure the site, the men, the work. Gather every detail before I speak. If Greaves has erred, I must understand the extent of the fault before addressing it. Prudence demands patience, and I will not rush this crucial task.

When the day comes, I will not shy away from the conversation. I will speak, even if the words are heavy with consequence. For in matters of safety, of life built upon mortar and stone, indecision is a risk I cannot afford.

Chapter Forty-Three

AUGUST 9, 2023

Nicole settled at her desk, sketchbook open but ignored. The glow from her laptop filled the quiet room as she scrolled through historical records and online archives. She wasn't looking for anything specific, just piecing together fragments, following the trail Greaves had left across time.

A headline caught her eye, small and easy to miss.

Mysterious injuries reported at Kingston construction site, 1832

She clicked on the link and scanned the article. Not a lot of information, but there was something about the phrasing, the mention of structural failure, that resonated with her. It wasn't a coincidence. Every piece was a warning, a safeguard, and now she had another piece of the puzzle.

Nicole took a deep breath and exhaled slowly. "Mitch," she whispered. "These are the things Greaves wanted us to see. These aren't just symbols. They're instructions and lessons from the past."

Her gaze remained fixed on the screen. History wasn't just on paper anymore; it was alive, whispering through time, waiting for someone to understand.

Mitch leaned against the doorway, watching Nicole scroll through her laptop, eyes narrowing at the words on the screen.

"Found something?" he asked, trying to keep his voice steady.

Nicole tapped the screen. "A report from Kingston, 1832 ... a building collapse. Nothing about cause or injuries, just says it was sudden and unexpected."

Mitch frowned. "So, it's a collapse, but it doesn't really tell us why."

"Exactly," she said, her tone cautious. "It's tantalizing, but it's not enough. I was hoping it might line up with some markers, but it's vague. Maybe I'll learn more tomorrow."

He stepped closer and rested a hand on the back of her chair. The candle on the table flickered, casting uneven shadows across the sketches she'd spread out. "Still," Mitch said, "it's a start. Something's there. And we're paying attention now. That counts for something."

Nicole smiled faintly, her fingers lingering over the keyboard. "It counts for something, but I wish it counted for more."

He nodded, swallowing the unease that twisted in his gut. "We'll keep looking. Piece by piece. Together."

The flickering light stretched across the room, and for a moment, the past seemed closer than it should, whispering its secrets, but still just out of reach.

Chapter Forty-Four

AUGUST 11, 2023

Nicole leaned closer to her laptop screen, squinting at the grainy digitized pages of the 1832 *Kingston Chronicle*. Her finger stopped at a headline in bold, ornate print.

TRAGIC MISHAP AT NEW WAREHOUSE — COLLAPSE CLAIMS LIVES

Her finger traced the words. The report described a partially built warehouse giving way, leaving several workers trapped. The collapse killed three people, injured many others, and critically injured one. Witnesses noted hasty construction and overlooked flaws, although no one formally recorded any blame. The air was thick with the smell of danger and the taste of suspense.

Mitch leaned over her shoulder. "This is it. The collapse. Whitmore went to see after hearing about it in the pub in Brighton. He didn't warn anyone beforehand. He went to document and understand what had happened." His dedication to preserving history was commendable, and it was thanks to him they were now piecing together the past.

Nicole's gaze dropped to a sketch reproduced alongside the article. "Wait … this looks familiar. Look at the lines, the support beams." She frowned. "It matches a sketch in Whitmore's journal." The realization dawned on her, sparking a fresh wave of curiosity. This could be a crucial link in the chain of observation and preservation.

Mitch nodded. "Exactly. He copied Greaves's original sketch. He wanted a record of what went wrong so he could study the collapse and preserve the knowledge for the future. "

Nicole exhaled, a shiver coursing through her. "So all those protective markers, the journals, the copied sketches ... they're a chain of observation and preservation. Greaves designed it, Whitmore documented it, and now we're piecing it together."

Mitch tapped the screen. "And the pattern spans decades, from Kingston to our house in Brighton and Morrisburg. Whoever follows the trail can see exactly where danger lurked. And where they took care to prevent it." The weight of this investigation was immense, but the potential to uncover the truth was even greater.

Mitch leaned back in the wooden chair and tapped his pen against the table. The newspaper clipping still glowed on the screen of Nicole's laptop, fading in a stark reminder that the collapse had really happened.

"Think about it," he said, more to himself than Nicole. "Whitmore didn't know what he was walking into. He just overheard a conversation in a Brighton tavern, then went to Kingston to see the aftermath."

Nicole nodded, her eyes straight ahead, glued to the screen. "And he copies Greaves's sketch of the structure. Every beam and every support. A record of what went wrong. Not his theory, but documentation."

Mitch traced the margin of the digitized clipping with his finger. "That's the thing. Whitmore's notes weren't just idle observations. They were careful, methodical even. He was preserving knowledge, but also ... warning future generations in a way."

He leaned forward, tapping another part of the clipping. "See these details here? Minor cracks in the walls, hasty repairs. This is the exact thing Greaves left markers for. He understood the weak points. Whitmore made sure the record survived, so no one would miss them."

Nicole tilted her head, and her fingers brushed against a faint symbol she had noticed in the Morrisburg attic. "So, all those scratches, etchings, even the things we thought were decoration ... they're a part of a continuum. Greaves designed them, Whitmore documented them, and now we're the ones deciphering them."

Mitch smiled faintly, the kind that comes with the quiet thrill of discovery, the kind that sends shivers down your spine. "And we're finally seeing the pattern. Not just a collapse in Kingston, not just a mysterious house in Brighton or Morrisburg, but a whole trail. Protective markers spanning decades. Whoever designed them expected someone to follow the path. And that someone, Nicole, is us."

He glanced at her, seeing the same mix of awe and determination in her eyes. "Looks like that someone is us."

Mitch stood and scrubbed his hand over his face. The glow of the screen made the growing stack of printouts beside him look more like a conspiracy board than casual research.

"Another distillery," Nicole said from across the table. The thick history book she had cracked open muffled her voice. She tapped a line with her finger. "Prescott had three, all busy in the 1860s."

Mitch exhaled through his nose. "Yeah, and they've flattened every last one of them. Parking lots, apartment buildings, nothing left to see." He flipped through another set of digitized property records, frustration prickling. "We're chasing ruins of ruins."

Nicole hummed and slid her finger down the page. "What about this?" She turned the book around for him to see. "The Moran-Hooker building, construction started in 1840. Still standing."

He pushed his chair closer and scanned the text. A warehouse used in the forwarding trade. Later, a Lifesaver Canada factory, a glove factory, and a pickle factory. The black-and-white photo showed a squat, yet imposing structure, shrouded in mystery.

Mitch's pulse picked up. "Doesn't name Greaves, but ... look at that." He pointed to the lintel over the window. "That's his signature curve. I'd bet my thesis on it."

Nicole smirked. "Better hope you're right, professor."

He ignored the jab, already reaching for his keys. "Come on. Let's check it out before I lose my nerve."

"It's late. Let's wait until tomorrow."

Chapter Forty-Five

APRIL 13, 1832

The sun cast long shadows across the scaffolding as Charles Whitmore approached the site. The hum of work carried on, but a palpable tension hung over the men. Their movements, usually fluid and coordinated, now carried a subtle stiffness. The glances that lingered too long on empty spaces spoke volumes.

Before he could even set foot on the main platform, Greaves was there, arms crossed and eyes sharp as flint.

"Young Whitmore," Greaves said, voice low, but laced with reproach. "Afternoon is no time to arrive at your post. And these past three days, I noted your absence. Explain yourself."

Charles straightened, masking the fatigue and unease that clung to him from Kingston. "I had business that required my attention. I regret the timing, but the work continues, does it not?"

Elias Greaves stepped closer, the taut lines of his stern face prominent. "The work depends on all of us. And when one vanishes without a word, the rhythm of the site suffers. I will not experience delays because of unexplained absences. Do you understand me?"

Whitmore nodded and chose his words with care. "Understood, and I assure you it will not occur again."

Greaves studied him for a long moment, then finally inclined his head. "Very well. Then let us see the progress made in your absence."

Charles followed him, scanning the men and materials, noting what had been done and what corners may have been cut. The shadow in Kingston lingered fresh in his mind. The cracked wall, MacCready's warning, but here, he needed to tread with utmost caution. Greaves had eyes like a hawk, and any hint of doubt or accusation could spark friction before he had gathered his facts.

He reminded himself to be patient, observe, and measure. The confrontation, where he would have to defend his actions, would come, but for now, he would watch and bide his time.

As Greaves, the seasoned overseer, moved from one group of men to another, the young apprentice fell slightly behind, his eyes sweeping the scaffolding, the timber stacks, and the freshly laid mortar. Everything appeared to be in order, yet subtle signs pricked at his trained eye. A joint too smooth, a beam set slightly off-centre, the faint smell of damp that suggested hurried work.

He crouched to examine a corner where the brickwork met the wall. A hairline fracture, nearly invisible unless you looked at it directly, ran along the edge. Too precise to be accidental, but no one seemed to notice. Whitmore made a discreet note in his pocket journal, careful that Greaves's sharp gaze did not detect it. He then pretended to adjust his boot, using the movement to scan the area for any signs of suspicion.

Footsteps echoed nearby. Greaves was moving back towards him, but the sounds behind him caught Charles off guard. A fleeting shadow in the corner of his eye made him glance up, only to find the area empty. He exhaled slowly and forced himself to focus. The mystery of Kingston's phantom footsteps had left a residue of unease he could not shake, adding a layer of suspense to the scene.

Whitmore observed the men as they worked. He listened to the rhythm of their hammering, the murmur of conversation. Minor details emerged. A mason hesitated over a joint; another wiped his hands on a coat that seemed untouched by sweat. Nothing overt, nothing he could confront immediately, but enough to keep him cautious.

Greaves returned, his voice low but firm. “Keep the pace steady. Do not rush the corners, young Whitmore. Check the men’s work yourself if you must. We can’t afford errors.” The tension between them was palpable, each word a silent challenge.

The apprentice nodded and tried to suppress the weight of his thoughts. He would follow this lead carefully, verify each detail and wait. When the time came, he would need every scrap of evidence to speak to Greaves without undermining authority or alerting the wrong men.

For now, observation was all he could manage. In the back of his mind, Kingston whispered, and the crack in the wall called him to uncover its truth. His determination was unwavering; his commitment to the task absolute.

Whitmore moved along the far side of the scaffolding, his gaze fixed on the mortar and timber. Their tasks absorbed most of the men so they remained unaware of his inspection. The shadowed presence of Greaves, a constant reminder of their strained relationship, kept him cautious.

Near the northeast corner, something caught his eye. A thin, uneven line in the fresh plaster, almost invisible unless the light struck it just so. He crouched and ran a finger lightly along the surface. Someone had hastily patched the plaster over a minor crack. Too neat and too deliberate. A worker had attempted to hide it.

His pulse quickened. This was no ordinary oversight. He made a discreet note in his journal, labelling it *Northeast Corner, a crucial part of the structure. Possible Stress Point.*

A murmur from the men made him glance up. One of the younger labourers had been whispering to another, glancing nervously at the boards above. Charles approached with measured steps, careful not to sound accusatory.

“Has this corner caused you trouble?” he asked softly.

The boy stammered and glanced towards Greaves, his nervousness palpable. "No, sir ... nothing serious. Just ... a little uneven, that's all."

Whitmore nodded, not pressing further, though the mind that had traced Kingston's collapsed wall now made the connection. Minor cracks hidden under carelessness, patched hastily, and left unchecked, they could become disastrous, a looming threat that he couldn't ignore.

He stepped back and took in the corner with a long, assessing glance. The evidence was subtle, but enough to confirm his unease. The same carelessness, the same hidden stress points he had seen in Kingston, seemed to echo here.

Greaves's voice cut across the site, clipped and commanding. "Keep your inspection thorough, young Whitmore, but do not linger in one place too long. There's work to be done."

He nodded again, masking the tremor of concern. Observation, careful note-taking, patience. The confrontation would wait, but the shadow of Kingston had arrived in Brighton. He would uncover its full story before Greaves realized the danger.

Whitmore continued along the scaffolding, inspecting walls, beams, and mortar with meticulous care. His experienced eye caught every detail, no matter how small. One corner showed a patched crack, another beam bore a faint twist, and here and there, the brickwork was slightly uneven. Each flaw alone was minor, perhaps within acceptable tolerances, yet together they formed a troubling pattern.

He paused to jot down notes in his journal, labelling each observation. *Southeast Wall, uneven joint; Beam 12 has a slight twist.* He had already recorded the patch in the northeast corner. The details mirrored the Kingston collapse. Hidden weaknesses, minor oversights, hastily concealed. A building might endure, or it might fail spectacularly.

A low murmur from a nearby worker made him glance up. The man avoided his gaze and shuffled his feet. He leaned in and whispered. "Was this corner difficult to align?" Greaves, the overseer of the construction, stood nearby, his presence a constant reminder of the delicate situation.

The worker swallowed, eyes flicking towards Greaves. "It ... gave some trouble, sir, but it's steady now. Nothing to worry about."

He returned to his journal and added to the southeast corner notation *potential stress point. Beam bowed slightly; patched with mortar. Observe for load tests.* This was a point that demanded careful observation and testing, a potential danger lurking in the structure.

As he watched the men work, Charles Whitmore sensed the human tendency to overlook minor flaws. He had seen it before. Repeated shortcuts, whispered assurances that 'it's fine,' the quiet hiding of errors rather than correcting them. Kingston had taught him the cost of ignoring those details.

Greaves's presence nearby reminded him of the delicacy required. He could not accuse. Not yet. Observing, recording, and gathering evidence was the path to take. When he confronted Greaves, it would not be rumour or fear that guided his words, but facts, patterns, and the knowledge of what could go wrong if ignored. One could not overstate the importance of gathering evidence in such a situation.

Whitmore straightened, looked across the scaffolding at the work in progress. The sun glinted off the beams and brick, ordinary and mundane. Yet, beneath those ordinaries lay a tension he could not dismiss. Every minor flaw whispered caution. Every patched crack told a story of potential disaster, a collapse that could cost lives and reputations.

He would wait, watch and record. The confrontation would come, but only when the evidence demanded it. When it did, there would be no doubt, and nothing left to hide behind.

Chapter Forty-Six

AUGUST 12, 2023

Mitch pulled his truck into the parking lot by the clock tower, shut off the engine and stared at the building across the corner diagonally from where they sat. It was the old Moran-Hooker warehouse, a place with a history as murky as the rain that had fallen east of Kingston. Although it wasn't a torrential downpour, he needed to turn on the wipers.

The stone steps were slick, and Mitch noticed the temperature drop as he pulled open the heavy door. The familiar thrum of voices, the comforting clink of glasses, and the inviting warmth of the pub washed over him, a stark contrast to the damp air outside.

The pub occupied the east portion of the basement of the Moran-Hooker, although 'basement' seemed incorrect. The ceilings were higher than those of most new builds, and the thick stone walls pressed in on all sides. Overhead, massive beams crossed like the ribs of an old ship.

Nicole slipped into a chair at a table against the far wall. Her eyes travelled upward. Mitch followed, scanning the room restlessly. The place smelled of yeast, wood polish, and river damp.

He tried to look casual as he sipped his pint, but his gaze kept snagging on the beams. Something about their scars didn't look random.

Nicole leaned forward. "Mitch, there," she said, her voice low. She pointed above the bar, where one of the old timbers caught the light the right way.

Mitch squinted. At first, the gouges looked like

the usual history of a working warehouse. Hooks, ropes, cargo impacts. But between the lines, a pattern emerged. A circle intersected by two faint triangles. A mark. His pulse quickened.

He jogged his chair back and tilted his head to follow the beam down its length. Another symbol surfaced, fainter, near the joint. Another still, half-obscured by a fresh bracket of iron that kept the timber in place.

Nicole's whisper carried across the small table. "It's the same as Morrisburg."

The din of the pub dimmed in Mitch's ears. The weight of the beams pressed down on him, and for the first time, he wondered if Elias Greaves's warnings hadn't been superstition at all.

"Shit." Mitch could not tear his eyes away. "He marked this whole place."

Nicole reached across the table and brushed his arm lightly. "Not random. Not vandalism. He was trying to protect it." Her words brought a new understanding, a light in the darkness of their investigation.

Mitch swallowed hard, a prickling awareness racing through him. They weren't just uncovering Greaves's past anymore. They were standing in it, their perception of the world around them forever altered.

Nicole turned her glass slowly, tracing the condensation ring on the tabletop. She tipped her head back, her eyes fixed on the beam above the bar. The carved shapes seemed to shimmer in the dim light as though the grain itself wanted to shift. She pulled a beer mat towards her, uncapped her pen and began copying one mark.

Mitch watched her at first with idle curiosity, but then something in her manner made the hairs on his arms prickle. Her hand moved with eerie precision, tracing curves and angles in long, unbroken strokes. Not the loose doodling he was used to seeing in her sketches. This was rigid, purposeful and almost mechanical.

Her face had gone slack, her eyes slightly

unfocused, as though she wasn't entirely in the room anymore.

He reached across the table. "Nicole?"

No response. Her pen scratched faster, the marks growing stranger, layered, and curling into one another, each stroke adding to the sense of impending mystery.

Suddenly, she stopped, blinked, and looked down as if seeing the coaster for the first time. Her hand had cramped around the pen, smudging ink across her fingertips. The coaster was no longer blank. Instead, intricate and tangled symbols covered it, overlapping in layers, each a puzzle awaiting a solution, and they seemed to pulse if she stared too long.

She drew a sharp breath. "I didn't ..." Her words trailed off.

"You were gone," Mitch said, unsettled. "Like, like someone else had hold of your hand."

Nicole flipped the coaster over, her heart pounded, and she swore the strange inked shapes pressed through the cardboard, etched deeper than the surface. She forced a laugh and tucked the coaster under her glass. "It's nothing. Just scribbles."

But neither of them could bring themselves to believe that.

Chapter Forty-Seven

APRIL 13, 1832

Whitmore stood at the top of the scaffolding, notebook in hand, eyes scanning the site one last time. He had noted each crack, each uneven joint, each hastily patched corner. They formed a pattern he could no longer ignore.

Greaves moved among the men below, assuring command, correcting measurements, his voice steady and unyielding. Charles watched him and weighed every gesture, every glance. The man's authority was absolute here, but the apprentice now carried a quiet leverage. Proof.

He exhaled to steady himself. It was time.

Descending the scaffold, he approached Greaves, keeping his tone even and controlled. "Sir," he began, journal in hand, "I've been reviewing the work, surveying the site, and I believe there are areas that merit closer attention."

Greaves looked up, brows knitted. "Observing? You've done nothing all afternoon but wander. What are you suggesting, young Whitmore?"

"Minor flaws, sir. Cracks, patched joints, and slight bows in beams. Individually, they are small. Perhaps negligible. But collectively, they resemble structural issues I've encountered before. Issues that if left unchecked can become dangerous."

Greaves's jaw tightened. "Are you questioning my oversight?"

He shook his head slowly. "Not questioning, sir. Reporting. Documenting. Ensuring that the work here is as secure as it must be. That is all."

A tense silence fell between them. Charles sensed the burden of Greaves's scrutiny and saw the careful assessment in those sharp eyes. But beneath the challenge, there was a faint acknowledgement. Whitmore had observed thoroughly, and he had evidence. The weight of this evidence added a sense of gravity to the situation.

Greaves finally inclined his head slightly, voice measured. "Very well. Show me these flaws, young Whitmore. I want to know whether your concerns are justified or merely imagined."

He nodded, and his relief mingled with caution. The confrontation had begun, but the work, the actual proof, would have to speak for itself.

Whitmore gestured towards the southeast corner, his tone careful and precise. "This area, sir. The beam where it meets the wall. Note the slight bow and patched joints. It may seem minor, but the pattern is concerning."

Greaves followed, eyes narrowing as he studied the corner. Charles remained quiet and let the man see the details. The hairline cracks hidden beneath fresh mortar, the subtle twist in the beam and the uneven alignment of bricks that someone had hurriedly smoothed over.

"Minor imperfections, young Whitmore," Greaves said at last. "Nothing that will compromise the structure."

He shook his head. "Individually, perhaps, but together they form a pattern. I've seen the consequences of such oversights before. A building compromised from within, collapsing when least expected."

Greaves's gaze hardened. "You refer to Kingston, I presume?"

After a brief pause, the apprentice nodded. "Yes, sir. I observed a collapse there, and the similarities are troubling. I would not bring this to you lightly, but the risk demands attention."

Greaves stepped closer and inspected the beam

more critically now. The air between them was taut, each aware of the other's scrutiny. Finally, Elias exhaled slowly, his voice measured, but it carried a trace of grudging respect. The apprentice understood the weight of that respect, a reminder of the power dynamics at play.

"Very well, young Whitmore. Show me everything you've noted. We'll examine each flaw, determine whether it is indeed a structural issue or nothing more than your imagination."

Whitmore's pulse quickened. The confrontation had moved beyond words. Now it was evidence versus authority, observation against experience. He had brought Kingston with him in his mind, and the shadow of that collapse loomed over Brighton.

As they began the detailed inspection, Charles kept his expression neutral, but inside, he was determined. He knew this was the moment truth would either surface or remain buried beneath stone and mortar, and he was not about to let it escape.

The apprentice took one last look at the repaired beam, committing every detail to memory. He nodded slightly to himself, satisfied that the men would now address the flaws. Without another word, he turned and walked towards the gate, journal tucked under his arm. The late afternoon sun cast long shadows across the site, and the distant sound of the nearby creek filled the silence he left behind, a sense of accomplishment warming his chest.

Greaves remained on the scaffolding, watching the young man's retreating figure. Pride and irritation warred with an unfamiliar tension that knotted his chest, a physical manifestation of his internal conflict. He had listened, dismissed, and finally, reluctantly obeyed. Yet, even as the men set to work correcting the flaws, Greaves could not shake the weight of his apprentice's calm certainty. Each command now carried a shadow of doubt, and for the first time in years, he experienced the gnawing awareness that he might have been wrong.

He muttered instructions to the men, but the words sounded hollow even to his ears. Had he overlooked something critical, as Whitmore had suggested? He prided himself on control, on knowing the building inside and out, but today, he sensed that control slipping.

Whitmore's parting glance lingered a moment too long, calm yet unyielding. It was not mockery, nor a challenge. It was conviction, the kind Greaves respected and resented in equal measure. And then the young man walked away, boots crunching over gravel, leaving a quiet emptiness in his wake, but a lingering influence in Greaves's mind.

Elias exhaled, a slow, measured release of air. Pride battled with reason. He would never admit his apprentice was right, yet he couldn't ignore the need to double-check the repairs, to ensure no shadow of failure remained.

As the men set to work on the corrections, Greaves watched from the scaffolding. Sunday would bring rest, yes, but the weight of the week still pressed on him like a heavy stone. Whitmore had warned him, and though he would not speak of it, the warning would shape every decision from this day forward.

Chapter Forty-Eight

AUGUST 12, 2023

When they drove to Prescott, they went straight through without stopping. It made for a long ride, so Nicole suggested they break it up on their way home with a stop in Kingston for a bite to eat.

Mitch navigated the city streets from the main highway until he and Nicole were almost at Lake Ontario.

"What about this place?" he asked as he stopped in front of the Merchant Tap House.

"Sure, why not?"

"Do you want to go in and grab us a table while I park?"

Nicole looked at the patio at the front and the side of the building. "I'll come with you," she said after a few moments of people watching.

There was a parking lot ahead, so Mitch pulled into it, grabbed the ticket from the machine and laid it on the dashboard of the truck.

Inside the pub, the air was warm with chatter, the delicious aroma of fries and vinegar clinging to the exposed stone walls. Above them, heavy beams stretched across the ceiling, blackened by time and scored with old tool marks. Vertical beams helped support the horizontal ones.

Nicole stared at the wood. Her eyes searched the timbers as though she expected a familiar pattern to emerge. The wood seemed to ripple with suggestion, every groove hinting at shapes she couldn't name. Her pulse quickened, and a ridiculous hope sparked in her chest that she might see one of those protective symbols again.

A member of the staff came and took their orders. Both chose fish and chips; Mitch ordered a pint of Rickard's Red for himself, and Nicole opted for Coors Light.

"Checking for doodles?" Mitch teased.

The corners of her mouth tugged into a grin. "Something like that."

He shook his head with a smile. Nicole's gaze lingered on the beams. To anyone else, they were just structural supports, relics of 19th-century craftsmanship. To her, they seemed like watchful sentinels, holding secrets etched into the grain.

The same person who took their orders returned with their drinks.

It wasn't until their food arrived that she finally pulled her eyes away, but a whisper of unease followed her through the rest of the meal. If the past was watching, how much longer would it wait before it revealed itself again?

Mitch leaned back in his chair, eyes drifting over the limestone walls and the heavy timber beams overhead. The place's history was rich, and the craftsmanship outlasted everything. Conversations hummed through the interior, forks clinked against plates, but to him, it seemed oddly hushed, as if the walls were whispering secrets from a bygone era.

A flash of bronze near the entrance caught his eye. A small plaque, engraved with the year 1836. He squinted and traced the numbers with his gaze. Old enough. It could be one of Greaves's earlier works. The thought of uncovering more about this mysterious building and its history piqued his curiosity.

His attention drifted upwards to the beams over their table. One had a shallow gouge, faint but deliberate-looking. A mark of craftsmanship or something else? He couldn't shake his anxiety, as if the building itself was trying to tell him something. He shook his head, trying to force it from his mind, but the unease lingered.

Nicole glanced up at the beams, her fingers brushing the rim of her glass absently. He kept his thoughts to himself, observing her. If there was something hidden in the wood, she didn't need to see it tonight. Not yet.

Buildings, old or new, seemed to remember everything. Every careless step, every whispered promise. Even the empty corners weren't truly empty. Mitch shook his head. Ghost stories weren't his style, and yet, he sensed it: a presence, subtle, but unmistakable. It was as if the pub itself was listening, waiting to reveal its secrets.

Mitch pressed his lips together and forced a half-smile. "Just thinking," he mumbled, more to himself than to her. The old stone walls and beams seemed to lean closer, silent witnesses to both past and present.

The question gnawed at him quietly and steadily. If this *was* Greaves's work, what had he built into it, and why?

They left The Merchant Tap House with the chill of the evening air nipping at their cheeks; the headlights cutting through the early darkness along the Kingston streets. Nicole sat quietly in the passenger seat, still glancing upwards now and then as if the shadows of the pub's exposed beams had followed her.

Mitch kept his eyes on the road, aware of the way she tapped her fingers against the notebook tucked in her lap. He stole a glance at her profile, then at the road ahead. He knew how old the pub in Kingston was. Four years older than the earliest portion of the Moran-Hooker building in Prescott. He said nothing. Not tonight. Letting her muse flow freely, he focused on keeping them both safe, even if the weight of history pressed uncomfortably against him.

"Everything okay?" he asked, his voice light, though the undercurrent of concern threaded through it.

Nicole gave a faint smile. "Yeah. Just thinking."

The rest of the drive passed in quiet

companionship, punctuated by the hum of the engine and the rustle of her pen moving over paper. By the time they pulled into their driveway in Brighton, Nicole had already begun to sketch, letting her hand wander almost of its own accord. Circles, triangles, faint arcs. The same symbols she had drawn in the pub in Prescott now emerged on the page with deliberate repetition.

Mitch watched her for a moment, his heart tightening. He didn't understand it, and yet he couldn't look away. Whatever was guiding her hand, whatever the protective markers meant, it was far from finished. Somehow, he knew they weren't either.

Chapter Forty-Nine

APRIL 14, 1832

Greaves stood at the edge of the scaffolding, hands clasped behind his back as he surveyed the men. Labourers mixed mortar in large wooden troughs, others lifted timbers with ropes and pulleys, and stone was reset where Charles had pointed out the flaws. He had barked the orders himself that morning, unwilling to give credit to his apprentice ... but the work was being done.

Out of the corner of his eye, he caught sight of Whitmore. The young man stood apart from the crew, journal tucked under his arm, gaze focused on the wall as though he alone could see its secrets. There was a composure about him, a maddening calm, as though he did not need to stay and watch the work.

"You've a sharp eye for cracks, young Whitmore," Greaves said at last, his tone edged and dismissive. "Though I sometimes wonder if you see shadows where none exist." His words carried a hint of challenge, a subtle invitation for Charles to defend his actions.

Whitmore turned and met his gaze without so much as a flinch. "Better to see a shadow before it becomes a ruin."

The words landed heavier than Greaves expected, and for a moment, a heavy silence stretched between them, charged with unspoken tension. Then the apprentice gave the smallest of nods, as if they had settled the matter, and turned away. No protest, no demand, no lingering claim of victory. He simply walked the length of the site, boots crunching over gravel, until he vanished.

Greaves's jaw tightened. He told himself the boy was a meddler, a nuisance who had pressed too far. Yet, as he looked back at the repaired wall, he sensed the undeniable truth settle over him. The house would stand stronger for Whitmore's meddling, a fact he would never admit openly.

He shifted his weight, barked an order to the nearest mason, and refused to look towards the road again.

Back at the boarding house, Whitmore, seated at the small desk, gazed out the window.

April 14, 1832
Brighton, this day,

The men labour without pause, as is the custom. Six days a week, with only Sunday granted for rest. I cannot fault them, nor the pace expected by Mr. Greaves. Yet, the flaws I have observed cannot wait. Each crack, each bow, each patched joint demands attention, and I perceive the weight of responsibility, a duty I cannot shirk, to ensure the work proceeds correctly.

The knowledge that Sunday will bring a brief respite to the men does little to ease the urgency. I can only hope they heard my guidance and earnest words before returning to what they must repair on Monday.

I have left the site, and with it the company of Mr. Greaves. Someone will mend the wall, not for my name's sake, but because we could not ignore the flaw once we spoke it aloud. He blustered, as is his manner, but the masons were ready to work. In that, I find a measure of peace, a soothing balm for my troubled mind.

It is not mine to remain. My presence breeds only friction, and I sense that pressing further would only close Mister Greaves's ears rather than open them. Better the work be done, however grudgingly, than my pride insist upon recognition.

I confess, as I walked away, I recalled the ruin in Kingston again. I see the crack still there, though it is long buried. It is possible my watchfulness now is but penance for something that I could not prevent.

Yet there is this comfort. I depart knowing the house will stand, not collapse upon those within it. That is worth more than any quarrel with a proud man who cannot abide correction.

So ends my work in Brighton.

Chapter Fifty

AUGUST 12, 2023

Back home, Nicole sank into the wooden chair at the kitchen table. The stack of notes and photocopies spread out before her. Mitch paced nearby, mumbling to himself over a set of Whitmore sketches. She wanted to focus, wanted to organize the clues from earlier, but her mind kept wandering back to the pub in the Moran-Hooker building.

She picked up a scrap of paper, a piece of an envelope she'd meant to use for a grocery list, and without thinking, picked up a pen.

As Nicole traced circles and triangles, her mind drifted back to the Merchant Tap House in Kingston. The exposed beams and limestone walls had pressed against her imagination earlier, and though she didn't know it, Greaves had once carved symbols into the timbers of that very building. Hidden marks meant to protect, to warn, to endure. They had arisen out of hard lessons. The collapse in Kingston years before, the groan of timber and stone under unforeseen strain, the cries of the men trapped and injured. Each line she drew echoed his careful intent, a thread spanning centuries, linking past and present, builder and observer. It appeared as if someone, or something, might yet be watching her every move. The thought sent a shiver down her spine, but her hand did not stop.

She didn't notice the minutes ticking by. The lines on the paper grew more intricate and layered, and they curled into patterns she didn't remember planning. Her fingers tingled with a strange energy; her hand moved faster than her thoughts could keep up, as if it had a mind of its own.

Mitch froze mid-step. "Nicole ...?"

She blinked and looked down at the paper. Ink sprawled across the envelope in a network of symbols she hadn't consciously drawn. Her chest tightened. This was the second time today that this had happened. "I ... I don't remember doing all that," she whispered, her confusion palpable.

Mitch's voice was low and careful. "You — you were gone for a while. Like back at the pub. Like someone else was guiding your hand."

Nicole pressed her palm against the paper, tracing one symbol with her fingertip. Her stomach churned. "It's like the building, or Greaves, is still here. Still reaching."

The room grew colder. Quieter. The house hummed around her, and for a moment she couldn't tell if the tingle in her hand was fear, excitement, or something completely different. The eerie silence added to the suspense. Nicole tried to shove the sensation down. But deep inside, she knew she hadn't finished the sketch. Not yet.

Mitch leaned over the table, careful not to jostle the envelope. The symbols sprawled across it were intricate and far more complex than what they had actually seen in Prescott.

"Do you still have the beer mat from the pub?"

Nicole reached into her bag, pulled it out, and set it beside the paper on the kitchen table.

He traced a finger along the lines, then stopped abruptly and dashed out of the room. Up in his office, he retrieved the Whitmore journal that they had received in the mail and Greaves's warped book they had brought home from Morrisburg.

Back in the kitchen, he set the two books on the table. "Nicki, look at this," he said and pointed to a symbol on the piece of paper. "See the arc here? And the intersecting triangles? That's straight from Whitmore's notes. The same protective pattern." He picked up the journal, leafed through it until he found the desired page. "He copied it from Greaves, I'll bet." Mitch set the first book down, then fanned through the pages of the other. Again, the same symbol. "And here's the master's version."

Nicole moved closer, still unsettled by how her hand had moved on its own. "But I didn't. I didn't consciously draw all this."

Mitch shook his head, awe creeping into his voice. "Doesn't matter. Your hand picked up the rhythm, the pattern. Whoever or whatever left those marks knew someone like you would follow the trail. This isn't just random."

He tapped the envelope. "So we know Whitmore copied these marks from Greaves's plans. He preserved them for a reason, and now we have another piece of the puzzle."

Nicole swallowed hard, and her eyes darted around the room as though the walls were listening. "So all the buildings ... our house, the collapsed structure in Kingston, Prescott and Morrisburg ... they're connected. He left a network of warnings. Protective markers."

Mitch nodded and said, "Not that they did any good in Kingston, but yes, that's it exactly. And this sketch — your sketch — confirms it. Greaves knew someone would eventually read them.And maybe Whitmore thought someone like us would finally understand."

Nicole exhaled, and the tension dissipated, yet a lingering shiver ran down her spine. Their house had undergone a peculiar transformation, now pulsating with a life she had never perceived. The old timber floors and dim corners were now charged with an enigmatic history. Deep within, she sensed the journey was far from over.

Mitch smiled faintly. "And neither are we."

Nicole leaned back, her gaze fixed on the journals that once belonged to the two men from the past, now resting on her kitchen table. The paper and the beer mat she had unconsciously sketched on flanked them. Were these her protective markers? But what were they guarding against? The collapse of walls and ceilings? The errors of long-forgotten builders? Or was it something more sinister, lurking in the hidden spaces these houses had kept secret for decades?

Nicole pressed her palm on the sketches she had drawn in a trance-like state, her fingers tracing the inked lines. Were these forces from the past, the unseen, or from entities that lingered just beyond her grasp? She couldn't explain her compulsion to continue, but a part of her instinctively trusted the guidance. Deep within, she knew this was only the beginning.

Looking towards the ceiling, she whispered,

"Is there anybody there?" said the Traveller,
Knocking on the moonlit door;
And his horse in the silence champed the grasses
Of the forest's ferny floor:

"You say something, babe?" Mitch asked.

"No, just thinking."

Mitch, with a keen eye, leaned over the table, poring over the intricate patterns Nicole had drawn. His finger traced the intersecting triangles and circles, comparing them with the faded notes and Whitmore's copied sketches in the journal.

"I know I've said it before, but these lines ... they're not random," he said. "Greaves or Whitmore planned this carefully. Each mark, each arc — it's all part of a network. A system of warnings, and maybe even a map."

Nicole watched him, her fingers brushing the edge of the beer mat. The hum of their Gothic Revival house seemed to settle around them, almost expectant.

Mitch tapped the page gently. "If we follow these, they might lead us to more. Other buildings, other markers ... whatever he was trying to protect."

Nicole nodded as the weight of history pressed in. The trail was far from finished. "We're to follow it, aren't we?" The potential danger of what they were about to uncover was palpable.

Chapter Fifty-One

APRIL 15, 1832

Whitmore sat on the edge of his bed in the boarding house; the quiet of the afternoon pressed against the thin walls. The echoes of hammers and saws from Brighton were gone from his ears, yet the memory of Greaves's calm, measured voice remained.

He had left the site the previous day, after laying out every concern he'd harboured. The flaws, the misaligned beams, the reminders of Kingston, had returned no more. The act of walking away felt final, but a hollow ache settled in his chest. Had he done right by himself? By the men? By the house that would rise without him?

His hands rested on his knees, fingers drumming a slow, restless rhythm. The tension lingered in his shoulders, even now, after the restrained, professional discussion about the house's structural integrity. Greaves had not argued, had only nodded, eyes unreadable, which left Whitmore with the weight of decisions unshared.

Did I act as a man of conscience, or merely a man afraid to shoulder responsibility?

He let out a slow breath and traced the ceiling's lines with his eyes. The sun dipped lower and painted the room in gold and shadow. Just outside Brighton, the work continued, but he was absent, a spectator to the house's fate. The memory of Kingston gnawed at him still. The splintered beams, the collapse, the lessons learned too late; the lives lost and the trust broken.

Whitmore picked up his journal and began to write, each stroke a quiet confession and a way to steady his mind. Notes, sketches, questions — all attempts to make sense of what he had witnessed and what he had left behind. The act of recording, he hoped, might be a shield against doubt, a way to honour both the craft and his own conscience.

He set the pen down and stared out the window as the evening shadows stretched across the town. He had made the decision. He had left Greaves's employ. Yet, the questions of safety, skill, and foresight, the very essence of his profession, would follow him long after the Brighton site faded from view, haunting him with the spectre of potential disaster.

Greaves stood in the fading light on the Brighton site, hands clasped behind his back, while his eyes traced the lines of the rising walls. The echo of Whitmore's boots had long since faded, which left only the steady rhythm of the men continuing their tasks. He had known the apprentice would leave eventually. The boy's conscience had always been sharper than most, but the finality of it still left a small, bitter weight.

The imperfections Whitmore had pointed out haunted him. Minor, yes, but reminders of human error, the limits of foresight. He had nodded when the lad confronted him about the structural issues, said nothing more than necessary, and maintained the cool mask that had carried him through decades of design and construction. And now the apprentice was gone, leaving Greaves to take the responsibility alone.

He turned, brushed dust from a timber and let his mind drift to Kingston, to the collapse which had sharpened Whitmore's fear and guided his own caution ever since. A careful plan and measures, including regular inspections and safety protocols, but each project bore the risk of human misstep.

Greaves exhaled, slow and measured and allowed himself a brief glance at the site as it stood. He could have reworked every beam, every joint, but such perfection was never feasible. The team noted, understood, and mitigated the flaws where possible. That was the only protection he could guarantee, a testament to the importance of foresight and diligence in his work. And the subtle guidance of his own markers, perceivable, served as a constant reminder of these qualities.

The sun slipped below the horizon, leaving shadows to stretch across the building site. Greaves straightened, squared his shoulders, and stepped towards the lean-to to gather his papers. Whitmore's absence would echo for him, too, but there was work to be done. Always work. And somewhere, in every corner, every mark, his care endured, a testament to the ongoing nature of his work and the persistence of his dedication, whether the apprentice remained to see it.

Chapter Fifty-Two

AUGUST 14, 2023

Nicole woke as the first rays of the sun filtered through the bedroom curtains, a familiar start to her day. She rolled over on her other side to snuggle with Mitch, but his side of the bed was empty. That wasn't like him not to come to bed. She knew the Morrisburg house preoccupied him. He'd made a mug of coffee when they got home, and she headed to the bedroom to preview the images on her laptop, a routine she had grown accustomed to.

She swung her feet out of bed and padded across the hall in her bare feet to the bathroom. This was the one room they had the most difficulty redesigning. She wanted retro, and Mitch wanted modern. Her logic was to keep the decor similar to the rest of the house, although the separate hot and cold taps on the old sink were a pain. Mitch wanted something newer because there was less chance of problems with new plumbing and fixtures. In the end, they compromised. She didn't know where he had found the old-fashioned toilet, which someone had completely modernised the tank. The clawfoot tub was better than the one it replaced.

Once she finished her ablutions, Nicole tiptoed past Mitch's office. The door was ajar, and he sat at his drafting table with his back to her. He'd set the table up so it overlooked the corner of the property where the Holbrook house had once stood. Why did he want to be reminded of where he nearly bled to death?

Pencil in hand, Mitch traced thick stone walls,

measured angles and noted window placements on the blueprints spread out across the surface. The Morrisburg house was stubborn, like a jigsaw puzzle missing pieces. The sealed room in the cellar, rumoured to hold the key to a long-forgotten treasure, and the concealed stairway to the tower, believed to be a passage to another world. None of these things showed on the original sketches he'd found in Greaves's notebook.

He rubbed his jaw, trying to imagine how the house looked when it was first constructed, long before layers of renovation and rot warped its shape. The Morrisburg property, a grand estate with a dark past, had seen generations of owners and countless secrets buried within its walls.

A faint creak echoed from the hallway, and he turned. Nicole stood in the doorway with a steaming mug in each hand. She approached and handed him a cup. "You been in here all night?"

"Yeah. This house. The one near Cornwall. I don't know if Elias Greaves was a genius or an imbecile. Nothing makes sense."

"Then how it is coming isn't the question to ask," Nicole said.

Mitch smiled. "Actually, better than I expected. The floor plans are starting to line up with what we saw. I think the hidden stairway might connect to a third-floor wing that was sealed off at some point."

Nicole stepped closer. "That fits with what Charles Whitmore wrote in his journal. The idea of secret passages and hidden chambers."

He nodded, shading a section of the blueprint. "I'm trying to recreate the original design, but there's something off about the proportions. Like the architect designed not with function but with symbolism."

Mitch set down his pencil and finally met her eyes. "We'll figure this out. Together."

The floor plans, spread across the table in the dimly lit room, depicted a house with a rich history. It was a place that had been reshaped by time and secrets, its shadows now captured in these intricate lines. Nicole traced the lines with her eyes, imagining the hidden stairway that spiralled upwards and the forgotten room beneath the floorboards.

Nicole stood in the doorway. Her fingers tightened around the frame. The ghostly presence she'd felt in the tower still lingered in her mind, unspoken but impossible to ignore.

"Do you think Elias Greaves knew what he was building?" she asked.

Mitch paused, his pencil hovering over the paper. "He wasn't just building. He was creating something. Something more."

Nicole nodded slowly, the weight of that thought settling deep inside her.

She took a deep breath. She still hadn't shown Mitch the pictures she had taken the previous day, the ones that revealed a hidden passage in the tower. Now, the weight of his words settled deep inside her, urging her to share her discovery.

Nicole took a deep breath, attempting to push down the unease creeping up her spine. "We have to find out what. Before it's too late."

Chapter Fifty-Three

APRIL 18, 1832

Whitmore sat alone in his room at the boarding house, the sounds of the town of Brighton muffled through the thin walls. Carriage wheels clattered on the cobblestone streets, a burst of laughter from the nearby tavern where he had first heard the rumours, which later turned out to be fact, about Greaves. His candle sputtered and cast more shadow than light across the page.

The journal lay open before him, and his pen hovered. The words wouldn't come easily. He had walked away from Greaves, from that strange house with the bizarre angles and symbols carved in beams. The memory clung to him like a burr. He still saw Greaves's steady gaze, unreadable, almost magnetic, as if the man were not so much speaking to him as measuring him.

He tapped the pen against the edge of the desk. Why had he stayed at that cursed place so long? Why had he listened to tavern gossip and then sought to test it with his own eyes? Curiosity, yes. But something else as well. A pull he couldn't name.

He bent his head and forced himself to write.

> *The man works with an intensity I have seldom witnessed. His signs, though meant for decoration, bear marks of intent beyond their surface. Symbols, shapes, flourishes. All repeated, as though a language lies beneath the brushstrokes. He claims nothing of it, but I*

cannot believe such patterns to be chance.

He sat back, the nib scratching to a stop. The room seemed colder for having committed those words to paper. His training urged him towards reason, to dismiss such suspicions as fancy, but the image of Greaves and his work lingered. The concentration, the way his hand seemed guided by more than skill.

With a sigh, Whitmore closed the journal. He pressed his fingers to the cover, as though sealing something inside. Tomorrow, he told himself, he would put Brighton behind him. Travel on. There are always other towns, other commissions, other work to be had.

And yet, as he snuffed the candle and darkness settled, the lines of Greaves's symbols seemed to float behind his closed eyes — insistent, unfinished, as though demanding to be seen again.

Chapter Fifty-Four

APRIL 22, 1836

The mist rolled off the lake, curling around the unfinished limestone walls like pale fingers. Elias Greaves stood on the damp ground with his hands clasped behind his back. His eyes traced every line of the rising structure, his meticulousness clear in every detail. The warehouse was modest in scale, but he treated it with the care of a cathedral. Every beam, every joint, every stone mattered.

He knelt briefly, tracing the grain of a heavy timber with a practiced finger. A shallow carving, almost imperceptible, already marked the beam. A triangle flanked by two arcs. Protective. These markings were not to keep thieves out, but to guard what he could not see. The walls themselves, the space inside, the people who would work here long after he was gone, provided a sense of security and foresight.

A shout drew him to the scaffolding. One labourer, a young man with an impatient streak, had wobbled while hoisting a beam. Greaves's sharp voice cut through the morning fog. "Steady. Mind the joinery."

The beam shivered under the worker's hands, and for a heartbeat, the air seemed to tremble. Greaves's stomach tightened. He couldn't help but recall the collapse in Kingston. Not this building, not yet, but the other one. The day had been chaos. The snap of wood, the groan of stone, the helpless cries of men trapped beneath timbers. He had survived, but the memory haunted him, a constant warning etched into his bones.

He turned his gaze back to the scaffold, slow and

deliberate, ensuring every handhold, every rope, every plank was secure. The weight of his responsibility was palpable. Nothing would happen here, not on his watch. Not this time.

By midday, the frame stood solid, each beam carefully aligned. Greaves ran his hand along the limestone wall, soothing dust and checking for flaws. Tiny cracks had already begun to form near the foundation, subtle but telling. He made mental notes, adjustments to be made before winter set in. The warehouse had to endure; failure was not an option.

As the workers ate their meal, Greaves lingered alone in the corner, scratching additional symbols into the timber with a hidden chisel. Circles and lines, almost invisible, but placed with purpose. Protective markers. He didn't know what dangers the years would bring, but his instinct told him to hide some vigilance and send warnings ahead, carving them into stone and wood for only the attentive or curious to notice.

He stepped back, surveying the space. The warehouse hummed quietly around him. The mist pressed through openings that had yet to have windows installed and carried the scent of the nearby lake and timber. Somewhere in the shadows, the past and future converged, and for a moment, Greaves felt it keenly. The building would last if he did his part. If not, well, that was a problem for someone who came after.

Greaves paused at the edge of the lake, and the morning mist clung to his coat. He surveyed the warehouse one last time; the timber frame was solid, and the limestone walls held firm. The workers were busy inside, unaware of the delicate balance that had kept them safe this morning. He allowed himself a brief, satisfied nod, content in knowing his work had been successful.

A chill swept off the water, crawling along the ground and into his boots. He shivered, though he told himself it was only the damp. Yet something in the air, something unseen, made him glance over his shoulder. Shadows clung to the far corner of the warehouse, deeper than they should have been, and for a moment, the faintest whisper brushed his ear. He couldn't name it, and he didn't try. The mystery of the warehouse seemed to deepen with every passing moment, leaving him with a sense of intrigue that he couldn't shake.

Turning away, he started down the path towards the road, the fog curling around his boots. Ahead, the world waited. Other projects, other buildings, other marks he would leave behind. Each one a warning, a safeguard, a message carved into wood and stone for anyone who might notice. His work, a blend of architecture and something more, was a secret he guarded fiercely.

And somewhere, in the quiet corners of the world, he knew his work would continue to echo long after he was gone. The shadows he left behind, the symbols hidden in timber, the whispers in empty spaces. These were not mere echoes, but the voices of those who had come before, trapped in the walls and floors of his creations. They would wait for those who knew how to read them.

Greaves quickened his pace, swelled by the mist and promise of more work, unaware that some marks he set someone would find generations later, guiding others to truths he could not yet imagine. The thought of future discoveries, of the secrets waiting to be uncovered, filled him with a sense of excitement that he couldn't ignore.

Chapter Fifty-Five

AUGUST 14, 2023

Mitch ran a finger along the edge of the old ledger, feeling the raised ink where Whitmore had copied sketches. Every line and symbol hinted at a mind both meticulous and secretive. He retraced the patterns, thinking about Greaves. Not just the man who built the Brighton and Morrisburg houses, but the one who built rules into the very walls, leaving warnings that spanned decades. The meticulousness was both fascinating and unsettling.

He leaned back and stared out the window. Between 1832 and 1870, Greaves had been everywhere, leaving traces of himself in every corner of every building. And somewhere along the way, he had vanished, leaving a trail of clues no one had thought to follow, until he and Nicole arrived. The mystery of Greaves's disappearance hung in the air, thick and palpable.

Mitch smiled faintly and shook his head. Even with all the newspaper clippings, journals and symbols, some of him couldn't dismiss the idea that Greaves still looked on. Maybe the man always would.

The shadows in the room deepened, and for just a heartbeat, Mitch felt the way Whitmore must have done centuries ago. Aware of something lingering just beyond sight. But he pushed the thought aside. Protective markers, hidden warnings, cryptic journals ... all puzzles. The protective markers etched into the walls seemed to guard secrets. The hidden warnings buried in the floorboards whispered of danger. And the cryptic journals held the key to the mystery. And Mitch liked puzzles.

But for now, the past could wait. The present was pressing, and Mitch could feel the weight of the mystery bearing down on him.

Chapter Fifty-Six

APRIL 30, 1836

The morning air was crisp and carried the scent of wet timber and mortar. Saturday work meant fewer hands on the Kingston site, but Greaves preferred it that way. Less noise and fewer distractions.

He paced along the newly laid foundation, his eyes scanning each joint and each plank with precision. Even the slightest misalignment was a thorn in his side. The men were steady enough, but caution was always necessary. A single misplaced beam could undo weeks of labour.

"Watch the brace, Harper," he barked as a young labourer lifted a beam too quickly. The timber wobbled and teetered at the edge of its cradle. Harper froze. Eyes wide.

Greaves moved faster than anyone expected, hand snapping out to steady the beam, and nudged it back into place. "Careful. One mistake and we'd be counting injuries instead of measuring progress." His tone was sharp but not cruel. There was a discipline to it. A lesson about foresight as much as safety, and the potential consequences of a lapse in vigilance. Harper swallowed, nodding rapidly. Greaves crouched and inspected the rope ends that held the scaffold. Frayed. A minor detail, easily overlooked, but enough to compromise everything. He jotted a quick note in his ledger, adding an extra brace and a new rope to the list.

As the men returned to work, Greaves allowed himself a moment to step back and survey the skeleton of the building. Even in the early morning light, he imagined it complete. Stone walls, timber beams locked together in precision. Each line, each mark, each beam carried intent, a testament to his crucial role in the construction.

His mind wandered briefly back to the Harrowick commission near Brighton. That project nearly ended in disaster from an accident similar to the one that almost happened here. With that in mind, he knew he needed to leave instructions, subtle markers, precautions, tiny messages for eyes that might not see for decades.

A sudden crack made him spin. The scaffold shifted slightly, and one man swore. Greaves strode over and examined the structure. Nothing broken. Nothing was lost, but the reminder lingered. Control was fleeting and vigilance eternal.

By the time the sun hit its peak, the foundation was steady, the beams aligned, and Greaves felt the satisfaction of a job done properly. As the men packed up, he lingered and scribbled a few final notes. Some would only make sense years from now, despite being visible.

He brushed his hands on his coat, his gaze lingering on the structure. Every building told a story. Every corner held a memory. And somewhere in the shadows, someone, maybe even Whitmore, would notice. He only hoped they understood.

Chapter Fifty-Seven

AUGUST 14, 2023

Mitch had sat hunched over the drafting table so long that his neck ached. The late afternoon sunlight spilling in through the window turned the paper into a warm gold, but his focus was on the pale blue lines traced across it.

Whitmore's journal lay open beside him, the spidery handwriting angled sharply across the page. Most entries were about measurements, deadlines, or Elias Greaves's moods, but a stray note caught his eye. Half-formed thoughts that didn't belong in an architect's log. One had stopped him cold.

Pattern repeats. Elias will not explain. Says it is an old truth, older than stone itself.

Mitch looked back at the roll of paper spread across the table. The surviving Brighton drafts Whitmore had worked on before he quit.

There it was again. Not obvious if you didn't look for it. The shape curved subtly through the decorative plasterwork on the main staircase landing. Another fragment hid in the tracery of the tower window. If you followed the arcs and interactions, they formed the same symbol that Nicole had photographed in the hidden room of the Morrisburg house's basement. A revelation that caught Mitch off guard.

A shiver crept up his spine.

If Whitmore had left Brighton before Greaves and his crew finished the house, then he'd only ever seen these early plans, yet he recognized the pattern as deliberate enough to jot down a warning in his private journal. And Greaves ... Greaves had carried that same pattern into his last known design decades later.

He glanced at Whitmore's journal again, wondering if Dan Brown had been onto something about hidden codes and symbols. Only here, there wasn't an ancient church or a priceless painting. Here, there were two houses tied together by a man who seemed to leave messages in the very bones of his work.

Nicole traced her fingertips over the corner of the old blueprint, careful not to tear the fragile paper. Mitch had rolled it out across the surface and weighed the corners down with a couple of his textbooks, the open Whitmore journal, and the worn book she had brought back from Morrisburg.

Now that he'd pointed it out, she couldn't unsee it. The lines and curves were so subtle they disappeared into the ornamentation if you didn't know where to look, repeated in the Brighton plans exactly the way she recalled in the Morrisburg house. This pattern, a mysterious and intricate design, seemed to hold a secret that had eluded even the talented architect, Greaves.

The chair creaked under her when she sat back. "So, Whitmore saw these decades before Greaves built the house in Morrisburg," she said, "and he still recognized it later."

Mitch nodded and pointed to the entry he'd shown her earlier. The entry itself looked innocent enough at first, with measurements and supply notes, but the last line carried an enormous weight. It read:

Pattern repeats. Elias will not explain. Says it is an old truth, older than stone itself.

The cryptic message seemed to contain the key to a truth buried for centuries.

An old truth. Those words gave Nicole a chill. It didn't feel like fear, but more like standing too close to something she didn't understand.

The house they lived in now, Brighton, had been Greaves's first, which survived. The one in Morrisburg was his last. If this pattern had followed him throughout his entire career, it wasn't a flourish. It was deliberate.

Nicole's eyes drifted from the blueprint to the warped book, a collection of Greaves's personal notes and sketches, sitting like an unanswered question on the table. "If Whitmore quit before they finished this house, he must have thought the pattern was dangerous enough to abandon Greaves entirely."

Mitch looked up. "Or dangerous enough to leave a warning for whoever found his notes next."

That thought prompted her to glance at the envelope that had earlier contained Whitmore's journal again. No return address. Addressed to The Occupant. She wasn't sure if it was luck or something else that had put it in her hands. But she had the creeping sense that they were stepping into the same puzzle Whitmore had tried, and failed, to solve.

Nicole let her gaze linger on the two sets of lines. The blueprints with their neat, measured strokes, and the Morrisburg book's looping, almost living symbols, each one a tantalizing mystery waiting to be unraveled.

She reached for the book, its cracked, worn leather cover warm from sitting under the light. The scent of old paper and dust rose as she eased it open. Mitch leaned closer but didn't speak, letting her think.

On the page before her, one symbol stood out. It was an interlocking curve like a stylized knot. She flipped back to the plans of their house and scanned the sweeping banister of the main staircase. There it was. Just below the newel post lamp. Not identical, but close enough that her pulse quickened. This symbol, she knew, was not just a decorative element. It was the key to a mystery that she and Mitch were just starting to solve.

"Might be a coincidence," Mitch said, though his tone made it clear he didn't believe it.

Nicole traced the knot with her fingertip. "Or maybe Greaves was hiding these in plain sight, over and over."

She thought about Charles Whitmore — young, idealistic, probably eager to prove himself — and how unsettling it must have been for him to watch the same symbol take shape in wood and stone without understanding why. She thought about his leaving before they had finished the construction of the house.

Her stomach tightened. "If something scared him enough to quit, what does that mean for us?"

Mitch closed the journal, tapping it against his palm. "It means we compare every symbol in this book with every line in these plans. If Greaves left a trail, we'll follow it," he declared with a determined tone.

Nicole nodded, though part of her wished she'd never seen the connection. The weight of the mystery, the fear of what they might uncover, and the determination to solve it all warred within her. Still, she turned the page, ready to mark the next match.

Deep down, she suspected Whitmore had been right. The pattern wasn't a decoration. It was a message, and they were finally beginning to decipher it, a sense of enlightenment dawning on them.

Nicole stood over the drafting table holding the blueprints for their house. This time, the book from the house in Morrisburg, a place where the mysterious architect Greaves had left his mark, lay open beside it. She held a ruler and moved it along the lines in search of any shapes that echoed in the strange symbols Greaves had sketched.

Mitch leaned over her shoulder. "Try the east wing. That's where the tower's foundation connects to the main structure."

Nicole adjusted the ruler and traced the curve of a narrow corridor. Suddenly, her finger paused. "Here."

She tapped a cluster of arches drawn faintly in pencil of a small, almost hidden alcove between two rooms. The shape of the hook matched one of the recurring symbols in the book. A stylized spiral that twisted inward like a shell.

Mitch's breath caught, and he felt a shiver run

down his spine. "That's the same symbol carved into the newel post at the house in Morrisburg," he said, his voice barely above a whisper. "And look at this ..." He pulled up a photo on his tablet of the faded carving, illuminated by a flashlight, from their first visit.

Nicole's eyes widened as she shifted her gaze from the blueprint to Mitch's photo. The realization hit her like a bolt of lightning. "This isn't just a coincidence. Greaves embedded this pattern in both houses. More than that, it looks like a map."

Nicole's eyes widened. "A map?"

Mitch nodded, his eyes sparkling with excitement. "A hidden one. The way the corridors and rooms line up with the spirals. Maybe it's a secret route or passage. It might show how to get from one place to the other."

Her pulse quickened. "Between the two houses?"

"Exactly."

Nicole reached for the Morrisburg book again and flipped through the pages more eagerly now. The two houses were connected beyond architecture. The fact someone had designed them to share secrets sent a chill down her spine.

They were standing at the edge of something much bigger, something shrouded in mystery. And the deeper they dug, the darker the shadows would become.

Chapter Fifty-Eight

MARCH 25, 1844

The Cobourg Courthouse rose from its foundation like a skeleton, its timbers stark against the pale spring sky. The clang of hammers and the rasp of saws carried across the square, where townsfolk gathered now and then to watch the progress. Elias Greaves stood apart, his sharp eye catching details no one else seemed to see. The way a joist sagged under strain. There was a faint crack in the ridge beam when the wind pressed hard against it.

"Mister Greaves," called one of the foremen, "shall we set the upper brace before sundown?"

Greaves gave a measured nod, his dedication to his craft unwavering, though the unease twisting in his gut deepened. The men went about their work with the confidence of the routine, but to Greaves, every structure bore the weight of Kingston. The memory of dust and cries, of stone collapsing like sand, haunted him still.

When the site emptied for the midday meal, Greaves remained, his actions shrouded in secrecy. He climbed the scaffold slowly, boots firm against the planks, and set his palm against the beam in question. It was solid, but not enough. Never enough. From his pocket, he drew a chisel; the steel caught the light as he pressed it to the wood.

The mark came quickly. Practised now. An interwoven knot, its lines straight and sure, a language no one else could read. Protection. Preservation. He carved another on the brace beside it, smaller, and hidden in the shadows.

Below, a boy no older than twelve, one of the apprentices, had returned early from his meal and looked up at the scaffold, his curiosity shining in his eyes. “What’s that you’re doing, sir?”

Elias descended, slowly and deliberately, wiping his hand clean of dust. “Builder’s shorthand,” he said smoothly. “Notes to remind me where we need to add strength.”

The boy nodded, wide-eyed, as if the explanation was enough. Greaves placed a hand on his shoulder before moving past. Yet, in his heart, the unease never left. He wondered how many more beams, how many more stones, would carry his secret language before someone uncovered the truth.

Greaves brushed the dust from his fingers. One day, someone might see them. Someone might understand. Until then, he would continue because he could not stop.

Chapter Fifty-Nine

AUGUST 15, 2023

Supper over, the dishwasher loaded, and the kitchen tidied, it was time to resume the search for the elusive Elias Greaves. Both Nicole and Mitch, fuelled by their unwavering determination, had their laptops set up on the dining room table across from one another.

Nicole scrolled, the glow of the screen washing her face in the dimmed room. "Here, look at this."

Mitch came around the table and leaned over her shoulder, his coffee forgotten. The page she'd pulled up was a heritage listing, a treasure trove of historical information that most people would overlook. But halfway down the text, the name *Elias Greaves* leapt out in bold, a significant discovery in their quest.

"He worked on the courthouse in Cobourg," Nicole said, reading on. "1844, design modification, something about adjustments to the stonework." She glanced at Mitch, her pulse quickening. "You don't suppose ...?"

Mitch rubbed his jaw, his mind already calculating the potential challenges. "If he left a mark there, it wouldn't be anywhere easy. That's a government building, reinforced, patched and re-patched. Whatever he tucked away, if he did, it's probably buried behind walls or under floors." The difficulty of the task ahead only added to the suspense and anticipation.

Nicole clicked open an old photograph from the archives linked on the page. The courthouse stood stern and immovable, its limestone walls catching the light in sharp planes. "It has the same feel, though. Look at the symmetry. The weight of it. It's Greaves."

"Yeah." Mitch leaned closer and pointed to the foundation. "If I were him, that's where I would put it. But nobody's getting in there, not without tearing the place apart."

Nicole sat back, her shoulders sagging. The photograph on her screen seemed to stare back at her, imposing and untouchable. For a moment, she let herself imagine it — the faint etching of a mark hidden in the wood, waiting for someone to see it again.

But that was all it might be. Imagination. Another door closed, another story sealed where they couldn't follow.

With a sigh, she shut the laptop. "We'll never know for sure."

He reached over and gave her hand a squeeze, but Nicole's gaze drifted towards the darkened window. She understood some truths would inevitably stay concealed, no matter how much one desired to expose them.

Mitch, his hand stroking her shoulder, observed Nicole. She remained fixated on the screen, her shoulders drooping under the weight of frustration.

"You know," he said gently, "maybe Greaves had a sense of humour. Hiding his markers where no one can reach? Kind of a centuries-old practical joke."

Nicole's lips twitched, but she didn't look up.

"I mean, he must have known someone stubborn enough would come along. Someone who wouldn't give up." Mitch brushed his hand against hers. "That's you, by the way."

Finally, Nicole looked up, her eyes meeting Mitch's, and a faint smile gracing her lips.

"Hey," Mitch said, softening the moment with a half-smile and a touch of humour, "if all else fails, we'll just admire the stonework and call it a field trip. Ice cream on the way home?"

She chuckled, a little breath escaping the tension.

They hadn't solved everything, but for now, it was enough.

Nicole let out a soft breath; the tension in her shoulders loosened just a fraction. Mitch's words, light as they were, brushed against the edge of her frustration and eased it.

A small smile tugged at her lips, more genuine this time. She glanced at Mitch, and something unspoken passed between them. Acknowledgement that even if some doors remained closed, they weren't standing still.

"Field trip and ice cream," she said, recalling family outings with her family and Mitch. And this time, the corners of her mouth lifted entirely, the memory bringing a warmth to her heart.

The courthouse could keep its secrets for now. There would be other days, and other discoveries. For the first time in hours, Nicole allowed herself to feel that even half a step forward was worth the journey, and that there was hope for the future.

Chapter Sixty

MARCH 27, 1844

The chill of the early spring air clung to the stonework, and dampness seeped into the mortar that was not yet set. Elias Greaves stood alone in the rising shell of the courthouse, and his boots crunched over scattered chips of limestone.

He ran a hand along the unfinished wall, his fingers tracing the clean lines. To anyone else, it was a proud moment in progress. The work that would outlive them all. But Greaves felt the weight of unseen eyes upon him, as though every cut of stone carried a question he couldn't answer.

The men had gone for the day, leaving their hammers and chisels stacked in neat piles. Silence pressed in on him. He crouched near the central beam and pulled a small tool from his coat pocket. With slow precision, he carved a mark, subtle and hidden beneath where the floorboards would later cover. Preserve and protect.

He lingered over the cut, his hand steady but his chest tight. It no longer felt like superstition, nor the whim of a cautious craftsman. The symbols were becoming something else. A charge maybe, or a promise binding him to the places he touched. If he failed to leave them, the building itself would betray its purpose, and him along with it.

The echo of Kingston still haunted him, a constant reminder of the stakes. He had sworn then he would never walk away without doing everything in his power to guard against such ruin.

Greaves straightened, set the chisel aside and gazed up at the skeletal frame around him. The courthouse would stand. It had to. This mark, unseen, unnoticed by all others, was his solemn vow, his unwavering commitment to its protection.

Greaves pulled his collar up against the wind and left the site. The fresh cut gleamed faintly in the dim light — a symbol of his commitment, a promise sealed in wood and stone.

Chapter Sixty-One

AUGUST 19, 2023

Mitch grabbed his keys off the counter. Nicole stood by the door, backpack loaded with her sketchbook, pencils and camera, her eyes bright despite the earlier frustration.

"Ready?" he asked, trying to sound casual. He was brimming with anticipation, and he could see it mirrored in her eyes. It was bad enough that they had to wait until the weekend to make the trip.

Nicole gave him a half-smile. "As ready as I'll ever be. Though I have an inkling, we won't get far inside."

"Then we make it a reconnaissance mission. Observe, sketch, and then enjoy the ice cream. Mutually beneficial."

She chuckled and slid into the passenger seat. Mitch started the truck; the hum of the engine blended with the excitement of possibility. Even if the courthouse didn't reveal its secrets, being there, seeing the stones Greaves once touched, felt like a step closer. Their emotional ties to this place fuelled their curiosity.

Some truths might remain locked away, but they could still chase the echoes, one road trip at a time. Their determination was unwavering, driving them forward despite the unknown.

The truck rolled to a stop at the edge of the courthouse lawn. Nicole leaned forward, eyes widening as she took in the building's stern façade. Limestone walls rose like a fortress, precise and unyielding, their symmetry meticulous down to every carved corner.

"Wow, it's ... imposing."

Mitch parked and shut off the engine, and the quiet settled around them. "Greaves liked his projects to make an impression," he said, his voice tinged with awe. "You can practically feel the weight of his hand in the design, his influence clear in every stone."

They walked up the stairs, the echo of their shoes on every step, a heavy, rhythmic sound that seemed to fill the air. Nicole reached out, brushed her fingers along the wall, warmed by the sun, and imagined the faint presence of a protective marker tucked somewhere inside.

"Do you think it's here?" she asked, her voice almost lost to the wind.

Mitch crouched to inspect the foundation. "If it is, it's buried deep. They've reinforced, patched, and maintained this building for decades. There's no way in without major renovations."

Nicole sighed and allowed her fingers to fall from the wall. The courthouse was magnificent but untouchable. Still, being here, walking the same steps Greaves had, seeing the lines she'd drawn, it was enough to fuel her insatiable curiosity.

She glanced at Mitch, a wry smile tugging at her lips. "Well, at least we can say we were here. Officially."

Mitch chuckled softly, the sound warm in the crisp air. "And I still owe you ice cream."

The two of them lingered a moment longer and absorbed the stillness, the rich history, and the invisible traces of the man who had left hints across generations. Some secrets were meant to be admired from the outside.

Back in the familiar embrace of her home, Nicole sank into her favourite chair, sketchbook on her lap. The day in Cobourg replayed in her mind. The austere limestone, the echo of her footsteps, and the impossible reach of whatever Greaves had left behind.

She flipped to a blank page and began to doodle absentmindedly, tracing patterns that had appeared in her mind since the Merchant Tap House. These were the same symbols she had felt at the courthouse, the ones that seemed to be a warning. Protective markers, yes, but now they felt less like cryptic symbols and more like a quiet insistence.

Watch. Remember. Safeguard.

Mitch's voice drifted from the kitchen. "Tea's ready."

Nicole paused, pencil hovering. She glanced towards the kitchen and smiled faintly. Even without solving every secret, there was comfort in being there, in following the trail, in understanding that Greaves's markers were more than just warnings. They were care, threaded across time, and a mystery waiting to be unravelled.

She scribbled one last tiny symbol on the page, a looped flourish that mimicked the curves of the courthouse windows. Quiet, protective, persistent. She closed the sketchbook and let the soft weight of understanding settle. Some things would remain out of reach, but the echoes of her experiences, the memories and emotions they stirred, were here, and she could hold them.

Chapter Sixty-Two

MARCH 28, 1844

The morning air was crisp and carried a faint tang of limestone and fresh-cut timber. Greaves stepped onto the Cobourg Courthouse site, boots crunching against gravel, surveying the scaffolding that rose like a skeleton towards the sky. The building would be grand. A symbol of law, order, and civic pride, but every stone, every beam, every joint whispered potential disaster if left unchecked.

He meticulously circled the framework, his eyes catching a slightly bowed joist and a gap in the masonry where the mortar had set unevenly. These were minor flaws, easily fixed, but his unwavering dedication and responsibility wouldn't allow him to ignore them. With hands on his hips, he inhaled deeply, knowing that a building's strength lies in the care unseen.

Greaves crouched beneath the rafters, unseen by the labourers, and carved a small, precise symbol into a timber beam. This symbol, a protective marker, was subtle enough to be overlooked but deliberate enough to preserve what otherwise might falter. It was a ritual now, part of his work, part of himself. A quiet convenience between builder and time.

As he straightened, his thoughts briefly wandered to Brighton and the collapse in Kingston, both of which had occurred years earlier. The memory of the calamity in Kingston, where a poorly constructed building had collapsed because of hasty construction, still haunted him, a silent warning echoing in every corner, scaffold, and stone. *Do not fail. Do not leave it to chance.*

A hammer rang out in the distance. He glanced towards the men, then back at his mark, satisfied. The courthouse would stand. It would shelter its occupants, witness history, endure storms and sun. But he too had left a part of himself in its bones. A quiet guardian for those who would come after.

By midday, with the men engrossed in their tasks, Greaves allowed himself a rare moment of reflection, his eyes lifted to the partially completed clock tower. In its shadow, he felt the weight of responsibility, a burden he carried with the strange exhilaration of leaving behind a trace that time could not erase.

"So I build," he said, "to preserve. To protect. To endure. To provide a sense of security that transcends time."

Chapter Sixty-Three

AUGUST 20, 2023

The next morning, Nicole sat at the kitchen table, sketchbook closed but still radiating warmth under her hands. Mitch poured coffee into their favourite mugs and set one in front of her, sliding his laptop across the table.

"Thought we'd pick up where we left off," he said, his voice tinged with anticipation. "Greaves didn't make it easy, but I think the trail is still there waiting for us to follow."

Nicole opened her laptop and pulled up a series of heritage listings, old construction records and newspaper archives. She scrolled past familiar sites — Brighton, Kingston — and stopped at a new entry. They had visited the Cobourg Courthouse the previous day.

"It's still inaccessible," she muttered, "but maybe there's something else. Another building, another clue."

Mitch leaned over her shoulder, his fingers tracing the screen. "Greaves left markers in more places than we realized. It's like he wanted us to see the care he put into his work. If we could just piece it together."

Nicole nodded, her eyes shining with determination. The protective markers weren't just symbols. They were a thread connecting him to the future, to them. And she was ready to follow wherever it led.

Nicole leaned back in her chair and continued to scroll through the archives. "Here. Port Hope. Look at this municipal building. Early 1840s, stone foundation, exposed beams inside. Still intact."

Mitch peered over her shoulder, his eyes narrowed at the cornerstones in the photographs. "Greaves's style," he muttered. "Subtle, deliberate. If he left a marker here, it won't be obvious."

Nicole's fingers hovered over the keyboard. "Exactly. But every building we've found him in before has had that same careful placement. It's like he's leaving a trail of breadcrumbs for someone to follow."

"Here's hoping we don't lose the trail like Hansel and Gretel did when the birds ate theirs." Mitch grinned. "Well, it looks like we're heading to Port Hope next. Another chapter, another puzzle piece."

Nicole closed the laptop, a flutter of excitement in her chest. Each building, each subtle clue, was pulling them closer to understanding Greaves's intent. And for the first time, she felt the weight of the thread, protective, deliberate, and reaching across time pressing insistently at her mind. The more they uncovered, the more they understood. And the more they understood, the more they wanted to know.

Mitch brought the truck to a stop at the edge of the quiet Sunday street, and Nicole felt a thrill of anticipation. The Port Hope building rose before them, its weathered stone walls marked by time, but still proud. The wooden beams were visible through the large open windows.

"This is it," she said, unfastening her seatbelt and climbing out. "The photographs didn't do it justice." Her eyes focused on the structure ahead. A former municipal building now served as a small, local arts centre. The mystery of the building's past piqued her curiosity.

"Looks like they've preserved a lot of the original architecture," Mitch said. "Exposed beams, cornerstones ... classic Greaves."

The front door was open, and a modest *Welcome* sign swayed in the breeze.

Inside, the vast hall revealed soaring ceilings, the original timber beams exposed and weathered. Exhibits lined the walls, showcasing local artists and historical artifacts. Nicole's gaze immediately drifted upward, tracing the beams, her fingers itching to sketch.

"See those notches?" she murmured as she crouched slightly to get a closer look at a carved symbol near the base of a supporting beam. "Another protective marker, just like the ones in our house, Prescott, and Morrisburg. He left them everywhere."

Mitch stepped closer, his brow furrowed in thought. "Always visible, yet hidden. Someone had to pay attention to see them."

Nicole's eyes followed another series of small carvings along the far wall. "It's like he wanted us to notice, but only if we were willing to look closely."

Mitch wore a mixture of pride and amusement on his face. "Well, we're willing. That's what counts." Their combined sense of accomplishment in deciphering the symbols was clear in their expressions.

They lingered, drifting through the space, eyes darting to every beam and cornerstone. Each symbol told a story, whispered across time, and Nicole shivered with excitement. The thread of protection was growing, weaving a map of Greaves's care that spanned decades, and they were understanding it, one marker at a time.

Mitch leaned against the doorway with his arms crossed, his brow furrowed in thought. Nicole sat at the kitchen table, her sketchbook open beneath her hand, pencil moving in steady, deliberate strokes. Her auburn hair spilled over her face. It was a familiar sight. One that usually calmed him, but tonight, something felt different. He couldn't shake the sense that she was sketching things meant for eyes other than his.

His thoughts slipped back to the way her voice had fallen into that poem without warning.

"Is there anybody there?" said the Traveller ...

The words had been soft, almost absent-minded, but they had stayed with him, worming their way into his thoughts since. He'd told himself it was nothing, just his wife being whimsical, poetic. But when he closed his eyes at night, the echo came back sharper and colder, like a question no one wanted answered, intensifying the unease in his mind.

Nicole looked up and caught him staring. "What?"

He forced a smile. "Just admiring the artist at work, that's all."

"You're always so sweet," Nicole replied, her voice warm and affectionate.

Her answering smile was quick and warm before she turned back to the page. The pencil moved again, looping its way into lines that seemed older than they had any right to be.

Mitch shifted his weight, a shiver running through him though the house was warm. Something about the air felt ... attentive. The shadows in the corners were too deep. He reminded himself he didn't believe in ghosts, that he never had.

And yet, the line came back, colder than before, and it lodged deep in his chest as if the house whispered it in reply.

"Is there anybody there?" said the Traveller ...

Mitch clenched his jaw and stayed by the kitchen door where he'd been, watching Nicole. Guarding her. But in that moment, he couldn't shake the unsettling certainty that they weren't the only two souls in that room, amplifying the sense of isolation in his realization.

Chapter Sixty-Four

JULY 3, 1844

The summer heat in Cobourg clung to the stone walls of the unfinished courthouse, the air thick with dust and the sharp tang of mortar. Whitmore adjusted his cravat, feeling out of place among the workers as he crossed the yard. He had come out of obligation, summoned to record the progress for his employers, but his heart was not in it.

And then he saw him.

Greaves stood on the scaffolding, brush in hand, his jacket discarded in the sun. The years since Brighton had not diminished him. If anything, his presence seemed sharper, more magnetic, his movements as precise and deliberate as ever. Whitmore froze when the old unease returned like an echo.

The journeyman architect's chisel arced across a panel destined for the judge's chamber, laying down what appeared to be an ornament, a flourish to soften the stone. Yet, his trained eye caught it at once. The repositioning of lines, the way the curves nestled into one another, formed something more than mere embellishment.

A memory of Brighton stirred. The tavern whispers, his own journal entries written in uneasy haste. He had left, telling himself he was free of it. But here it was again, waiting.

Greaves descended the ladder with the ease of a younger man, though silver threaded his dark hair now. He spotted his former apprentice and smiled as if they were old friends.

"Ah, young Whitmore," he greeted warmly. "You find men the midst of work once more. What do you think? Will this house of law approve of a touch of grace?"

Whitmore inclined his head stiffly. "The judges may appreciate the ornament. The people ... I am less certain."

Greaves chuckled. "People see what we show them. Rarely more, young Whitmore."

The words spoken so casually sent a chill down Charles's spine. He longed to press him, to demand what purpose lay behind those marks. Instead, he opened his notebook and made a brief, mechanical sketch of the scaffolding, unwilling to meet Greaves's eyes.

When he looked up again, Greaves had returned to his work, chisel strokes flowing with uncanny assurance. Whitmore's hand trembled as he recorded the scene. He knew then he would never be free of the man, nor of the designs he left behind.

Chapter Sixty-Five

JUNE 12, 1858

The mid-afternoon sun struck through the half-finished rafters and painted the floor in sharp gold and shadow. Greaves knelt, chisel poised over a beam that had already borne three sets of marks from his hand. Each line, each cross, each subtle flourish was no longer casual or fleeting. They were obligations. Vows. He carved slowly and deliberately, measuring the depth, the angle, and the space in between.

The surrounding men laboured on, unaware of his attention to these invisible lines. To them, he was a perfectionist, an exacting master. To himself, he was a custodian of something far older than the time or stone, a legacy of craftsmanship and responsibility that had been passed down through generations. Something that demanded care beyond the skill of carpenters and masons.

A shiver ran down his spine. He paused, hands hovering over the wood, and recalled the collapse in Kingston. The wobbled scaffolding, the screaming labourers, the moans of the dying ones taking their last breaths. Even now, decades later, it clung to him, a shadow he could neither shake nor ignore.

Greaves set the chisel aside and traced his fingers over the marks, committing them to memory once more. Preserve, protect, and endure. They had become more than instructions. They were warnings. A conversation across time, and he was the unwavering messenger.

The day pressed on; the sun inching westward. Sweat stained his collar and ran down his back, but he did not stop. He couldn't. Not yet. Not until each beam, each joist bore witness to his diligence.

And when the men finally left, tired and laughing, Greaves remained. Alone, he inspected every hidden corner in the structure, noting where his hand would need to mark again, where shadows might gather and harbour misfortune. He was no longer building a house, or a warehouse, or a courthouse. He was negotiating with the unseen, the intangible forces of memory and consequence, bargaining with them to ensure the safety and longevity of his creation.

As twilight settled, he stepped back, chest tight, and his eyes scanned the skeletal walls. The structure stood for now. But he knew he must return, carve again. Mark again, or risk the weight of every past mistake he had ever witnessed falling into ruin.

Chapter Sixty-Six

AUGUST 22, 2023

Nicole gathered the journals and her sketches, stacking them on the table. Her fingers lingered on the edges of the paper, tracing the symbols she had connected moments before.

Mitch stood nearby, toolbox in hand, his attention no longer on the upcoming job. He kept glancing towards the hallway where the sound had come from, his body tense and rigid with a palpable unease.

"We should double-check the windows and doors," Nicole said casually, even though she flinched at a faint creak from above. "Make sure nothing's loose."

Mitch nodded, though neither moved immediately. Instead, they stood together in the quiet kitchen and listened. The house held its breath; it seemed.

Another soft, barely audible noise echoed like the scrape of a boot against the floorboards. Nicole's hand shot up and clutched Mitch's arms, her fingers digging into his skin. "It's nothing," she said, but Mitch knew from the tremor in her voice it was something.

His jaw tightened. "The past might be checking in." He'd tried to shrug it off, half-joking, half-serious.

Nicole gave him the side-eye. "Or it's just reminding us we're not done yet."

Mitch didn't answer, only glanced towards the shadowed hallway once more. The unease lingered, crawling over his skin like a draft he couldn't shake, growing stronger with each passing moment. He hated that it felt real. Hated that he could feel it at all.

Yet, somewhere beneath the tension, a spark of resolve flared. They had the journals, the symbols, the connections. Whatever was waiting, whatever had left the markers, they would face together, their determination shining through the darkness.

But as Mitch watched Nicole straighten the sketches, he couldn't help but notice the faintest shift in the light across the wall behind her, subtle and wrong. He blinked. Nothing should have been there.

And yet ... it was.

Nicole's eyes remained fixed on the sketches as she leaned back in her chair. The lines, the symbols, the remaining markers. They all finally clicked. Brighton to Kingston to Prescott to Morrisburg. Every mark was deliberate, every curve a warning, a safeguard.

Mitch stood behind her, hands resting on the back of her chair. He didn't touch her. He didn't need to, but his presence was a tether, grounding and protective. He'd watched her struggle, watched her doubt herself, and now he felt a profound sense of relief. She'd done it. She'd solved it.

"He wasn't just decorating ..." Her voice trembled with the weight of understanding. "He was protecting. Anticipating danger, leaving warnings in plain sight, coded in a way only someone paying attention could understand."

Mitch swallowed hard. "And now we know," he said, his voice low. "We can do something about it. Whatever it was, we can handle it. Together."

Nicole turned her head back and forth. "There's more," she said. "Something Greaves wanted us to see last. Something final."

A sudden draft made the papers flutter, and they both froze. Just the house settling, Mitch told himself, but Greaves had built it in the early 1800s so it should be long since settled. The shadows seemed heavier than they should have been, longer. He shifted slightly, his protective instinct flaring, even as rational thought told him there was nothing.

Nicole's hand hovered over the last symbol, and a

shiver ran through her. Mitch leaned closer and brushed a strand of hair from her face. “We've got this,” he said, voice low but firm. “No matter what.”

Her eyes met his. “I know.”

As they returned their attention to the last marker, the faintest, impossible sense brushed at the edges of Mitch’s awareness, as if the past was watching, waiting, acknowledging that they had understood, and that the story was still unfolding. The anticipation of what was to come was palpable.

Mitch’s jaw tightened, and his mind raced as he tried to ground himself. Protectiveness and dread intertwined, a quiet certainty that they were now fully part of whatever Greaves had left behind. And that the past hadn’t finished with them yet.

Chapter Sixty-Seven

FEBRUARY 28, 1870

Whitmore sat at his desk in the dim lamplight, the smell of coal oil permeating the room. His hand hovered over his closed journal. Should he even bother to document this latest news? He didn't work for Greaves anymore. What difference did it make to him if the man was building again?

He opened his journal and dipped his pen into the inkwell. Every time he thought he had freed himself of Greaves, something brought him back to the forefront. This time it was more town whispers. The man was building again, this time in Morrisburg, a house purported to be the grandest the town had ever seen.

Whitmore scribbled the date at the top of the page, then began to write, measuring each word with care.

> *They say Greaves has taken on another grand project. They have laid the foundations, or will do so soon. Already there are murmurings among the workers that he leaves marks, subtle but deliberate, in the timber. Some claim it's superstition; others, a sort of craft he alone understands. I saw him working. Precision beyond reason. Caution bordering on obsession. Yet, there is foresight. A method I can neither emulate nor fully trust. I must watch from a distance to see what may come of this Morrisburg venture. Something in me fears that those who follow in his footsteps*

might stumble if unaware.

He leaned back, eyes narrowing as he traced the shadows flickering on the wall from the lamplight. Greaves's name felt heavy, weighted with both admiration and unease. Whitmore set down the pen and rubbed the bridge of his nose.

I will write as I can, but I know the truth may not reveal itself for decades. And yet ...

He tapped the page lightly with the pen, as if to mark the words with intention. "I will record it for those who come after. Perhaps they will understand what I cannot."

Outside, the night pressed close to the windowpanes. Whitmore listened to the wind rattling the eaves and wondered if Greaves's hidden message had already begun, somewhere unseen, waiting for the right eyes.

Chapter Sixty-Eight

MARCH 31, 1870

The winter chill had only just begun to loosen its grip when Elias stood inside the half-built Morrisburg house, boots dusted with sawdust and mortar. The timber frame was skeletal, shadows stretching long in the faint light through the open windows. Each beam, each joint demanded meticulous precision; one slip could undermine months of painstaking work.

These marks were no longer simple precautions. They had become a language, a careful dialogue with forces he could feel but never name. He retraced the symbol slowly, pressing the chisel into the grain with a kind of reverence. Each cut was a prayer etched into the wood. Preserve. Protect. Endure. Not only the house, but the people who would live in it, the memories it would hold, the shadows it might shelter.

Elias ran a hand along the rough-hewn beam at the corner of what would become the library, the grain abrasive beneath his fingertips. There, a subtle notch, almost imperceptible to anyone else. A marker, not for decoration or pride but for protection, intended for those who would come after him long after his hands were gone.

The labourers moved about, unaware of the gravity in the space between hammer and nail. Greaves barely acknowledged them; his attention fell to corners that would never see light, to walls that would hide secrets, to floorboards above which something invisible might linger. From beyond the site came the bark of a dog and the lowing of cattle, the everyday chorus of nearby farms mingling with the industrious rhythm of hammer and saw.

He paused at the staircase, and bent low to inspect the stringer's angle. A tremor of worry tightened his chest: a man had nearly lost his footing the day before, and the thought of a fall haunted him more than the biting cold. He made a mental note to adjust the supports, to reinforce the rails, to leave invisible warnings in the open for those who might follow. These small cautions, invisible to the untrained eye, were his way of safeguarding lives.

Outside, the snow was melting, and a pale grey sun glinted on the river beyond. Elias pulled his coat tighter and exhaled, letting the quiet settle over him. This would be more than bricks and timber. It would be a guardian of sorts, a silent sentinel etched with his care.

A faint chill swept through the hall, carrying echoes of Kingston, Brighton, Cobourg, every site where he had left part of himself in timber and stone. He remembered the collapse, the frightened eyes, the terror that had scorched itself into memory. That memory had become a compass guiding his hand: do it right. Do it carefully. Do not fail.

Returning to the plans on the workbench, he traced a pencil lightly over a beam in the drawing. Another subtle mark, another hint of foresight. When they finished the house, it would hold not just walls and ceilings, but centuries of watchful thought, waiting for the right eyes to understand.

Elias moved among the men with a palpable sense of authority, inspecting their work without a word at first. A misplaced plank here, a skewed post there, nothing escaped his eyes. One of the younger labourers, Thomas, wiped sweat from his brow and glanced nervously at him, sensing the gravity of Elias's presence.

"Sir?" He ventured. "Do you want me to redo the north wall support? It's ... a bit off?"

Elias crouched to measure the joint, pencil

tucked behind his ear. “Yes,” he said finally, his tone firm but not unkind, “it must be straight. Every beam, every angle, must bear the weight exactly as drawn. A slight mistake now could be disastrous later.”

The men exchanged wary looks, knowing that Elias’s exacting standards were as much a part of the house as the timber itself. One of the older workers muttered under his breath about the man’s obsession with perfection, but Elias caught it and merely nodded. His relentless pursuit of perfection was not a burden, but a testament to his dedication. He didn’t need their understanding; he needed only their skill.

He moved to a corner where a beam would eventually meet the ceiling and traced a subtle notch with a sharp chisel. Another protective marker. No one saw it. No one would notice unless they knew where to look. Elias stepped back, considering how the lines of the house interacted, how light and shadow would fall across each floor and hallway.

A sudden clatter from the scaffold made him turn. A labourer had wobbled while carrying a heavy beam. Elias’s hand shot out, steadying the man before he could fall. “Careful,” he barked. “The wood can wait. Your footing cannot.”

The man nodded. Greaves straightened and brushed sawdust from his coat. “I will not be the one to curse this house,” he mumbled. “Not while I can prevent it.”

And with that, he returned to the plans on the workbench, already thinking several steps ahead, placing unseen warnings in wood and ink for the future, driven by a mixture of foresight and obsession. His ability to anticipate potential issues and his meticulous planning left the men in awe of his foresight.

When the men departed for the day, Greaves remained, a figure of secrecy in the dim light. By the lantern’s glow, he retraced the hidden lines, planning the secret room’s entrance, imagining the trap door above it, and visualizing who might someday find it, and what they would understand.

He paused, hand resting on the floor where the door would be, and whispered to himself. If the walls could speak, would they warn? Would they protect? He did not wait for an answer. The ritual was his, the covenant between builder and time, shadow and light, past and present.

As night settled over the construction site, Greaves finally allowed himself a deep breath. For now, the house was as it must be. He would return tomorrow and every day after that, eagerly awaiting the day when every unseen corner bore his careful signature. Until he accounted for every shadow until the house itself knew to watch and guard.

Chapter Sixty-Nine

AUGUST 23, 2023

Nicole traced the last symbol on the page, her eyes shining with a mix of triumph and disbelief. "That's it," she said as she gave a fist pump. "It wasn't just random ..." It had led her to this conclusion all along.

Mitch entered the dining room. "You been at this all night?" he asked. He leaned on the table and studied her face more than looking down at the papers spread out. "So, I wasn't completely off base, then," he said, pausing briefly. "When I thought it looked like a date."

She looked up, surprised, then laughed softly. "You weren't wrong. It *is* a date. But not just numbers carved into wooden beams or stone. The markers finish it. They're the other half of the code."

Mitch straightened, folded his arms and kept his eyes fixed on the notes. "Figures. I was chasing shadows without the entire picture."

Nicole shook her head. "No. You had the first piece. If you hadn't seen that pattern, I don't think I would've realized what I was missing. Greaves ... he left it broken on purpose. A fragment here, a symbol there. Like he knew it would take more than one person to piece it together."

Mitch let out a breath, heavier than others, allowing his shoulders to ease as if he'd been carrying the weight for too long. "I needed to hear that," he admitted, his voice low. "That I wasn't just ... reaching. That I actually saw something real."

Nicole's gaze softened. "You did. And you gave me

the spark. I just carried it the rest of the way." Their mutual support was a testament to the strength of their bond.

For a moment, silence stretched between them, neither uncomfortable nor weighted with understanding, but filled with it. Their shared understanding deepened the connection between them. "That's closure enough for me," Mitch said.

Nicole studied him, catching the faint tremor of vulnerability beneath his usual steadiness. She hadn't seen it in him for a long time. Not since he was a teenager and the death of his parents in the 1998 plane crash. Now he was protective, watchful and may have been a little unsettled, but she let him be. He had his part and she had hers, and somehow Greaves managed to bind them into the same story.

Mitch set the last piece of trim against the wall, lining it up with the others. Busy hands kept the mind quiet, or they should have, but Nicole's breakthrough kept threading its way through him, tighter each time.

She had been right about Greaves, about the care he'd taken. About the responsibility he passed on. She had done what he couldn't. She strung the markers together, coaxed the meaning out of them when he'd been circling the same half-answer for weeks. He wasn't bitter about it. Not even close. He was proud of his wife. Proud and a little protective, although he doubted she'd ever welcome that word. Nicole was strong, sharper than she gave herself credit for, and he respected the hell out of her. But part of him still wanted to step in, shield her from the weight of what they had uncovered.

He rubbed sawdust from his palms, frowning at the silence. The shop wasn't usually this still. The clock ticked, and the rafters gave their familiar groan. But underneath it, something else, low and steady, seemed to hum.

He stood still with his hand hovering above the extension cord. The air had shifted. Cooler somehow. Sharper. He turned.

Nothing.

Still, a prickling worked its way up his arms. The kind you couldn't reason away. He tried. Draft, insulation, settling boards — take your pick.

But then, faint as breath, came the squeak of wood creaking. Not the rafters nor the wall. Behind him.

Mitch wheeled around. The workbench stood bare, tools in their proper places. Other than him, the shop was empty.

He laughed, though it landed flat. "I need sleep."

As he shut off the lights and left, the uneasy thought clung to his skin like sawdust. If Greaves had left all those markers, maybe it wasn't only to tell a story. Perhaps it was a warning, a chilling possibility that sent shivers down Mitch's spine.

And for the first time, Mitch wondered if disbelief would be enough to protect him, a chilling realization that left him vulnerable and exposed.

Chapter Seventy

APRIL 6, 1870

The fog rolled in off the St. Lawrence River that morning, curling low over the fields. Greaves stood at the edge of the property, boots sinking into the damp soil, and studied the skeletal frame of what would become the grandest house in Morrisburg.

It was all angles and ambition for now. Lines chalked in the dirt, stakes marking where walls and wings would rise. He pulled his notebook from his coat pocket and flipped to the page with his own hand-drawn designs. This house, more than just a home, was a grand statement, a testament to his ambition, and a legacy in the making.

And although no one else knew it yet, it would be something far older.

Greaves glanced over his shoulder. The men who unloaded timber at the far end of the lot were locals with strong backs and wary eyes. They didn't know him beyond being *the man with the plans*. And for Greaves, that was how he liked it.

He drew the small leather case, which held the brass compass and the folded sheet of symbols, from his other pocket. These were not just tools for construction, but for something far older and more mysterious. The compass needle wavered, hesitated, then swung towards the centre of the plot. Perfect, the alignment was exact.

A shadow shifted at the edge of the fog. It appeared to be a man wearing a bowler hat, but when Greaves blinked, the figure was gone. The supernatural seemed to be at play, adding a mysterious element to his unfolding story.

He exhaled slowly and returned the symbols to his pocket. Some things had to be done before the walls went up. Some marks, ancient symbols of power and protection, had to be set where no one would see them again.

By the time the fog lifted, the men were already hammering the first boards into place. Greaves kept one eye on his plans, and the other on the shadows, the shifting forms that seemed to be more than just tricks of the light, as if he expected them to move again.

The clanging of hammers and the groan of timber being shifted filled the air. The workers had nearly finished the foundation trenches and neatly stacked the stone blocks beside them. Greaves paced along the edge, directing the masons with clipped instructions.

The men worked in sullen silence, their chisels biting harder than needed into the stone. "I tell you, it's Kingston all over again," one grumbled. "Mark my words, he'll bring this place down the same as he did there."

Another spat into the dust. "Strange signs and scribbles, that's no way to shore a wall. Saw it before and saw men buried for it."

They fell quiet when Greaves's shadow crossed the scaffolding, but the tension lingered, thick as mortar.

Then one of the younger men, a lanky lad barely out of boyhood, stopped mid-swing. "Sir," he called. "You'd better see this."

Greaves's stomach tightened.

The boy moved out of the way and showed a flat rock that someone had flipped over in the foundation trench. The underside bore a series of carved symbols — shallow grooves worn smooth with age.

Greaves crouched and brushed away the clinging dirt. Yes, he set one of his marks exactly where it needed to be before the digging began. But there was a problem. He should have buried it deeper under another layer of stone.

"You know what this means?" the boy asked, his eyes narrowing.

"Old masons' marks," Greaves lied and forced a faint smile. "Superstition from a century ago. Nothing more."

The boy didn't look convinced. He spat into the dirt, muttered something to the man beside him, and the pair exchanged a look Greaves couldn't quite read.

By midday, two more workers had quit without collecting their pay. Others kept their distance from him, their murmurs adding to the growing sense of unease.

That night, long after the men had put their tools away, Greaves returned alone. Lantern in hand, he lowered himself into the trench and replaced the stone. As he did, the fog rolled in again, thick and silent.

From somewhere beyond its veil came the sound of a slow, deliberate footstep, a sign of impending danger.

Chapter Seventy-One

AUGUST 23, 2023

Nicole spread the Whitmore and Greaves journals across the dining room table, side by side; their cracked spines and frayed corners formed a crooked line. The wood beneath them was cool and scarred and seemed to bear the weight of centuries of secrets. And just in Nicole's genealogy, there were plenty related to this house. She pulled her hair into a ponytail, tucked a pencil behind her ear, and turned on the table lamps at either end of the sideboard for additional light.

Afternoon was sliding into dusk, and the house had that heavy, listening stillness she knew too well, a stillness that seemed to swallow every sound.

She inhaled the faint scent of old leather and mildew. Her heart thudded with the same restless energy that had been dogging her since Kingston, when they stopped at the Merchant to break up the trip and have a bite to eat. Mitch had brushed off the cornerstone with one offhand comment and then said nothing more.

"All right," she said to the empty room, her voice filled with determination. "Let's see if you've been waiting for me all along."

She began with their house. Whitmore's scrawled account of his first day and later finding the problems with the workmanship, which were hastily covered up.

The following entry held the drawing she'd copied weeks ago. A simple diagonal slash, three dots tucked in its angle. She pulled out her own sketchbook and laid her rubbing beside it. The faint lines matched Whitmore's description exactly.

A shiver ran down her arms. "Marker one. Not decoration. Not random."

But even as she wrote the word Brighton beneath the sign, doubt coiled through her. Perhaps she was forcing the connection, desperate to make meaning out of scratches that could have been anything.

She rubbed her eyes and exhaled slowly. "No, keep going."

She flipped through the pages of Whitmore's journal until she found the reference to the building collapse in Kingston. His words described scaffolding, noise, and men hauling stone. Then, as if slipped in sideways, a line.

> *Greaves marked the beam, carving a circle with a line drawn true across its heart. It was to no avail. The building came down with injuries and loss of lives.*

Nicole, with a passion for unraveling mysteries, looked at her notes; her hand trembled as she redrew the shape. A bisected circle.

Whitmore's doubt echoed faintly in her head. Decoration or device? But by now, she had a growing understanding of the symbols, no longer believing in coincidence.

Brighton's diagonal with three dots. Kingston's circle and line. Her throat tightened. Greaves had carried something forward. Every stone was more than mortar and weight. They were promises, safeguards. She could almost hear him murmuring. *Never again.* The emotional weight of these symbols was palpable.

Nicole reached for the Morrisburg sketch, the one she'd made from memory after crawling out of the hidden room in the basement with Mitch.

Her pencil tapped against the edge of the paper as she studied it. A mark carved at shoulder height, half faded by time. Two nested triangles. She had thought it nothing more than idle scratching. Now, with Whitmore's words open before her, it blazed like a flare.

Marks not made as decoration but as a warning.

Nicole swallowed hard and copied it into the growing row beside the others. Diagonal with dots, circle with line, nested triangles. Three pieces. A progression.

Her pulse quickened.

For a long time, she sat motionless, listening to the sounds of the house. The rafters creaked as though someone shifted their weight in the room above. A chill draft brushed her ankles.

"Is there anybody there?" she asked, half-remembering the words from that poem, *The Listeners.*

Her voice startled her. She laughed shakily and pressed her palms flat on the table. "This is ridiculous. I'm just stringing together shapes."

But when she leaned forward again, aligning the pages side by side, the truth refused to vanish.

Brighton's marker angled downward like a warning sign. Kingston's circle with its line, balance, structure, and strength. Morrisburg's triangles, layered, shielding, nest-like guardians. These were not just random shapes, but a thread. Not superstition, nor accident. A language of care, a deliberate communication from the past.

A thread. Not superstition, nor accident.

Nicole's breath caught in her throat. She whispered the words as they formed. "Care. Foresight. Responsibility."

Her vision blurred. She pressed the heels of her hands against her eyes, but the tears came anyway. After all the doubt, all the fragments, she finally understood. Greaves wasn't arrogant. He wasn't hiding from his mistakes. He had spent the rest of his career making sure no one repeated them. This realization, this understanding, was like a weight lifted from her shoulders, a clarity she had longed for.

"Me," she murmured. "He left them for me."

The thought made her laugh.

The lamplight wavered, shadows creeping long across the floor. Nicole gathered the three symbols together in her notebook, drew a line connecting them, then another and another until the page looked less like scattered shapes and more like a map, a protective weave stitched across time.

Her chest loosened for the first time in weeks. She sat back, pencil sliding from her fingers, and let the silence of the house fold around her.

Greaves had carried Kingston's dead with him. Whitmore had carried Greaves's puzzle. And now, she carried them both, the thread unbroken, reaching across nearly two centuries. She was not just a bystander, but a part of this intricate web of history and care.

Nicole closed her eyes and whispered to the stillness. "I understand now. I won't forget."

Chapter Seventy-Two

MAY 15, 1870

By now the walls had risen, brick against the spring sky, and the roofline had taken shape. Inside, the air smelled of lime and plaster dust, mingling with the sweet dampness of freshly turned soil.

In the cellar, a young labourer hauled a load of rubble towards the stairwell, wiping sweat from his brow.

"You've a steady hand," Greaves said, stepping closer, his voice low and deliberate. "And a sharper eye than most."

The boy straightened, uncertain whether he was being praised or tested. "I do what's asked of me, sir."

Greaves nodded towards the far wall, where a faint seam in the stone that had been closed up weeks before. "There are places in a house where spaces aren't meant to be lived in, nor even known. Do you understand?"

The youth frowned, shifting from one foot to the other. "Like a vault?"

"Something like that." Greaves's eyes lingered on the wall. "A chamber meant not for things, but for moments. A place to disappear into, should the world above grow ... dangerous."

The boy gave a short nervous laugh, unsettled by the intensity in Greaves's tone. "Strange business, that."

"Strange, yes. Necessary, too." Greaves let the words hang, then clapped the lad on the shoulder with a sudden, almost jovial force. "Go on, then. The stone won't shift itself."

As the boy trundled back towards the stairwell, muttering under his breath, Greaves remained by the wall, fingers brushing the faint ridge of mortar. Soon he would fashion the trapdoor above and the recess would be complete. A house needs its hidden bones as much as its proud ones.

Elias crouched beside the freshly installed beam, his chisel poised with a practiced hand. The afternoon light filtered through the cellar windows, catching the dust motes that swirled around him. He glanced at the young labourer, Samuel, who had been assigned to help with the final reinforcements around the hidden room.

"Remember what I said about the priest hole," Elias said, tapping the chisel lightly against the beam. "This isn't just timber or stone. Every corner, every seam ... it has a purpose. Not everyone will understand, but someone, one day, will."

The labourer nodded; unease flickered in his eyes, but he said nothing. Elias let the silence stretch, broken only by the creak of timber settling and the distant lowing of cattle from the nearby farms.

He traced a subtle mark along the edge of the beam, almost invisible, but deliberate. "These symbols, they're not for decoration. They're for guidance, protection ... a way to safeguard what must be kept safe."

The young man's gaze followed his hands, intrigued but unsure. Elias straightened, brushing sawdust from his coat. "You'll see," he said softly, "this house will carry more than walls and beams. It will carry foresight, warnings, and a measure of care from me, for anyone who walks its halls long after I'm gone."

A quiet resolve settled over him, as it always did when he worked in this secretive space. The priest holes, the marks, the hidden precautions — each was a thread in a careful tapestry, a dialogue with the future that few would ever perceive. Yet he knew, deep inside, it was all necessary. Every cut, notch, hidden mark was his responsibility. A silent promise etched in wood and stone.

The workers had departed hours ago, leaving the house hushed except for the whisper of spring wind through the unfinished windows. Elias stood in the room on the north side of the house, directly above his hidden space he had designed.

He knelt beside a section of the floor, his hands caressing the timber that would soon conceal the entrance to the priest hole. With meticulous care, he measured, adjusted, and finally pried a loose board free. Greaves had fitted the trapdoor into place with such precision that it would escape even the most discerning eye.

Sliding a small latch into position, he tested the mechanism.Silent. Secure. Invisible. A subtle curve in the wood's grain masked the seam, and the dim lantern light barely touched the faint markings he had carved nearby. Guides that only someone trained to notice would understand.

Elias exhaled; the weight of the responsibility settled heavily onto his shoulders. This was no ordinary construction task. It was a solemn promise for the future. Whoever came after him, whoever understood the signs, would find a sanctuary, and perhaps answers to questions he could not yet foresee.

He stepped back, brushed the sawdust from his hands, and whispered to the empty house. "Safe ... and waiting for the right eyes."

The trapdoor, flush with the floor, remained unnoticed beneath the shadows, a hidden portal into the secrets of Greaves's design. Elias extinguished the lantern, and the house fell into silence, its secrets locked away for decades.

Chapter Seventy-Three

AUGUST 23, 2023

Nicole sat at the table with her sketchbook open and pencils scattered around her. She should have been working on CNC IT Solutions business, but these symbols and ciphers had her fascinated. The previous night's discoveries still hummed in her mind, a quiet energy she couldn't shake. She traced one of the protective markers she had copied from the Morrisburg notes, following the curves and notches with her fingertip. Each line felt deliberate, weighted with care.

Mitch moved about the kitchen, unloading and reloading the dishwasher. He hummed softly, a sound meant to ground them both. Nicole looked up and smiled faintly. "You're trying to keep me from imagining ghosts again, aren't you?"

He shot her a glance over his shoulder, eyes soft but firm. "Possible. Or I'm just reminding you there are living, breathing problems, too."

Nicole chuckled, but it didn't reach the tension in her shoulders. She leaned back and let herself breathe. "Everything connects now. The markers, the journals, the buildings. I can almost hear him speaking through the wood."

Mitch crossed the room and rested his hand on the back of her chair. "Then listen carefully," he said. "But don't lose yourself in the echoes. We face it together, remember?"

A sudden creak from above made them both freeze. Mitch's jaw tightened, but he didn't let it show.

Nicole's fingers hovered over the sketchbook, trembling slightly. They shared a glance, and then Mitch offered the faintest shrug. "Old house. Old floors. Nothing more."

Nicole nodded, willing herself to believe him, but inside her heart raced. The markers weren't just designs; they were warnings. And the house seemed to agree.

Mitch stood at the foot of the stairs, leaning against the newel post, and watched Nicole move about the kitchen. She had a quiet focus, methodical and precise. Her hands traced the edges of the sketches and journals as if each line held a heartbeat. He swallowed against the lump in his throat. She made it all seem possible, even when the house's creaks and sighs reminded him of how old it was, how much history it held.

He picked up one of her sketches from the hall table, fingertips brushing the inked symbols. Protective markers, she had said. Warnings. Cautions. He tried to imagine the hands that had carved these into the timber, the care, the foresight. And he felt something shift within him. A weight, heavy and unseen, that made him both protective and restless.

A floorboard groaned upstairs. Mitch's hand twitched; his instinct to defend kicked in, though the rational side of him knew it was probably nothing. Yet the unease remained tangible, a thread that wound around his chest.

Nicole looked up, catching him staring at her work. Her eyes softened, and she gave him a small smile. "You've got that look," she said. "Thinking too much, as usual?"

He forced a grin. "Possible," he said, lowering the sketch. "Or I'm just making sure nothing gets past us. We're close, Nicki. Really close."

She nodded, returning her attention to the papers. Mitch leaned against the newel post a moment longer, letting the quiet settle. Protectiveness, anticipation, and a quiet, gnawing dread tangled together in front of him. He couldn't shake it, but he would face it with her.

And when he finally stepped back to the table, picking up pencil and notebook, he allowed himself to feel a spark of excitement. The next day would bring more clarity, more understanding, and whatever waited in the shadows; he would meet it head-on.

Nicole lingered over the table, her fingers hovering above Whitmore's journal as if touching it could draw out its secrets. She traced the curves of the symbol again, whispering the line from *The Listeners* under her breath. "Is there anybody there?" The words didn't belong to her, and yet they resonated, as though the house might answer.

A shiver ran down her spine, but she pressed on. Each mark. Each sketch felt like a puzzle piece finally sliding into place. She looked at Mitch, who was leaning against the newel post, jaw tight, eyes scanning the room as if he could see the ghosts of the past.

"Acting as a protector again?" she teased, though her voice wavered.

Mitch offered a faint grin, but didn't answer. She smiled softly and returned to her work, heart racing with the anticipation of discovery. The markers were more than history now. They were a bridge. And soon, she hoped they would understand everything Greaves had left for them.

Chapter Seventy-Four

AUGUST 24, 2023

Soft golden morning light spilled across the kitchen table. Nicole traced her fingers over the sketches from the night before that she had brought in from the dining room. The lines of symbols and markers were still fresh in her mind. The journals lay open beside her, but today she didn't feel the weight of history pressing down. Instead, it hummed quietly, like a chess match waiting for the next move.

Mitch had said little about the workshop when he returned last night, and she didn't press him. She knew he had a way of carrying unease silently, letting it settle before he addressed it. But something lingered in the air between them, a tension she felt as she reached for her pencil.

Her hand hovered above the paper, then she began to doodle again, the symbols spilling out without thought. Each curve and line flowed naturally. As she worked, the first line of *The Listeners, "Is there anybody there?" said the traveller* drifted back.

A shiver ran down her spine. Not fear, but a sense that the past hadn't finished speaking. She glanced towards the window, towards the quiet road outside, and wondered what Greaves might have meant when he left these markers — warnings, messages, protections.

Nicole tucked her pencil behind her ear and shook her head. Whatever it was, she and Mitch would face it together, their resolve like a beacon in the gathering darkness.

But even as she thought that, she couldn't ignore the faint tug at the edge of her awareness, as if someone, or something, were just beyond the threshold, a silent observer in the shadows.

She pushed the papers aside, intending to tidy the table. That's when she noticed it. A slight shift in the light on the windowsill, a shadow that shouldn't have been there. She blinked. Nothing. The sun hadn't moved enough to cast an extra shadow.

Her curiosity prickled. She leaned closer to the symbols she'd drawn, tracing the lines again, and thought of the Merchant Tap House, the Morrisburg house, the Moran-Hooker building in Prescott and their own home. Each marker seemed to hum with intention, as if someone or something guided her hand.

A soft scrape behind her made her freeze. She told herself it was Mitch coming in from the workshop, or a chair settling on the floorboards. But the hairs on her neck stood, anyway.

She straightened, scanned the room and whispered, almost in challenge. "If you're here, show me," her voice a simple declaration of her refusal to be intimidated.

And in that quiet moment, Nicole realized the markers hadn't finished. They had one more message to reveal.

Nicole leaned over the table, her eyes scanning the patterns she'd drawn, again. Something about the spacing, the way certain symbols repeated, tugged at her memory. Kingston, Brighton, Prescott, Morrisburg. Each site had carried a fragment of the puzzle. And now in her sketches, the pieces had started to fit.

She picked up one journal and flipped to the pages Whitmore had copied from Greaves's own hand. Words about walls, beams, and precautions jumped out in a new light. The protective markers weren't just warnings. They were a map of care, a sequence Greaves had left behind to anticipate mistakes, missteps, even accidents.

Nicole's heart raced as she realized the symbols

on the paper were not just random marks. They were instructions, a guide. The thrill of discovery surged through her, igniting a fire of determination.

Nicole grabbed her pencil and cross-referenced her doodles with the journal notes. Slowly and methodically, she started connecting lines and symbols to specific dates, locations, and even structural elements in the buildings. Each stroke made the pattern clearer.

Mitch appeared in the doorway. “Found something?” he asked.

She looked up, a small triumphant smile forming. “More than that. I think I finally understand what Greaves intended. It’s not just history. It’s a safeguard. He was leaving a way for someone like us to follow, to see what he saw, and maybe avoid what went wrong.”

He stepped closer, his expression a mix of relief and awe. “You did it. You figured it out,” he said, the weight of the revelation settling on his shoulders.

Nicole nodded, her eyes returning to the table. “And it makes sense now. All of it. The Kingston collapse, the construction on this house, Prescott, and even the Morrisburg house. The markers weren’t just for protection; they were a message. A story in symbols. And it wasn’t finished until we pieced it together.”

Mitch’s jaw tightened as he studied her. “I can’t believe how clever he was ...”

Nicole met his gaze, her expression steady but thoughtful. “Clever, yes, and cautious. But also, maybe warning us that the past doesn’t always stay behind,” she said, her voice filled with caution caused by the unease lingering in the air.

The air between them shifted, heavier now, charged with understanding, mixed with a quiet hint of unease. Somewhere deep within the house, the shadows seemed to press closer, as if they knew someone had solved the puzzle.

Nicole set her pencil down, and her fingertips lingered on the edge of the paper. “We need to document all of this,” she said. “Every symbol, every marker, every connection before it disappears again.”

Mitch nodded. “Agreed. And we stay together.

Every step of the way."

For the first time since Nicole had placed the journals together on their table, the past felt alive. Both of them understood Greaves had left more than symbols. He had left a responsibility, a duty to uncover the truth and prevent history from repeating itself, and now they were part of it.

Then, just as Nicole stood to gather the papers, a faint sound, almost like the scrape of wood against stone, drifted from the hallway. They froze.

"Did you hear that?"

Mitch shook his head. "Probably just the house settling."

But neither moved to check, because deep down, Nicole and Mitch knew it wasn't just the house.

Chapter Seventy-Five

AUGUST 29, 1870

The late August sun poured through the tall, nearly finished windows, casting warm rectangles across the dust-strewn floors. Elias moved through the house with quiet precision, boots brushing over sawdust and plaster fragments. He had set the roof, plastered the walls, and laid the floors, but each corner still demanded his careful attention.

He paused in the hallway, tracing the grain of a beam that had once seemed ordinary but now bore the subtle markings only he could read. Preserve. Protect. Endure. These were not idle symbols. Each one was a reminder, a silent instruction for the future occupants.

In the kitchen, a young labourer adjusted a cabinet panel. Elias approached, crouching to inspect the joinery. "Careful there," he said, pointing out a slight misalignment. "The wood has its own memory. Respect it, and it will serve you well."

The worker nodded, unaware of the greater weight behind Greaves's words. Outside, the village hummed with activity. Carts clattered down the roads, dogs barked and cattle lowed in the distance. Inside, Elias felt the house shift beneath his feet, alive with hidden purpose.

He moved to the staircase and ran his hand along the banister. The protective markers he'd placed months ago seemed to vibrate under his touch, a reassurance the house would guard itself, and those who lived within it, if they knew where to look.

Pausing in the library, Elias allowed himself a

moment to survey the nearly finished space. The house was no longer a skeletal frame but a living structure, ready to embrace the stories it would hold. And somewhere beneath the polished floorboards and plastered walls, the hidden room waited quietly, its secrets locked away, a silent promise preserved for the right eyes.

Chapter Seventy-Six

AUGUST 24, 2023

Mitch had shoved the coffee table tight against the couch and sat on the living room floor. Notebooks and sketches surrounded him like a map of their discoveries. He traced the lines of the protective markers Nicole had copied, his mind turning over possibilities. Each notch, each subtle curve, he understood they weren't random. Elias Greaves had been careful, precise, and almost ... reverent.

The air in the room felt thick, heavy with unspoken warnings. Mitch shook his head, trying to dismiss the chill crawling along his spine. He didn't believe in ghosts, in spirits lingering in the corners of old houses, but he couldn't deny the tension that threaded through the wood and stone of these places.

Nicole moved behind him, carrying her sketchbook and leaning over to lay it beside his notebooks. "You're still working?" she asked, voice quiet, but tinged with the same anxious curiosity that he felt in every nerve.

He looked up and smiled faintly. "I can't stop now. Not with everything we've found. I need to see it all together."

She nodded and settled on the floor beside him, pencil poised over her own sketches. They worked in companionable silence for a while, occasionally exchanging thoughts, hypotheses, or just a word of encouragement. Mitch kept glancing towards the windows, half expecting the shadows outside to shift unnaturally. He hated admitting it, but a sliver of dread had wormed its way in.

When Nicole traced the curve of the last symbol, she exhaled. "I think we're ready," she said. "Ready to go back."

Mitch's fingers hovered over a notebook, then he closed it decisively. "Saturday, then," he said. "We go back to Morrisburg. We see what Greaves left, what he wanted us to find. And we're prepared this time."

Nicole leaned back, resting her head against his shoulder. Mitch felt the warmth of her presence, a tether against the unease that lingered in the corners of the room. "We'll be okay," he said, more to himself than her. "We'll face whatever's there. Together."

Outside, the late afternoon sun cast long shadows across their property. Inside, the markers, sketches, and journals waited, silent witnesses to the careful attention of their creators, and to the next step in uncovering a story that had waited more than a century to be understood.

Chapter Seventy-Seven

SEPTEMBER 29, 1870

Sunlight caught the copper on the roof in glints that almost blinded Greaves as he approached the main entrance.

Inside the plasterers worked methodically, smoothing walls that would hold the secrets and symbols he had carefully embedded in the beams. Each brushstroke of lime and sand felt like a gentle covering over something not meant to be immediately seen. He lingered at a corner, running his fingers along the recently installed panelling. The subtle notches he had carved, the protective markers, were hidden now, but their intent remained potent. Preserve. Protect. Endure.

He paused at the staircase, where the carpenter had secured the stringers and polished the banister by hand. A small pang of memory struck him. Kingston, Brighton, Prescott, Cobourg, Port Hope. Every site where he had left a part of himself, and yet here in Morrisburg, he felt the weight of finality. The house was no longer a project but a culmination.

The trapdoor hidden in the library remained perfectly flush with the floor. He crouched, examining it as he had done many nights before, ensuring the latch was secure and the markings nearby unobtrusive. Whoever came after him would find it only if they knew how to look, and perhaps that was the point. Secrets had power only when preserved carefully and intentionally.

Elias rose and walked to the north-facing window. The river beyond reflected a low September sun, golden and steady. He exhaled slowly, letting the warmth wash over him. The exterior and the roof were complete, and the house would not just hold his craft, but his foresight, his care and a trace of the unseen forces he had always felt.

As he returned to the plans laid across the workbench, he ran his hand over a pencil mark tracing the final beams. One by one, the house's bones would cover and hide, but the intent would remain embedded in every notch and corner, waiting for the right eyes to understand.

Chapter Seventy-Eight

OCTOBER 31, 1870

Elias Greaves moved through the Morrisburg house, a place that seemed to breathe with a life of its own. His eyes traced every beam, every arch, every hidden line of his design. The wind whistled through the gaps around the windows, carrying whispers that seemed to echo his own words, adding to the eerie atmosphere.

No apprentice watched over him. Whitmore left before they completed the Brighton construction.

The young man seemed unwilling, or perhaps unready, to follow Greaves's chosen path. The house was his alone now, alive with the symbols and secrets he had embedded within its walls-cryptic markings that only he could decipher, and hidden chambers that held untold stories.

As he ascended the central staircase, a chill filled the air. Shadows shifted unnaturally, stretching and twisting across the floor and beams. Greaves felt a pull, as if the house was tugging him towards some hidden truth — a truth that lay buried in the very foundation of the house, waiting to be unearthed.

When he reached the tower staircase, the shadows moved faster, curling and pressing closer. A whispered half-threat, half-warning wafted through the empty halls. *The past must remain. The house must endure.*

Before he could step back, a cold force swept over him. The wind howled, the shadows converged, and Greaves was gone. No body. No trace. Only a faint coppery scent lingered, like the aftermath of a long-forgotten tragedy, and the faintest outline of a figure in the light. The man was forever bound to the house, waiting for those who could read the shadows through time.

The workers below said it was an accident. Some swore they had seen him moments before. Others insisted the man had vanished as if swallowed by the very walls he had built. The Morrisburg house stood silent, its secrets intact, its creator gone but never forgotten.

Chapter Seventy-Nine

AUGUST 26, 2023

The road to Morrisburg stretched ahead. The four-lane highway made for a boring drive. Mitch could have taken the slower route along the river, but with the late start they got, this was the fastest way to get there. He kept his eyes on the road, but glanced at Nicole occasionally. Her mind was elsewhere, as was his. "You excited to get back in there?" he asked, voice low, as if speaking too loudly might break the spell.

She turned towards him and grinned. "More than I thought I'd ever be. And this time, we have the notebook." Nicole patted the worn, warmed leather-bound book resting between them, a symbol of their mission. "We're going to return it to its place. Properly this time. No matter what."

Mitch's jaw tightened. "Seems ... right, I guess. Closing the circle."

A thunderstorm blew in from somewhere, almost as if it had followed them. The rain pelted the truck, making it difficult to hear. The windows fogged up from the difference in the indoor and outdoor temperatures. They had to stop by the real estate office first to get the key, and then it was on to the house.

When they finally reached the town, Mitch parked the truck as close to the realtor's as possible so that whichever one drew the short straw and had to dash in for the key didn't get totally soaked.

Nicole leapt out of the truck before it came to a complete stop. She was only gone an instant, but to Mitch it seemed longer, the suspense building with each passing second. When she returned to the truck, she held the key high in the air, a triumphant smile on her face.

Nicole and Mitch stood before the massive Victorian house. It appeared familiar yet different somehow. Older, wiser, and holding the weight of its secrets more heavily? Nicole's stomach fluttered. Every step they had taken had led them here, and yet she knew the markers still held one last message.

Mitch parked the truck at the end of the walkway to the front door. The engine ticked as it cooled, leaving a quiet only interrupted by birdsong from the trees. Nicole grabbed the notebook carefully and ran her fingers over its cover, feeling the rough texture of the leather and the faint indentations of the embossed symbol. "I hope he'll approve," she said, the words barely audible over the rustling leaves and the distant chirping of birds.

"I think he already does." Mitch squeezed her shoulder.

They stepped out, loose gravel crunching under their feet. The hidden room beckoned like a secret they had finally earned the right to uncover. Nicole's heart raced, a potent mix of excitement and reverent caution. Every symbol, every sketch, every page of the journals led to this moment, and the anticipation was palpable.

As they reached the front door of the mansion, the rain stopped briefly, and the sun peeked out. Nicole thought she saw a faint shape in the corner of her eye.

Mitch placed his hand on the doorknob. "Ready?"

Nicole nodded. She held the notebook like a talisman. "Ready."

He unlocked the front door, and they stepped into the hallway, making their way to the room with the trapdoor in the floor.

Nicole knelt on the uneven dirt floor in the hidden room nestled in the cellar of the Morrisburg house. She carefully placed the notebook on the wooden bench, her fingers trembling with anticipation, and swept away a layer of dust that had settled over the years, revealing the secrets of the past.

Thankfully, it hadn't sold and was still on the market, so they could visit one last time. Nicole's flashlight shook in her hand. Mitch hovered close, his breathing steady while his eyes scanned the shadowed corners of the subterranean chamber.

"This has to be it. Everything Greaves ever drew points here." She ran her fingers over the sketches she'd made and compared them to what she had just traced on the wall. Each mark now made sense. Preservation. Protection. Foresight. And now at last she could trace the full intent of Greaves's message.

A sudden hush seemed to descend over the small underground room. The air shifted, the temperature dropped, and there was a faint metallic scent and a weight that pressed against her chest. Mitch noticed it, too.

A faint shimmer coalesced near the far wall. The figure was tall and imposing, but not threatening. Elias Greaves. His eyes held the calm of a man who had seen the future and left his instructions for it. Nicole held her breath.

"You've understood." Greaves's voice was low, echoing as if carried across time.

Nicole and Mitch exchanged a glance, and his hand found hers, forming a silent anchor in the strangeness. "All of it ...the markers, the warnings, the protections," she said.

Greaves inclined his head, and a faint smile touched his lips. "Yes. You followed the path. You see what I intended, what I could not finish. You completed what I started and respected it."

Mitch stepped closer. "We didn't do it for you," he said in a low but firm voice. "We did it because it mattered."

Greaves's gaze softened. "And that is why it matters still. The past is never truly gone when someone understands it."

Nicole's fingers lingered on the notebook, tracing one last symbol. "Preserve. Protect. Watch. Learn. That was the message."

Greaves nodded once in quiet affirmation. A soft breeze, impossible in a sealed chamber, brushed against their cheeks. Greaves smiled faintly, then faded, leaving only the warm smell of wood and candle smoke that seemed to linger in the air. The room felt lighter, yet alive and charged with memory and care.

Mitch exhaled. "It's done," he said.

Nicole understood it wasn't just about closure, but about a profound responsibility that had grown between them through their shared understanding of the past. She smiled faintly. "We have understood. And now, it's our duty to carry it forward."

The two rose together, letting the silence settle around them. Mitch placed a hand on the ladder that led up from the secret room. "Time to close this chapter and maybe open a few new ones. Who knows what other mysteries we might uncover?"

Outside, the rain had stopped entirely, and the sun was out, casting long shadows in the late afternoon. But inside, the past had spoken, and they had listened. Their understanding had not only preserved history but also connected them to a legacy that would continue to guide them.

Back at their home in Brighton, Nicole picked up her sketchbook and opened it to the last page. Nicole's careful lines sketched the Morrisburg tower, demonstrating her dedication. The symbols were there, subtle and elegant, creating a bridge between eras. She closed it, and a quiet calm settled over her. Each line, each symbol now had a story. The dual timelines had converged. Greaves's past, Whitmore's apprenticeship, the hidden rooms and their modern discoveries.

As she gazed at the gleaming tower, past and present collided. Shadows through time had revealed the truth, and the forgotten still lingered. Mitch wrapped his arms around her from behind, and for the first time in weeks, they simply stood together and allowed the quiet triumph to wash over them, the past honoured, the present secured and the echoes at rest. "We did it.

We figured it out. Everything."

"And survived," he said with a grin, his voice carrying a palpable sense of relief.

Outside, the sunlight caught the tower of their restored home, glinting on the copper roofs and casting long, silent shadows. For the first time, the echoes that lingered had settled, bringing a profound sense of closure.

And somewhere, just beyond sight, it felt as though the house itself exhaled and settled into its centuries-long vigil, content that everyone had finally heard its story, and that the echoes of the past had finally rested.

Epilogue

OCTOBER 31, 2023

The scent of fallen leaves filled the crisp autumn air as Nicole stepped back, hands brushing the plaque she had designed. For now, it remained hidden behind a burgundy-coloured piece of velvet fabric.

Mitch stood beside her, fingers intertwined with hers, a smile forming on his lips. "This is the moment we've been waiting for," he said, his eyes reflecting the anticipation that filled the air.

Nicole nodded, a mixture of pride and reverence warming her chest. "It feels ... right. Like we're closing the circle."

A small gathering of neighbours, friends, and Nicole's brothers had come to witness the unveiling, but Nicole's eyes lingered on the house itself. From the foundations to the tip of the tower, the house stood as a metaphor of lasting strength. Every beam, every corner, every hidden symbol had a story, and for the first time, that story was complete.

With a gentle tug of the covering, the plaque revealed itself. A masterpiece of artistry and history, it paid homage to Elias Greaves's foresight, his care, and the hidden protections he had left behind.

The copper letters and motif gleamed in the morning sun, each one a reflection of the protective symbols and subtle markings that adorned the house, bridging the gap between past and present.

While the crowd murmured appreciatively, Nicole only had eyes for the house, and for the past she and Mitch had brought vividly into the present.

Mitch leaned closer and said, “He would have been proud.”

Nicole smiled and let the warmth of the day and the sense of closure wash over her. “We are.”

For a moment, the world seemed to pause, and in the quiet, the echoes of Whitmore’s and Greaves’s journals, the whispered markers and the careful hands of Elias Greaves resonated through time. The house had kept its secrets, but now, finally, it told its story.

As the autumn wind danced through the yard, the shadows and light mingled across the plaque, carrying the memory of care, protection, and generations bound by hidden hands. Finally, they unveiled a lasting bridge between eras.

As the crowd dispersed, a single autumn leaf drifted down from above and tumbled across the plaque. For a fleeting moment, sunlight caught the edges of the copper letters, and a shadow traced one of the hidden symbols as if acknowledging its legacy. Nicole smiled softly, sensing the quiet presence of those who had come before. A gentle reminder that the past was never truly gone, and that care and foresight could ripple across generations.

THE END

<<<0>>>

Also by Melanie Robertson-King

Short Stories

The Consequences Collection
Cole's Notes (A Short Story)
EFD1: Starship Goodwords – a cross genre anthology(Carrick Publishing, 2012)
Cole's Notes (Revised version)

Children's Books

Tim's Magic Christmas
All Aboard the Canadian with Buddy and his Four Fantastic Furry Friends!

Time Travel Romance

A Shadow in the Past (second edition)
Shadows From Her Past

Sweet Romance

It Happened on Dufferin Terrace
It Happened in Gastown
It Happened at Percé Rock
It Happened at Lake Louise
It Happened at Niagara Falls
It Happened in Lunenburg

Dual Timeline Novels

WHISPERS THROUGH TIME
ECHOES THROUGH TIME

Romance with heat

The Secret of Hillcrest House
YESTERDAY TODAY ALWAYS
(King Park Press)

MELANIE ROBERTSON-KING

https://melanierobertson-king.com

Melanie Robertson-King has always been a fan of the written word. Growing up as an only child, her face was almost always buried in a book from the time she could read. Her father was one of the thousands of Home Children sent to Canada through the auspices of The Orphan Homes of Scotland, and she has been fortunate to be able to visit her father's homeland many times and even met the Princess Royal (Princess Anne) at the orphanage where he was raised.

www.ingramcontent.com/pod-product-compliance
Lightning Source LLC
LaVergne TN
LVHW091113080826
845145LV00008B/1893

* 9 7 8 1 9 9 0 3 7 1 1 6 5 *